# The Scarred Viscount's Redemption

A Clean Regency Romance Novel

## Martha Barwood

# Table of Contents

# Prologue

The house smelled of nothing, a smell that James could never get used to. All his life, scents always assailed his nostrils. Perhaps it was the buzz of activity in the house when his father used to be around, or the sweet smell of tea leaves simmering in a teapot when he was a child. But this time, it was nothing. And the thought of nothingness made him feel much more alone than ever.

A sigh escaped his lips as he reclined further in the chair, fingers skimming over the soft linen napkins and ornate cutlery. Just seeing them took him way back to when he served his country, spending his time hidden under the mud-covered battlefield, the acrid smell of gunpowder filling his nostrils.

He had been on the battlefield when the news came - something so terrible that he sank to the ground in pain, eyes brimming with tears. James forced himself not to think about those awful memories, to allow himself to enjoy the life he had now. A life he never wanted.

"Alice, you have to stop sulking," his mother's high-pitched voice rose in the room, a careful soprano that reminded James of all the times he had been scolded as a child.

It had only been eighteen months since he returned home, and a part of him yearned to be carrying a weapon. To fight for his country and not just sit at home and sip tea like people of the ton. James stifled a yawn, closing his eyes for a brief moment, and let himself wander through his memories. Vivid ones of him carrying a musket, his hair smeared with mud...

"James," his mother called out to him, her voice taking a low tone now. "Your breakfast is getting cold."

For one, James was not interested in eating. They had come to London only a week ago, and he hated everything about it. The noise, hustle, and bustle of carriages along the cobblestoned streets, all of the people in Hyde Park, and the horse-riding men on the tracks. James had been surrounded by noise all his life, and now that he was at home, he craved some quiet.

More than anything, even breakfast, he wanted to be back in the countryside. James yearned to be back on his horse - he had named it Helios - and ride down the large estate, to feel the wind in his hair as he let himself get lost again. It was his way of having fun. Being alone and surrounded on all sides by nothing but greenery, to talk to himself about things he would not tell anyone else. Not even his mother.

"Do you want something else?" his mother, Lady Hamilton said to him from across the dining table. "I can ask the maids to prepare something else."

James shook his head softly, and his ash blonde hair fell over his face. He pushed them back, not even attempting to touch the food. He wanted to tell his mother that he wanted nothing more but to return to the tranquillity of the countryside, but James knew that the probability of that happening was so low that his mother would allow horses to prance around in the drawing room than allow him to leave London.

And that was all because of his sister, Alice. It was early spring, and the Season was just beginning. Every ambitious mama would come to London with her daughters, thrusting them in the path of eligible bachelors. Also, they came for the juicy gossip that the Season provided, of news that happened between the time that the last one ended and this one began. Like all mamas, his mother brought his sister for the Season. This was Alice's third one and somehow, she had not been snatched by an eligible man.

James knew that more than anything, it was his duty to get Alice married this time. He was now Viscount Hamilton and not just James. At the thought of the responsibility that came with the name, he wished that his brother was still alive. His brother was trained by their father for this role. The perfect gentleman now lay in rest at their countryside home, just near their father.

"Duty," he muttered under his breath, raising his head to stare at the white high vaulted ceilings and the ornate chandelier that hung from it.

James never liked the word when he was at home. Instead, he preferred it when he was rolling in mud, serving his country, and making sure that everyone was safe. At least it was better than sleeping in till midday and visiting clubs. More than a decade ago, James wanted that life. The one his brother had.

He wished to fill his belly with whiskey, to laugh with friends as they talked about horses and bets, boxing rings, and champions. More than anything, James wanted to be acknowledged by his father. All his life, they poured their love and attention on Ned, his older brother and James felt like a third wheel in his own home.

But he had found his friends while he was away from home. Second-born sons like him recounted how much trouble they gave their families because they wanted to be noticed. And after spending so much time fighting and drinking ale, James began to see the world in another light. Being a second-born son did not mean that he was not noticed. It meant that he was free to do whatever he wanted. Unburdened by responsibility, James could soar, travel, fall in love and grow.

"James, is there something on your mind?" his mother asked, not raising her nose from the sheet in her hand. "Perhaps you would like to talk about it?"

Alice snickered, her bright green eyes shimmering in the sunlight that came from the window. She was the youngest in the family, and James could recall what a petulant child she'd been. Alice had always been interested in art, spending her time in the small gallery, her hand splattered with watercolor. Even now, he could see her fingers trailing listlessly on the white cloth that covered the table as if she were trying to paint something.

"Nothing Mother," he replied, looking out the window and unconsciously rubbing his hand on his cheek.

The scar.

His hand passed over the crater on his face, and it sent a tingling through his body. A wide mark ran down the side of his face, twisting down the cords of his neck, and disappeared under the dark green cravat. James had looked in the mirror that morning, knowing that society would never accept him as he was.

The jagged pink scar was a reminder that no matter how elegantly dressed he was, the ton would never accept him as one of their own. It was a mark of honor among soldiers, evidence that he fought tooth and nail to serve his country. But for people who fed on gossip and scandal, who viewed riches with envy, his scar only made him seem like a reprobate.

"Brother," Alice said for the first time that morning, "perhaps we should go to the park? I am tired of sitting in this house all day."

James shook his head. There were too many people in London. Those that would see him and balk, cowering because of the hideous scar on his face. No, he would rather remain in the house, loitering away as he counted the days till they could return to the countryside.

"I am sure Mother would like to show you around," he replied softly. "I have not been in London for many years, and I do not want us to get lost."

"Nonsense," his mother retorted, holding up the sheet of paper. "You are the Viscount now, James. Viscount Hamilton. And your sister is in your care. You must see that she is matched by the end of the Season. If you do not take a walk with her, how do you expect to do that?"

Duty or not, James did not want to venture past the wrought-iron gates that were crawling with bougainvillea. In the house, even the servants stared at him like he was some stranger, merely staying for a few weeks before departing. Little did they know that he was here to stay.

"Say, Mother, You are the best at matchmaking and all things involved," he replied in a bit to flatter his mother. Flattery made Marcia bluster and smile. "And it is tradition for mamas to accompany their daughters, as I would merely scare them off."

Alice watched them with interest, a smile playing on her lips. James noticed it and bit down on his lips to stop himself from smiling. In his mind, he hoped that his mother would take the bait and accompany Alice to the park instead.

His mother sighed dramatically, dropping the silverware ceremoniously on the napkins. "You should consider putting yourself out too, James. The Season's balls should start in a few weeks or less, and eligible debutantes would come swarming. You can find a wife for yourself."

"What?" James exclaimed, utterly bewildered by his mother's words. "Get married?"

Lady Hamilton nodded subtly. "Do not look at me as if my words are new. You are the Viscount now, James. It is your responsibility to make sure that the family name continues. Do you want some evil cousin to encroach on everything your father built?"

James could not believe his ears. Ever since he returned, his mother had not said much to him except to remind him that he was now the man of the house and he had a responsibility. A duty to uphold. He knew how titles moved from father to son, but he had never imagined getting married. Not with the scar on his face.

When he did not talk, his mother continued. "Even the gossip sheets are talking about you, James. This one says that: Viscount Hamilton has returned from serving his country and all the ambitious mamas are out to take him for themselves. With such fortune, it is no wonder why everyone wants him. And after hearing tales of his charm and form, every debutante will be out for him. But will the viscount succumb to matrimonial bliss this Season? You know what they say about eligible bachelors. The more they make themselves unavailable, the harder the mamas go after them. It is -

"Mother, please stop," he said, unable to hide his embarrassment. "Any more and my ears will bleed."

Alice laughed. "His charm and form? The author of that sheet must be talking about someone else."

James bristled at his sister's words. Before the scar, he was known as the cunning of the two brothers, strikingly handsome with his ash blonde hair and piercing blue eyes he got from his mother. Also, he was a consummate sportsman, riding the horses on hot sun-beaten tracks and bringing them to victory. The ingenious streak still resided somewhere within him even though he knew that when he left to join the war, that part of him stayed back at home and was now covered in cobwebs.

"Everyone knows that you have returned to take over as the viscount," his mother said. "Getting married is the next thing to do. Have children and continue the Hamilton name."

James sat there, unblinking. He wanted to argue, to tell his mother that he would never marry. At least, not with the jagged scar on his face. But from a young age, he knew that his mother loved arguments, even more than juicy gossip. He uttered not a single word, remaining silent for the remainder of breakfast.

No matter how he tried to look at it, James was well aware that he had lost his charm. No lady would be willing to marry a gentleman with scars. With that in mind, James knew that the issue of marriage would die down soon. And he would be able to go back to his quiet life in the countryside.

# Chapter 1

Genevieve was happy. At least she knew that much about herself. It was the start of a new season and that meant new dresses from the modiste, boring lectures from her mother about how a proper lady should behave before a gentleman, juicy gossip from her friends and spending time with them, and most of all, new books from her father. It was the latter that she enjoyed the most.

She ran a slim finger over her fuchsia dress, the silk swimming between her fingers. It was part of the collection from the last Season, the very gown she had worn to the Vauxhall ball - the biggest of the Season. She had been the center of admiration, her gown shimmering gold under the soft lights that lit up the open-air ball.

But even with all of the dresses, Genevieve was still unmarried even with the many offers of marriage she had received. As the daughter of the Duke of Montmere, her father had high standards that most of the eligible bachelors of the last Season did not meet. Even though it saddened her that a few of her friends were already married, she knew that her father's judgment was right. He wanted something great for her and she would gladly wait until the right gentleman crossed her paths.

"This Season is going to be the best one yet," Elizabeth said, carefully dropping the porcelain teacup on the newly waxed oak table in the drawing room. "I have heard that bachelors would be coming from all over the countryside."

Kitty waved her off with a slight gesture, rolling her eyes dramatically. "Elizabeth, you said the same thing last Season. And look at where we are. Still unmarried."

Genevieve laughed lightly, her voice carrying on the light spring breeze that wafted in through the windows. Her friends were the absolute best, and all of them made their debut in society last Season. The Queen even named Genevieve the diamond of the Season - the most honorable title a lady could have for the entire Season. With that, many men visited and brought gifts, flowers from all over London, and many more even offered proposals.

She hoped that this Season would be the same. All of them

did. Staying unmarried for two seasons might be disastrous as the new bachelors would be younger. And that might be cause for trouble.

"We were not named diamond of the first water," Elizabeth countered in a smooth contralto. "Even Genevieve is not complaining."

"I am," she said suddenly, surprised by the firmness of her voice. Then she loosened up a bit. "I mean, last Season had wonderful gentlemen. Remember Lord Montgomery? He bought almost all of the florists to deliver to my house every morning."

Kitty laughed. "And the dismay on his face when His Grace rejected his proposal? I heard he moved to the country this Season and will not be here till the end of the Season."

"End of the Season?" Elizabeth chimed in. "Who comes to London after the Season has ended?"

Kitty shrugged. "I have no idea. Maybe bachelors that want to visit White's. But then, they should have enough whiskey in the countryside."

"I wonder how they drink that vile poison," Genevieve said and let out a strangled cry. "Every drop is regrettable."

They all laughed and went back to sipping tea and helping themselves to the delicious sponge cake that Genevieve's house was known for.

"But really," Kitty spoke up, breaking the silence that stretched between them, "this Season must not pass us by like the last. I do not want to become an old maid by next Season."

Elizabeth laughed. "We are still very young, but Kitty is right. We are not getting any younger. By next Season, I will be one and twenty."

"For this reason, we have to make plans," Genevieve said. "For the audacious mamas, finding the perfect husband seems to be child's play."

"And yet, we seem to find it so difficult. But we are different from the insipid wallflowers of last Season. Imagine last Season when Estella wore an old cream dress to the Vauxhall ball."

Genevieve stifled a laugh. Estella was far older than them and had seen more Seasons than they had. Everyone knew that Estella hung around at balls, moving around in the dark and leaving even before the dance was over. Almost no one knew her because she kept to herself, and now, she was married. To a fine gentleman by the name of Lord Ferguson.

"She is married now, Kitty," she replied, watching the dust motes dance in the rays of sunlight. "I know that there must be something wrong."

Kitty smiled. "And what might that be?"

"I do not know yet," Genevieve replied with a small but fulfilling smile on her face as she brought a small sheet of paper from her reticule.

She had been working on it after last Season's disappointment, and the pages were smudged with ink. Nevertheless, she showed the paper to her friends with an aura of superiority around her. Genevieve had thought about the previous Season when her family retired to Stonehaven, their estate in the countryside. All the gentlemen that turned to her had certain qualities that her father did not approve of.

So Genevieve had written down all of those qualities, hoping to find someone that might have none of them. But in the end, she knew that it would be close to impossible. Instead, she wrote all the qualities she expected in the perfect husband, and she was determined to find a man that matched all of those qualities this Season.

"This here," she said, holding the paper out to her friends, "is my ticket for this year's Season."

Kitty read it over, her eyes were wide with incredulity. "Blue eyes?"

Genevieve shrugged, pouting slightly. "Blue eyes are rare but beautiful, Kitty. I mean, have you ever looked at someone with those dazzling eyes? I wish to be looked upon by them, is all."

Elizabeth groaned. "And that stands at the top of the list? Surely, eyes are not the only prerequisite to marrying ."

"Of course not," Genevieve stated, stifling the mirth that bubbled in her throat. "But I fancy those bright eyes. Think of a summer night when you just lay awake and gaze into your husband's eyes. Pools of blue, just pulling you towards them."

Kitty laughed again - a high-pitched one that rang through the room. "Those books are responsible for your fantasy, Genny. This is the first time that you do not have that impossibly thin nose of yours between the pages of a book."

Genevieve smiled, taking Kitty's words as a compliment. "If you say so, then my father is responsible. He does not want to have a daughter whose mind is only on watercolours and gossip."

They continued to talk about books for a while, about how Genevieve sometimes got lost between the pages of a book, caressing the spine and immersing herself so much that she sometimes forgot the world around her. While they spoke, Genevieve wondered how people could not like books.

For her, the pages were a means of transport, taking her to worlds unknown. Through the leathery smell of the pages, Genevieve found a whole new world waiting for her. The sumptuous letters slowly fed into her mind, and from when she laid her hands on her first book, she found a new kind of intimacy. One that not even friends could provide. On sunny days, she got lost in the cavalcade of healthy spines and yellowed pages. In winter, she lay under heavy sheets and eiderdown, staring at the pages until she drifted away into sleep.

It was why she found gossip sheets to be exceptionally boring. One time, Kitty had asked her why she did not read them with such joy as the rest of the ton did. But Genevieve had just waved her away with an excuse. Deep down, she did not see the relevance of the words on those silly pamphlets. None of the authors provided the same feeling as real books did, how they helped her journey into worlds unknown.

"I went about the previous Season the wrong way," Genevieve said, shifting on the ornate brocade chair and feeling the silk of her dress rustle under her. "There were several offers for a proposal, but every one of them was turned down by my father."

"We know all about that," Elizabeth said softly. "Finding a solution to this problem is of utmost importance if you do not want to remain unmarried this Season."

She let out a sigh. "This time, I will not only put my needs but also my family's as well. A perfect gentleman that will not only be eye-catching but dutiful as well. Nothing like Lord Hastings who was nothing but talk."

They all laughed at the joke before Genevieve continued. "Before he even makes calls to our home, I will present his name to my father and mother first for their approval. That way, things can go more smoothly than ever."

"Knowing you, whichever gentleman you decide to marry will have to be nothing less than perfect," Elizabeth drawled, shifting away from the rays of sunlight.

Genevieve nodded with a sly smile on her face. She had inherited that trait from her parents, and it was a habit of hers that her friends found to be quite frustrating. She liked perfection and would do whatever it took to attain it. Genevieve was fastidiously neat, even without the help of her lady's maid, Jenny. Even when she learned to paint and dance, she perfected both arts to the point of exhaustion.

Last Season, her quadrilles and waltz impressed all the gentlemen that had the privilege to dance with her. Some stepped on her feet, but she hid her horror with a small smile and when the music finally stopped, she got away from them at the first opportunity. And now, Genevieve craved perfection. More than anything else. She wanted the man she would spend the rest of her life with to be compatible with her if not perfect. So much so that she made a long list of the qualities she wanted. And among them was the ability to dance well and read just as much.

Genevieve had seen some marriages crumble and she did not want to become a stranger in her own home. She knew in her heart that if she found the perfect gentleman, their marriage would be perfect as well. They would not just be husband and wife, but friends and lovers. Till death do them part.

"Making a list is not too much work," she said, gesturing to Elizabeth. "I got this list down in less than a fortnight!"

"You must know what you want," Kitty put in, eyes shining. "But I agree with you, Genevieve. Making a list is a very good idea."

"Enough about these lists," Elizabeth groaned, ringing for some cakes. "This is the start of a wonderful Season and we will begin by attending dinner at my parents' manor this evening."

"Nobody told me about that," Genevieve moaned in distress. "The modiste has not finished my dresses yet."

Elizabeth smiled - a sly one that pulled her lips into a wicked look. "You still have all your dresses from last Season. Or have you given them out so fast?"

Genevieve shook her head. All her clothes were carefully arranged in a closet, and she hoped to give them out to anyone who needed them by the end of the Season. She did it every year, helping the maids and usually letting Jenny pick her choices first.

"They are still gathering dust in the closet by the window. I have not opened that box in months," she replied painfully.

Kitty spoke softly. "Then you will have to make do with one of the dresses. Elizabeth has invited us two weeks prior. It would not be fair to cancel now, would it?"

Genevieve grumbled in her seat and reached for the book on the small stool. She wound her fingers around the spine, carefully tracing the stenciled edges. "Fine. I will have Jenny pick out the best one for tonight. And I will have to go to Madame Bellatrix's shop for my dresses. They should have been completed since the previous week."

"In as much as we share your grievances, we all know that Madame Bellatrix makes dresses for most of the ton. Seeing as this is the start of a new Season, she has her hands full. I visited her just a few days ago as well."

Genevieve let out a sigh. "Then she should get more apprentices to help. At least, that will make her work a bit faster."

Elizabeth stared at them as they bickered before sliding into the conversation. "Before I forget, a distant cousin of mine will be attending as well. He is from my maternal side, and his name is Viscount Hamilton."

Kitty's eyes widened. "Viscount Hamilton from Lady P's gossip sheets? The eligible bachelor with the wit and charm?"

"Lady P has it all wrong," Elizabeth stated, her voice hoarse. "From what I heard, he is a recluse and prefers to spend all of his time in the countryside."

"Even with all of his charm?" Genevieve asked.

Elizabeth rolled her eyes. "Mother told me that he has a scar on the right side of his face. A scar he got from the war. Maybe that is why he spends all of his time alone."

Kitty sighed heavily, the sound echoing through the now silent drawing room. "We should applaud him for his great service to all of London. It cannot be easy to fight a war much less carry a heavy scar on your face for the rest of your life."

Genevieve nodded wistfully, her heart going out to the young man she had never met. As she sipped the last of her tea, she wondered how he must feel. Perhaps like a bird with broken wings, unable to fly. She pushed the thoughts out of her mind, wanting to make her heart light again.

"We must leave now," Kitty said, looking outside the window. "Time is really moving fast. My house is quite far away, and I have to prepare for dinner. I just hope that Dorothy has picked out a dress for me."

The sun was receding into the horizon now, lighting up the skies in pink and orange, and gold. Time had run out fast, just like it usually did when Genevieve was having a conversation with her best friends or when she was reading a book. She looked out the window, hoping there was a little more time for her to snatch a few words from the pages of the book beside her.

"Mother needs me to help show the viscount around the house," Elizabeth said, getting to her feet and smoothing the creases in her dress. Then she turned to Genevieve. "Do not be late."

She laughed and bade them goodbye, watching their figures fade and slip out the large door. With a sigh, she ambled up the stairs with the book in hand, unable to read a single word before the day ran into darkness and starlight.

# Chapter 2

James wished that the night would never come. It came too soon, hanging over his head like an overcast cloud, covering the whole world in a darkness so tight that it made his head swim. Suddenly, he wished for the blue-grey dusk of London afternoons, the color and hazy light that came through the slim windows of the Arlington manor. Without thinking, he caressed his right cheek, his hand running over the long scar that marred his face.

The night hung like a threat all day, with every passing hour reminding James of the ordeal he would have to face at dinner. His mother had been invited to the Arlington manor earlier in the week for a dinner, one to commemorate the start of a new Season. When the letter came in a yellow scented envelope with an ornate wax seal, James wanted to tear it up into little chunks and toss them into the flames in his study.

But his mother, Lady Hamilton, sat there while he cut the wax open, watching him carefully as he tried to read the contents. At the sight of the name, Marcia - his mother's name - James cringed at the informality that he knew stemmed from more than three decades of friendship and familiarity. He could recall that the whole family used to go there but they had been kids then, running up and down the stairs, trying to see who wouldn't be out of breath. Eventually, they would lay on the carpet at the bottom of the grand staircase, their eyes gazing at the vaulted ceilings and hearts pounding in their chests.

He shook himself awake, separating his thoughts from his reality. James tended to mix them now, the hours crashing into themselves as days crawled slowly past. He indulged himself with whatever book he could find in the library - a way to get past the reclusive lifestyle that had been chosen for him by his circumstances.

There used to be a time when James did not have to go through the laborious chore of straightening his cravats or pulling his breeches. For a long time, he did not even wear cravats. He considered them a waste of accessories, the thin slips of fabric around the necks of gentlemen. Instead, he preferred the breezy feeling of an open shirt, of riding through the fields until his hair was matted to his scalp with sweat and he had to feed his horse some sugar cubes for the journey back home.

James wished for that life once more, wishing he could just reach out of the window and pull it back to himself. But years had passed since he had ridden a horse for the fun of it. Even when he returned to take over his brother's position as Viscount Hamilton, he only rode horses because his mother asked him to stretch his legs. They seemed stressful on his tailbone now, each jolt of animal muscle sending pain through his spine.

Soft hands pulled at the fabric of his coat in a bid to straighten it, and slowly, a smile came to his face. When he arrived back home, a valet had been assigned to him by the name of Peter and soon, James had found a friend. They talked about the war and James' memories, of the acrid smell of gunpowder and the noise that came with gunshots.

He found it easier to speak with Peter than anyone else in the house except his sister. Sometimes, they just exchanged a few words and Peter left him to attend to the affairs of the house. Checking accounts, appending signatures on bills, and making sure that the family was staying afloat even with the exorbitant expenses of buying new dresses and attending functions. Other times, they spoke till the clock struck twelve, the candlelight burning low as he faced the window.

"Is this okay, my lord?" Peter asked in his usual gruff voice, straightening the fawn-colored waistcoat and its gold buttons.

James replied with a simple 'yes' before allowing the real world to fade all around him again. He wondered why he was getting dressed so much when this was supposed to be a family dinner. At least, that was what his mother said and a part of him wondered if she said those words just to alleviate his worries about socializing with members of the ton.

He knew that he was not yet ready to meet other people that were not part of his family. The doctor had told James that he would get used to the scar with time, but he still felt it tingle and itch every other day, and sometimes it became raw with pain. He silently hoped that today was not one of those days where he would keel over in pain, clawing at his face to make the pain stop.

After the scar that forever changed his life, James had not met other people except his mother and sister, the maids that roamed around the home, the valet, the butler, and a few other people in the house. Not one of them was an outsider. They all knew him before the scarring - the handsome young man he was turning out to be. Even though James did not want to meet other people, he knew that sooner or later, he would have to socialize. At least for Alice's sake.

Barely following the sound of Peter's low humming, his thoughts drifted away to memories of his brother, Ned. Even though their father treated them differently, James and his brother were still best of friends. They looked almost alike, with their ash blonde hair they inherited from their father, but while James had striking blue eyes, Ned's was a grey like steel but soft and filled with happiness. They went everywhere together and talked about everything.

When the letter arrived at the camp that Ned was gone, James did not know how to feel. At first, it was terrible anger, a tidal wave of horror that threatened to wash him off the face of the world. His brother had died of an illness after spending so many weeks in bed and paraded by physicians. The anger became sickening grief, one that kept him down for days on end. Even now, at the thought of Ned, he blinked back tears.

James knew that if Ned were still alive, he could decide to skip the dinner entirely and settle down at White's, filling his lungs with cigar smoke or warming his belly with whiskey. For a long time now, James disliked the vapidity of family dinners, sometimes speaking rather pugnaciously in a bid to excuse himself from his father's watchful gaze. Ned would shoulder all of the responsibility as he had always done, shifting the attention to himself so that James could slither away unnoticed.

Ned's words were usually smooth and kind, enthralling people the moment his mouth opened. It worked on their father every time James did something wrong like gambling with almost everything he had in the boxing ring and losing it all. Ned would apologize and their father's heart would soften. James was always the troublemaker, and he did all of this to make his father acknowledge him. He was tired of being treated like a spare; like he did not matter. Like he was not worthy of their father's time and attention.

At the time, it hurt so much that James sometimes resorted

to doing something much worse than he had done before. When he decided to leave the house for the battlefield, he could see the secret happiness on his father's face. And for that, he resolved to never come back home. But here he was, his cravat straightened by Peter's expert hands.

"Hope this is not too tight," the valet said, pulling the cravat fabric a little stronger.

James spared himself a glance in the mirror, amazed at Peter's efficiency and skill at making him look presentable. Now, he donned a white inner shirt made from linen, the material soft on his body. A proper waistcoat followed, brown and dark, a memento of his brother. The tailcoat was ivory, double-breasted, and fitting him perfectly. The cravat was a matching brown, contrasting with the paleness of the coat. In more ways than one, James finally looked less like the troublemaker he was and more like a viscount.

Until he turned the side of his face. The candlelight illuminated the scar, making him look ghostly. His skin was a bit tanned, courtesy of spending his time under the countryside sun, sinking himself into the books from the large library. But the scar was pink, a jarring contrast to his face and he rubbed it slightly, tracing the path it took from his face and down to his neck. All of his fears started rushing in, further worsened by Peter's histrionic gestures when he straightened the back of his coat.

"Leave it," he said, walking away from the mirror and watching the muted twilight blue of the sky.

"Yes, my lord," Peter said, leaving the room at once.

In the silence that ensued, James sank into the chair by the open windows, watching the curtains flutter in the light spring breeze. He was Viscount Hamilton now, a position he never wanted. One that only Ned was the perfect fit. His brother was handsome and intelligent, striking in a way that responsibility and duty came easily to him. But he was different. A troublemaker at heart, following the twist and tumbles as life led him on.

A soft sigh escaped his lips after he took in a mouthful of air. "I am Viscount Hamilton."

The words were an affirmation of his position, his way of telling himself that he had a family to take care of and a responsibility to tend to. He knew that wallowing in self-pity and trying to deceive himself would only amount to nothing. The mantle was on him now, and there was no other choice.

It was Alice's third Season, and as the viscount and head of the house, he had a duty to make sure that his sister was matched by the time the Season came to an end. Also, he wanted her to be happy. Just like his parents were. Even though their father did not like him very much because of his incorrigible knack for mischief, he loved their mother.

Sometimes, they would sit in the belvedere overlooking the messy tangle of trees, talking to one another like old friends. James would watch them from afar, his gaze held by the tranquility and affection that his parents showed one another. When his father passed away, it had been a horrible time for the family. Mother locked herself in her room, slowly turning into a shell of who she used to be. Her skin turned a sickly gray, eyes sunken from starvation. And James was grateful that Ned was there. To comfort her and bring her from the brink of nothingness.

He had a duty too, to make sure that Alice was well taken care of. That she was happy with whomever she decided to spend the rest of her life with. James wanted her to be loved and at the thought, he felt an unfurling inside him as he touched his scar once more.

With a grunt, he flipped his pocket watch closed and roused from his seat by the window.

*** 

For the first time in a while, James felt safe among people. He was in the drawing room at the Arlington Manor, engaged in a conversation with the Marquess of Arlington, Lord William Arlington. James was never one for conversation but when the older man spoke to him, he was soon carried away.

Lord Arlington talked about himself with gusto, determined to tell James everything he needed to know, all at once. At first, it was frightening, but it later occurred to James that Lord Arlington probably never had any company except older men like himself. He spoke of his days in Eton and Oxford, surrounded by people who thought of him as brilliant. Lord Arlington talked with an uncluttered simplicity, one that James enjoyed as much as reading a book.

"How are you enjoying your stay in London?" he asked, dabbing at his face with an embroidered handkerchief even though the windows were open.

"Very well," James replied courteously and with a smile that he hoped did not make him look as roguish as he saw himself in the mirror. "Although I quite prefer the quiet of the countryside to the bustle of these streets."

Lord Arlington laughed, one that made his pudgy face even pudgier. "Don't we all? This Season has been uncharacteristically dull. If not for my wife dragging me all the way here, I would just continue enjoying my stay at Venus Hall."

James smiled easily. "We both have a responsibility to make sure that your daughter in your case and my sister in mine, get matched this Season."

"As much as I would like to speak about the marriage mart, I have to change the subject for my wife will intrude on our conversation if she hears about such a topic," he replied, patting his greying hair. "Perhaps we should talk about business?"

James nodded, thankful that the topic was about to change. For one, talking about marriage seemed to bring back his mother's comment some days ago. And even though he did not voice his disinterest that day, a part of him wished that he had.

"I heard that you are in the tea trade now, having moved away from your father's heavy wheat production," Lord Arlington said, sinking deeper into the velvet-covered furniture. "How has it been?"

"Flour is still an important consumable in homes, but tea seems to have a lesser workload and higher profit," James stated proudly. "But the better the quality of the tea leaves, the tastier and more expensive it becomes."

"Ah, I see. I once heard from a scholar that tea is better than wine for it causeth not intoxication. And I must agree that he is quite right. But the importation of tea is quite expensive don't you think? Your mind must be running helter-skelter to put such investment on such a lucrative enterprise."

James looked at Lord Arlington's slackened jaw and waved away his distrust. "Importing is rather expensive just as you have stated. Instead, I purchased a large piece of land in Cornwall when I returned to take over my position as the head of the house. The weather has been favorable and I have hired plenty of peasant farmers to tend to the land and grow the leaves. By the end of the Season, we should have our tea primarily in all of London."

"Magnificent!" Lord Arlington exclaimed. "I would never have thought that we could grow tea here in England."

"It is not a straightforward process," he said, "but it is very possible. And I have some connections with the Queen. When the first batch of tea leaves is harvested, they will go straight to her. A kind of incentive to allow me to distribute to all of England. And maybe with time, we can be looking at exports."

"Surely, we will need to talk about this more. Perhaps I can even invest in this trade and tell all of my friends about it. I am quite sure that Lord Snell and Lord Mallen will see the tea trade as a profitable venture. Even His Grace, the Duke of Montmere would be surely interested."

James smiled at Lord Arlington, his heart giddy with excitement. "We should meet over drinks then. I will make sure to send for someone to bring a sample from the first batch."

Lord Arlington replied, but around James, the world was fading away again. He looked to his left and saw his mother speaking animatedly with Lady Arlington - whom she called Cynthia when they were together - and Alice had stalked off to the window, staring at empty space.

James smiled at Lord Arlington, knowing that he made a great decision by coming over to their house for dinner. He would never have thought that the marquess would want to become an investor in his business. James knew that having Lord Arlington on his side would strengthen his business, and his jovial demeanor was sure to bring more potential investors that would make his trade even better.

He had stopped producing wheat a few weeks after his brother had passed away, noting that it used too much manpower and after paying off his workers, the profits were usually low. His mother had told him to increase the land used in producing wheat so that they could harvest more, but James knew that meant they would have to hire more people, and the profits would remain the same.

When he told the workers to cease production, his mother

had been aghast. But James had a plan, one that would increase their profits tenfold without so much need for menial labour. From removing a huge amount of money to purchase the land in Cornwall, to importing seeds and planting, it had not been easy for James. Filling his late brother's shoes while starting from scratch was tough, but he proved that he was tougher.

Starting out, he needed a few investors so that he could get money to get more seeds and start bigger, but everyone he met did not trust him because of the hideous scar on his face. To them, he had been involved in some illicit and unsavoury business and not defending his country from invaders. But now, things were finally looking up.

Lord Arlington and his friends had large fortunes, and James could use their connections to reach more people. The people of London imported tea, but now, he would be the only producer in the whole country. It was a massive untapped market, and he hoped that everything would work out just the way he planned.

"My lord," the butler bowed beside Lord Arlington, his voice ringing through the room. "His Grace, the Duke of Montmere, Her Grace, the Duchess of Montmere, and Lady Genevieve have graced us with their presence."

Lord Arlington shot to his feet and James did the same, curious as to who Duke and Duchess were. He had never seen them in his life, and he watched as everyone straightened themselves out. With a smile on his face, he hoped that the night would not become a disaster because he had not been expecting visitors as he thought this would be a family dinner.

# Chapter 3

Genevieve was at least glad that something had gone well that night. She wanted to lose herself between the pages of a book, to read about real love that happened down in Messina, of the deepest relationships that wrung people's hearts and took their souls to places that their hearts would have never imagined.

After Kitty and Elizabeth left, Genevieve had spent the remaining minutes of dusk in the library's alcove, staring at the muted violet sky, inhaling the leathery scent of paper, and looking through the list of qualities she wanted in a gentleman. More than blue eyes, she wanted to marry someone who was her friend. Who she could talk about prose and poetry to for hours without either of them getting tired, who would not give tepid comments and instead be more interested than she was. Like her parents, she wanted a gentleman without debts, who was kind and enigmatic, full of charm but also someone who liked to stir things up.

As the stars winked into existence, her mother had come to call her from the library, talking about how Jenny had almost searched the whole house for her. Genevieve laughed at her mother's jokes, wondering how she could still have that light-heartedness for so many years. Most women were turned bitter by marriages, but her mother still floated around the house, smiling and waving. At that moment, Genevieve decided that she wanted a gentleman that could make her happy for the rest of her life.

Most times, Genevieve thought of a simple life in a manor in the countryside, a crab apple tree by her window so that petals would drift in from time to time when the summer breeze blew. She yearned for a transparent commitment, of how her parents wore their unrequited love like a heavy cologne. She wanted to spend her winter weeks by the fireplace, huddled closely with books in their hands that they would talk about until darkness fell.

When she returned to the room, Jenny had laid out an amber gown that just arrived from Madame Bellatrix. It came with an apologetic note, informing Genevieve that the rest of her dresses would be ready by the end of the week. But none of that mattered as the evening gown before her was so beautiful that her gaze was fixed on it for several minutes.

The amber silk seemed to shimmer in the candlelight, turning gold when Jenny brought the light close. Tulle crisscrossed the slight indecent bosom, compensating for the low neckline. The inside was soft lace, almost floating on her skin as Jenny helped her into the dress. All the anger at Madame Bellatrix for the delay dissipated when Jenny combed the tangles out of her blonde hair and matted rose oil into the strands. It took a while to get the stubborn curls straight, and Jenny piled them atop her head, the light making her hair look like spun gold. A smile crossed her face as she twirled in the mirror, the jade earrings gleaming on her lobes.

As they stepped into the Arlington manor, Genevieve was surprised at the amount of redecorating that had been done. She had been close friends with Elizabeth since they were children, and her father was a close friend of the Marquess, Lord William Arlington as they had gone to Oxford together. Genevieve and Elizabeth had played in the manor, running around and hanging on the balustrades to see who could hold themselves longer.

But now, bougainvillea wrapped around the polished silver gates as their carriage rode in, and the light scent of flowers filled the air. It was so much different from the smell of sugar and baked goodies back in the day, but mesmerizing nonetheless. Where there was a lawn, a hedge of roses grew, their petals dark and silvery under the wan moonlight.

"William sure spends a fortune to make his house look even better every Season," her father said gruffly, his eyes almost glowing in the darkness.

She heard her mother's airy laugh. "I am sure Lady Arlington is responsible for the changes. Which man pays heed to flower arrangements when they have glasses of alcohol and business to talk about?"

"True," her father commented. "I hope he has some fascinating new enterprise that I can invest in this Season. William has a good eye for thriving businesses."

"I have heard some gossip that he is the only debt-free marquess in all of London. His fortune even rivals that of Plowden."

Plowden was a Duke well known to members of the ton as irresponsible. He was young, and some even called him immature. He spent most of his time with a flask in his jacket, half drunk, and visiting gambling dens whenever he could. He had friends that were just as silly and vain as he was, all of them wasting their money and letting time just slip by.

Genevieve had been quiet the whole journey, saddened by her inability to bring a book along on the carriage. Her father had talked endlessly about how the event was just a small dinner of friends and family, not some excuse to slip away to the perch on a brocade chair and lose herself in the words again. But at the thought of spending time with Elizabeth, she brightened.

"William!" Genevieve's father, the Duke of Montmere said boisterously, his voice ringing through the room. "When last have we met?"

"I believe we met last autumn, Your Grace," Lord Arlington replied with a smile of his own, bowing.

"You do not need those formalities now, William," the Duke said. "Remember when I poured fire ants in your bed because you would not share your pillows?"

"Of course!" he replied, a wicked smile on his face that made everyone laugh. "How could I ever forget that? I had pock marks all over my skin from the onslaught. You could have just bought your pillow from the Covered Market a few yards from Buckingham Palace. But you decided to spend all of your allowances at the gentleman's club."

Genevieve watched as her parents fell into easy conversations with the hosts. Elizabeth's mother, Lady Arlington had greeted her and turned to her mother to talk. They had been friends since they were little, often fighting when they were younger. But now, they were closer than ever, both of them sharing gossip and trying to match their children to honorable gentlemen.

At the thought of marriage Genevieve recalled the list laying on the small desk by the window in her room, held down by the ink well and paper cutter she had gotten the last time she went with Elizabeth and Kitty to buy a few things from the stalls on Piccadilly. She hoped that this Season would at least be favorable, and she might find someone who checked all of those boxes in her heart.

"Your Grace, I want you to meet someone," Lord Arlington said rather suddenly, his voice like thunder but tinged with joy. "This is Viscountess Hamilton, a distant family member. And here is her daughter, Miss Hamilton."

Genevieve looked at the two women, both of them exuding elegance. But while the older woman's own was imposing, Miss Hamilton's was subtle. With her delicate face and dark blue dress, she looked like she wanted to melt into the shadows. Her demeanor was slight and friendly, blonde hair spilling down the sides of her shoulders. She looked disinterested in the conversation and her eyes darted too many times toward the painting in the corner of the drawing room. One that screamed of youthful exuberance in shades of teal and burnt orange, incorporating sepia tones into vivid landscape colours. It made Genevieve want to be friends with her at once.

"Your Grace," Miss Hamilton said and curtseyed, carefully lifting the sides of her gown. "It is my pleasure to finally meet you. Lord Arlington has spoken of your gestures of goodwill."

Genevieve watched her father laugh - one that bordered on amusement. "William is merely trying to tone down the list of his sufferings in Oxford. If I begin counting, dawn would soon arrive and I will not be through at all."

Everyone laughed, and through all the amusement and conversation, Genevieve heard it. A low voice tinged with amusement, a soft baritone that made her suddenly feel aware of herself.

"Your Grace," Lady Arlington said softly as she bobbed a curtsy. "I am sure William has forgotten to tell you about Viscount Hamilton. He is merely carried away by his goal for retribution."

And that was when Genevieve saw him. It irked her that she did not notice him earlier because he was not one that eyes passed over without second or third glances. He was tall, towering above her father whom many considered to be tall indeed. From where she stood, his hair looked grey, with bright undertones that reminded Genevieve of a field of wheat in the summer. His grey hair did not reek of age as other men did. Instead, the locks were healthy and quite long, curling around the sides of his ear.

"Your Grace," he said, his baritone echoing through the now silent room and making Genevieve shudder. "It is such an honour to meet you."

Genevieve watched as Viscount Hamilton greeted her father and placed a kiss on her mother's gloved hand. When he turned to her, she froze, her emotions overpowering her ability to think clearly. She was soon overwhelmed, her breath coming out in soft gasps.

She held his eyes with her own, her belly simmering with a lot of emotions that she had no words to describe them. His eyes were pale and dark all at once, and it filled her with a sort of longing that she had never felt before. The startling blue of his eyes filled her vision and reminded her of the ocean, the crests and troughs as the blue waters faded into the horizon. When he turned his head to the side as a gesture of wonder, Genevieve saw his eyes darken and glow, and for a moment, they were frozen in time.

"Lady Genevieve," he breathed, the air from his mouth warm against her skin.

It thawed her, bringing her back to life. She watched him bow slightly to her, his hair falling over his eyes. When he straightened, Genevieve saw the scar on his face, pink and raw in the golden light from the chandelier. She had the strangest urge to reach out and touch it, to cradle his sculpted face in her hands and banish the scar away.

"I am most pleased to make your acquaintance," he said, eyes wild with humour.

She suspected a deep intelligence in the manner of which he spoke, each word enunciated and sweet, sending a tingle through her back. Genevieve tried to nod, but every movement felt strained and her body struggled against her will. In the end, Genevieve brought herself under control and smiled as he drifted away again, slowly melting towards the darkness. Even as he stood there, broad shoulders dressed in an ivory tailcoat, he had an aura of mystery that Genevieve wanted to unfold. She was suddenly caught up in a whirl of excitement watching him speak with her father with ease, a certain fluidity that almost no one else had. Not even Lord Arlington.

Turning away from him, Genevieve felt her heart race. The stark blue of his eyes was forever etched into her mind and she wanted to get lost in the ocean, in the dark color of his hair - a mix of grey and white and gold. It made her think of winter. Of the grey skies and dusting of snow on the streets and flowers, of lush warmth and dreams of heat.

Elizabeth was a few strides away, leaning casually against

the cornflower blue wallpaper of the drawing room and staring at her. Genevieve felt her cheeks flush with embarrassment and she turned away at once, many thoughts rummaging through her mind. She wondered if her friend had seen the way she looked at the viscount, or had felt the same rush she felt as well. It was all so confusing for Genevieve, so much so that she felt charmed and helpless.

"Dinner is ready," the butler said from the arched entryway that led to the drawing-room, his voice hoarse as if he had been speaking all day long.

In a short minute, everyone was seated at the table, watching as the food was being served. By some intervention, the viscount was sitting opposite her now, his eyes glowering. The smell of roast duck did nothing to alleviate the growing worry in her mind. She wished that someone would at least break the uncomfortable silence, to indulge her in a conversation.

"Have you seen the gossip sheets?" Lady Arlington said, her voice rising through the heavy silence. "I heard that the Vauxhall Gardens will be the most memorable this Season. The Queen has been making preparations for a ball there."

Her mother, the duchess, laughed slightly. "I need to know who tells these authors about the gossip. They seem to be reporting the same thing these days and milk us of our five pennies every week."

"Such an exorbitant fee for gossip," Lord Arlington said, helping himself to more peas and roast duck. "What does anyone need the gossip for? Is it not better to just watch things unfold?"

Lady Arlington scoffed. "Let things unfold? Being caught by surprise is mostly a result of scandal. It is better that we know these things before they happen."

The Duke laughed. "Women and their gossip sheets. I am sure that the maids have a pile of paper to throw out soon from all the sheets we have purchased last Season."

"I heard that a lot was going on in London last Season," Lady Hamilton chimed in. "A lot of scandals to go around. And particularly at the Vauxhall Gardens."

"More reason why the Queen is hosting it this Season," Elizabeth intoned. "This season, there would be no masquerade ball at Vauxhall to hide anyone's identities."

Lord Arlington laughed. "Finally, less money will be spent this Season. Some masks cost quite a fortune!"

"But there are more events this Season," Genevieve spoke for the first time, her voice tense. "Lady Pemberton is hosting a ball this year as well. Apparently, I heard that Lord Pemberton's business with the mines in Georgia is flourishing."

"It will never hold meaning to me why people waste the returns of their business investments on hosting balls," the Duke said. "It is just a show, nothing else."

The Duchess shook her head. "It is showing the ton how blessed they are. More dresses and hosting balls equal the ability to pay a handsome dowry. And that means more offers of proposals from whoever is hosting the ball."

"The Suttons are not excluding themselves this Season," Lady Arlington said. "A ball will be hosted at their manor, and I heard that Lady Sutton wants to do her best to outshine the Queen. Little does she know that the Queen holds all of the fortune."

They all laughed, and Genevieve watched the viscount from the corner of her eye. He had not said a word all evening, his mouth only opening when he tipped the fork towards his lips.

"More gentlemen for the taking this Season," the duchess announced. "I hope that my Genevieve gets married soon enough. I do not want her to spend another Season in that house."

A blush crept on her cheeks. "Mother!"

"The same goes for Elizabeth and Alice," Lady Hamilton said. "I read in some sheet that most men are returning from their sojourns this Season. It is only wise that we help them take advantage of the Season. By making them new dresses and letting them attend balls, we further increase their chances."

"The Countess of Kenford is hosting a soiree at their manor tomorrow," Lady Arlington said. "And I heard the juiciest news that the Earl of Kenford will be in attendance!"

Genevieve tried to put on a smile. Almost every unmarried lady in London knew about the Earl of Kenford. He had traveled a few years ago, claiming that he wanted to see the rest of the world. Ever since, he only returned to London once a year to see his mother, the Countess. Genevieve had heard from Kitty that the earl only came in the dead of night and left before dawn. He was every lady's dream gentleman, hers included.

From all the news she heard, the Earl of Kenford should be nine and twenty, and ready for marriage by the society's standards. She had seen him once, and he was handsome with a shock of sandy-colored hair and skin so pale and smooth that it looked like milk. Genevieve had seen him from afar, so she could not recognize the color of his eyes, but she hoped that they were blue. Like the viscount.

"Everyone knows the Countess and the Queen are close friends. Surely, her soiree is going to be lavish," the duchess said. "A grand event to officially open the Season."

"I have to tell Madame Bellatrix to be on schedule. There is no way any of our daughters are missing this soiree. If the earl will be in attendance, I am sure that many gentlemen will be too," Lady Hamilton said with a soft smile on her weathered face.

As they discussed the rest of the events for the Season, Genevieve could not help but wonder if the Earl of Kenford would meet her expectations. She recalled her list of qualities on the desk, saying each one under her breath.

"Blue eyes, he must be a graceful dancer, handsome and honorable, a man with a kind heart, and someone willing to talk to me about books and literature."

She stopped muttering, and her eyes hovered over the viscount's. He did not seem to notice her, and Genevieve stared long and hard at his scar, wondering if there was a way to help him get rid of it.

# Chapter 4

James was unsmiling, still slightly bewildered that he had no idea about the plans made for dinner beforehand. Usually, he did not like being around people anymore, knowing that they would only stare at him like he was some sort of exotic animal, strange with an air that told him he did not belong to the crowd.

So he sought his fun inside the confines of their home in the countryside, eating scones and drinking tea while looking outside the window at the garden, his eyes partially on the book laid out before him. It was a drastic change from the man he used to be. Wild, turbulent, and interesting. James was nothing like the perfect gentleman. Instead, he was quite the opposite.

Where his brother, Ned was calm, James was loud and boisterous, filled with boundless optimism that even thinking about it now was astonishing. The change had come with the scar on his face, the jagged pinkness contrasting with his sun-tanned skin and making it stick out even more.

So when everyone started talking about the Season's events at the dinner table, James kept mute, quietly helping himself to the food. He was at least glad that his mother did not drag him into the conversation for he knew nothing about the latest news and events, or how the Vauxhall gardens was home to the finest balls ever hosted in London's history.

Since he returned home, James had been doing more listening than talking except when he was in Alice's company and she was explaining the difference between ochre and burnt sienna or sea green and Baltic. Even now at the dinner table, he listened with rapt attention at the peals of laughter, at the words that floated seamlessly through the small crowd present. Of the Pembertons and Suttons, of the Queen's decision to host this Season's Vauxhall ball, of everything else.

He registered the names in his mind, hoping to send letters to them about investing in the tea trade. No one but him and now Lord Arlington knew how lucrative the business was and he was sure that soon enough, the Duke of Montmere would know all about it. Tea was a perennial plant that did not do well in the muted skies and rainy days of London. But with effective research,

James would be able to make a name for himself in a few months. And unlike wheat, tea could last for years without the need to ever plant more. He was sure that the next generation would benefit from the tea trade as more time went by.

James helped himself to more roast duck, astonished by the inherent taste of the meat. Perhaps it was because he had spent so much time eating from cans that he did not quite recall how great the kitchen maids made their food. A small sigh left his lips as his thoughts drifted, carried on the wings of heavy conversations and loud laughs.

Slowly, James began to think of other things. As usual, his mind did not dwell in one place for a long time and soon, he began to think of the reception he got from the Montmeres. The Duke was cheerful, even more friendly than Lord Arlington had portrayed him. From the small conversation they had, James found out that Lord Arlington and the Duke had been friends for quite a while, and they spent their latter days in Oxford, taking their time to bet on boxing matches and sometimes sabotaging each other.

The Duchess was a slight woman, covered with bloodless elegance. Her complexion was well-preserved and full of health, and her fair hair was held up in an elaborate fashion like other ladies of the ton. Her eyes were a criss-cross between blue and green, shimmering as he greeted her. She had a type of amusement about James, and her smile was dazzling as he straightened himself from his bow.

And then, there was Lady Genevieve. The look on her face was of shock as if she had seen something that she was not supposed to. At first, James could not determine if he should be offended because of the strange way she regarded him. In the end, he decided to remain neutral, seeing as he was used to people looking at him that way. He was tempted to bring a hand to the scar, to rub it out of existence. If only he could.

She was speaking now, talking about how Lady Pemberton wanted to host a ball in a bid to show off their newfound wealth from the mines. He was surprised that she did speak after all. When he greeted her, she just stared at him with empty eyes and nodded. The shock on her face soon melded into something else, an embarrassment that came with disgust.

James couldn't blame her for looking at him that way.

People were often disgusted by his appearance and it was the main reason he decided to stay in the countryside, to have his fill of whiskey whenever he wanted, to get himself lost in the tempestuous waters of life. It was better than being stared at as he got down from his carriage and walked into the gentleman's club.

He was sad that even gentlemen like him stared long and hard as if trying to enmesh an image of him into their minds so they could turn the other way whenever they saw him coming. The thought reminded James of his older brother and his handsome appearance.

When Ned turned four and twenty, the gossip sheets spoke much about his charm and good looks, his fortune, and his title as Viscount Hamilton. For generations, the ton knew that a great fortune was associated with the Hamilton family name. All the mamas thrust their daughters in Ned's path, eager to let their daughters become Viscountess. At balls, the ladies flocked around him, and James recalled one time that a lady swooned, hoping to be caught by Ned but was instead saved from falling by another gentleman. She left the man and came back to meet Ned, batting her eyelashes.

They talked about it for weeks, laughing in the study. Now, James knew that while some of the young ladies wanted to be viscountess, many were even more interested in his good looks and charm than his title. They wanted him to be their husband so they could show him off to the rest of the ton and make other ladies green with envy.

James was handsome too, having stared in the mirror a lot while he was younger. But Ned was more handsome, even bordering on beautiful. Where James' face was manly and defined, Ned's face was slim, almost cherubic. He had large doe-eyes and an intoxicating smile. Delicate cheekbones accentuated the softness of his face, and his jawline was straight, reminding James of all the old roman statues they used to have in the gardens.

And now, there was a huge scar on his face. He knew that most ladies would run away from him because of his appearance. When he stared in the mirror earlier, he looked ghoulish and evil, and James had come to a realization that titles were never enough. Among the ton, appearances did matter, and Genevieve had looked at him, frozen like he was less human.

He dropped his silverware gently on the linen napkin, already having his fill for the night. James already decided that Genevieve was also as superficial as the rest of the ton, people who stared at him like nothing else about him mattered except the scar on his face.

"Lord Hamilton," the Duke called, and before he could say anything, James interrupted him.

"Please, Your Grace, call me James."

"Ah!" he exclaimed softly. "Only if you decide to call me Edmund."

James nodded with a smile on his face. The Duke was a humble man, one who did not care about titles.

"I heard that you served as a soldier," Edmund said, voice filled with concern. "I want you to know that the whole country is forever indebted to the likes of people like you."

James heard the pity in Edmund's voice and he cringed even though he tried his best not to show it. He had heard people tell him that over the years. Of how much he must have suffered, rolling through mud and eating non-quality food. Of how the soldiers suffered from anxiety and tried to distance themselves from life in general even after they came back retired.

But he wanted none of the pity. He became a soldier of his own accord, walking up to the conscription center in his dark blue coat and bright silk cravat, his eyes filled with determination. James still recalled that moment like it was just yesterday, standing before the officer and asking his name to be put down. The older man had asked him if he was drunk or trying to play tricks on them. Only commoners registered of their own free will because soldiers were paid handsomely and all the payment went to their families.

Seeing someone from such a fortunate family disoriented the officer. He continued to stare at James as he picked up the quill and dipped it in ink, his mind made up as his delicate handwriting was scrawled on the paper. He had found friends on the battlefield, people he trusted with his life. Even now, he recalled all the times someone saved him from certain death, shielding him from gun pellets with their bodies.

Sitting in that room and eating roast duck made his heart twist with betrayal. James had betrayed his comrades when he came back to his life of comfort, knowing that they would never have the same opportunity he did.

"It is an honour to serve this great country," James managed without sounding forced.

Composing himself proved to be difficult but he managed it anyway, clenching his fists under the table until his nails dug into his palm. The memories of war still assailed him and at some point, James almost believed that he smelled gunpowder in the air.

"He has sacrificed so much by going to join the war effort," he heard his mother say, holding her hand over her chest in mock horror, and James almost lost his composure. "I was terrified when I heard of his conscription, Your Grace."

Edmund smiled. "He knows what he signed up for. And he is a good man for following through and protecting the well-being of this country. We are forever in his debt."

James stomped his feet, his calm performance slipping through his fingers. It was almost noiseless, but a heavy silence fell over the room. It looked like everyone heard it. Or rather, they felt it. James wanted to yell that it was his choice to become a soldier. That he hated being the second son, his life meaning nothing to his father. For the first time in his life, James knew that his life meant something to his comrades.

The silence stretched for minutes, tense and heavy as soon as it descended. James kept a watchful eye, his muscles straining. He wanted the conversation to start again so that he could melt peacefully into the background of it all, unbothered by whatever topic they were speaking of.

"Gentlemen," Edmund said finally, dabbing at his mouth with a napkin to remove the stripes of gravy on his chin. "May we retire to the parlour and leave the women to their antics? We have business to talk about."

James was relieved at once, the tension easing from his veins. Everyone resumed talking when he, the Duke, and Lord Arlington roused from their seats. As they left, he heard them talk about how they would all visit the modiste's shop to get their dresses in time for the soiree. He sighed at the ostentation of it all, knowing that he wanted something more than accompanying the women in his life - his mother and sister - to balls and social events.

On getting to the parlour, James took a seat by the window where he watched the night skies and the twinkling stars. He wished to return home to his study so he could write about how the clouds scudded across the star-ridden sky, about the bliss of silence and the anguish that came with pity. James rubbed the scar on his face lightly and felt it tingle.

"I just heard of this prospective business investment," the Duke said, his eyes gleaming with satisfaction as he balanced himself on the brocade chair close to the fireplace. "Tea trade?"

Lord Arlington spoke quickly. "It was an overview. I intended for James to explain the details. But it is expected to be highly lucrative."

And so, James explained everything about his new business. Buying the huge piece of land in Cornwall, importing seeds from across the ocean for planting, the need for less labor and higher profit margins, and every other thing he could remember.

"I can say that I am certainly impressed. You planned all of this on your own?" the Duke asked, astonishment written over his features.

James gave him a small smile. "Yes, Your Grace. I noticed how much tea was valued in London and decided to singlehandedly create a market for it."

"You see what I told you about the viscount's ingenuity? I would have never thought of something like that!" Lord Arlington exclaimed.

The Duke nodded, putting his finger on the cleft in his chin. "Ingenious indeed! The whole of London would only be able to buy tea from you. A marvelous plan! And I already intend to put a fortune on the trade!"

"Thank you, Your Grace. I also believe that the more, the merrier," James replied, his heart quickening in anticipation.

"Never worry about that. I will inform all of my acquaintances about this! You can be sure to buy more pieces of land in Cornwall. Even Lord Pemberton would want to invest."

"What about the mines in Georgia? Surely -

James was interrupted by Lord Arlington. "Anyone with the right stand in business will understand your position, Lord Hamilton. As for the mines, there are many jewelers in London. There is less profit if you consider how much the gemstones are sold."

And they talked on and on about the business and forging

new connections to ensure the betterment of the trade. James watched them speak, gaining useful insight about running a large-scale business like that. His father had never bothered to teach him because of Ned, and he needed it now more than ever.

Also, he was glad that throughout the entire conversation, the issue of the war or stomped feet was not brought up. In more ways than one, he was glad to heed his mother's advice to visit the Arlington manor.

# Chapter 5

Genevieve had been sitting by the open window for a long time now, her body still wrapped with the sheets she pulled away from the bed. The warm breeze, heavy with the scent of roses filled the room and assaulted her nose.

Usually, she sat there with a book she got from the library the day before, reading the words and flying seamlessly through the pages. But this time, there was no book on her desk. Instead, her mind was wrought with thoughts. And not of gold and rust from the book she read last, but of dazzling blue eyes that reminded her of the ocean and warm summer skies in the countryside.

Her face was flushed with embarrassment even though she was alone, at the thought of Elizabeth noticing her reaction towards the viscount. Genevieve berated herself for freezing before him, his soft gaze holding her own. And when he spoke to her, the calmness of his voice surged a tempest within her, one that she had only read in books.

"Be still," Genevieve muttered to herself, eyes closed as the breeze warmed her skin.

It was hard not to think about the viscount. With his hair like grey threads intertwined with white and gold, blue eyes so tranquil that they held her gaze, a mysterious air surrounding him that made her want to know him, his broad shoulders straining against the coat, his soft smile as he regarded her.

The thoughts consumed her wholly, drenching every other thought. Genevieve let the sheets slip from her shoulders, to see if the warmth of the breeze might pull her away from the thoughts of Viscount Hamilton. Not only was he handsome, but humble as well, asking her father to call him his given name and not by title. And when he said her father's name in return, it was accompanied by a strange familiarity and newfound friendship, only serving to bolster her father's boundless energy and cheery demeanor.

She picked her list from under the inkwell, turning the paper in her hands. There were a few splotches here and there but none of those mattered. What she wanted to see were the words on the page; words she had written whilst she was happy and optimistic about what the next Season might hold.

Genevieve held the list to the light, watching with careful fascination as the light flooded the paper, rays of healthy sunlight bursting through the words. She turned it down again, reading the words on the paper. Qualities she wanted the perfect gentleman to have. The gentleman of her dreams. She had always wondered afterward why she had written the list. Doubts clouded her mind from time to time, a growing restlessness as the days crawled past that she would never find the perfect gentleman.

"Blue eyes," she said softly, closing her eyes once more to revel in those two simple words.

No matter how simple they felt, Genevieve knew in her mind that finding a gentleman with that quality would be hard in London. She had seen gentlemen with washed-out blue eyes like Lord Candlethorpe, with blue-grey like His Grace, the Duke of Hastings, or the same blue-green eyes that she inherited from her father. But the viscount's eyes were a dazzling blue, so startling yet amazing, Lucent pools that shone under the light like liquid gold, that darkened when he regarded her. Genevieve had never seen eyes like that. And at that moment when she saw him, she knew that those were the kind of eyes she wanted in a gentleman.

Throughout the rest of the dinner at Arlington Manor, she expected him to say something to her. Perhaps to start a conversation about his time as a soldier but when her father talked about it, he stomped his feet on the ground. It was quiet, but she felt it. She had a feeling that he was disinterested in talking about the horrors of the battlefield and also about the upcoming social events.

When they all talked about the soiree that the Countess of Kenford was hosting, the viscount did not utter a single word. He lifted his silverware laden with food to his mouth, eyes soft and swirling. From their short stay at the manor, Genevieve had the feeling that he was a rather quiet person, preferring to keep to himself than associate. Elizabeth had told them that he was a recluse, and now, she believed it as well.

Her thoughts drifted back to his eyes and mannerisms, the gentle way in which her name rolled off his tongue. Frozen was not the word she could use to describe the way she felt. Genevieve felt more lost than frozen, wandering into his dark blue eyes. Viscount

Hamilton fit the first quality on her list easily, capturing her mind with just a gaze.

But there was the problem with his face. The jagged scar stood out on his right cheek, almost spreading towards his nose and running down to the side of his neck, and disappearing under the high collar of his coat. At dinner, she imagined how his face would look without the pink scar marring his skin. He would look more handsome than most gentlemen, with his defined jawline and aquiline nose, and broad shoulders that boasted a strength she could not fathom.

Even with all of those marvelous qualities, Genevieve could still see the scar in her thoughts, standing out on the burnished skin of his face, taking away all of his good looks and confidence he must have had before all of it. She thought about how he must have gotten the scar, the pain of the wound flaring in the cold camps during the war. She shuddered, mind wistful at everything the viscount must have gone through before coming home.

"My lady," Jenny's high-pitched voice that resembled a screech pierced through the comfortable silence that had already woven around Genevieve.

She tucked the paper under the inkwell once more, the page folded to hide her words. Jenny's presence was great that morning- a distraction to take her mind away from the viscount and his suffering.

But even as Jenny led her to the bath, she could not take her mind away from the startling blue pools of mystery.

***

Descending the stairs, Genevieve lifted the hem of her morning dress. It was an old one, a gauzy dress made from emerald green satin that shimmered when she stepped into the sunlight. The puffy sleeves and flowing lines clung to her body, and it was the evening gown she wore for the last soiree of the previous Season.

With the dress, Genevieve had earned a lot of compliments from gentlemen and ladies alike with the latter group asking for her modiste. She had brought Madame Bellatrix to the limelight, showing off all the dresses she had made. Now, she hoped that the modiste would bring her clothes in on time and not disappoint her.

It was time for breakfast, and Genevieve felt her stomach scream. Blood rose to her cheeks at the sound and she hurried down the marble staircase to the large dining room in her home. Jenny was still upstairs in her room, helping her to pick the best outfit for the soiree that she would be attending at high noon.

She smiled as she walked into the room and her father was smiling as well. Genevieve placed a kiss on his cheek and sat beside him, and her mother looked elegant as always in a violet dress that accentuated the color of her eyes.

"I want you to extend an invite to Lord Hamilton," the Duke said after a small sip of tea, gesturing to his wife. "I need him to grace our upcoming dinner ball."

The Duchess' face was one of incredulity. "What?"

"Sybil, I am sure that you heard me the first time. Invite the viscount and the rest of his family to the ball."

Genevieve's lips curled into a smile at the banter. Her father never called her mother by name except when he wanted something. But he said it with such affection that it made her blush. But when she saw a frown form on her mother's face, Genevieve knew immediately that something was wrong.

"I have invited other Dukes and Duchesses to the ball," Sybil replied, her normally mellifluous voice rising a note higher. "Invites have been sent out at the start of the Season to the most prominent members of the ton. Even Lord Arundel did not get such an invite."

"Then send an invite to Viscount Hamilton specially. I want to get to know him better at the ball."

"You seem to forget that we have appearances to uphold, Edmund. I will have no -

The Duke sighed dramatically, burying his face in his hands. "You can forget about appearances, Sybil. Who cares about appearances if you have no money to back it all up? I am seeking to invest in his trade, and it is a very promising one."

Genevieve watched her mother's frown deepen. "Fortune? We have enough -

"I want to go into business with the viscount, Sybil. Send an invite to him as soon as possible," the Duke said with an air of finality and left the table.

Genevieve watched her father amble away, leaving her

mother frowning at the table.

***

The music room was airy and bright thanks to the large arched windows on the topmost floor of the manor. A grand old apple tree was growing by the window, letting its scent into the house. When her father brought the deed to their countryside manor, Genevieve had been more than happy to choose a room by the window and another for her music room.

She had finished learning from a tutor for years now, and most times, Genevieve even created her songs on the pianoforte. She was good at it, better than all of her friends by a wide margin, and every morning, she played perfect tunes. Just like her mother wanted.

Usually, Genevieve loved the fruity smell of the apple tree, reveling in it as she played whatever song came to her mind. But today, she smelled nothing. No particular song came to her mind as she was still worried that her parents might get into their very first argument. She had watched as her mother spoke about the viscount and rage surged within Genevieve, raw and unforgiving as it spurned from the pit of her stomach.

Never in Genevieve's life had she ever imagined that her mother would say such words. Just the night before, she smiled at the viscount and said such kind words. Even when they bade the family their goodbyes, her mother greeted the viscount separately, thanking him for keeping her father company while the women talked about the Season's glamour and events.

But now, the unbridled bitterness and hatred in her words stung Genevieve like a sack of needles. She knew that her mother was a perfectionist, fussing over the flower arrangements and making sure that the parquetry was polished to its finest. She complained over the smallest dust motes floating near the windows, the grime on the floors at the back of the manor, and almost every other thing. Genevieve was genuinely surprised that her mother did not complain about the Arlington manor and its colorful spaces.

The word 'appearances' still echoed in her mind as she set her hands to the keys of the pianoforte. Slowly, she let her hands dance like they had done a hundred times before, playing a classical chord that she had spent almost three months trying to

43

learn. It lacked all the fluidity she normally had and soon, the song suddenly went a note higher than usual.

"You have played this song a hundred times over, Genevieve," her mother chided, her nostrils flaring the way they usually did when she was annoyed. "Remember that you will be entertaining our guests with the pianoforte in our upcoming ball. It is your chance to get the gentlemen to notice you."

Genevieve bit back her words, pushing them down her throat from whence they came. She nodded glumly, wondering whether her mother finally sent the invitation or had disregarded her father's words entirely.

"I am sorry Mother," was all Genevieve said, trying to bring her mind to focus on the keys.

"Your pianoforte needs more practice," her mother stated dramatically, dropping the small sheet of printed paper in her hand. "I will schedule a few more lessons for you before the ball. We will do nothing less than perfection."

Genevieve nodded and went back to playing the pianoforte, wondering whether the viscount would attend their ball or not.

# Chapter 6

James was staring at the cup of tea before him, admiring the new teacup pieces his mother purchased when they came to London. He was awash in the hazy glow of the morning light, his hair slightly ruffled by his long walk through the garden by dawn.

He had been unable to sleep, and he spent the whole night staring at the high ceilings and rolling in the eiderdown. His mind was a mess, and he tried to push out the bad memories in his head. Memories that he buried back on the battlefield when he received the letter that contained the sad news of his brother's passing and informing him of the vacant viscount position that would now be his.

Reluctance and grief had filled him when he read his mother's delicate handwriting, a gentle cursive that had been developed over years of training and propriety. Even as he lay down on his bed after the exhaustion of being around the Duke and Lord Arlington, the grief snuck up on him again, entangling him in a snare so complicated that he was unable to extricate himself from it.

Even as he stared at the cup of tea that was growing cold and the small bowl laden with biscuits, the grief still gnawed at his heart. A pang of guilt that came from assuming the position that was Ned's. In another world, he dreamed of his brother being alive, challenging him to grueling horse races that made their tailbones hurt even with the soft leather of the saddles. But in this world, Ned was gone and James was filled with a longing for something he could never have. His brother's laugh and gentle smiles, his pleasing demeanor which brought the young ladies of the ton a running.

It had been quite a while since Ned passed from an illness, but the grief did not dim with time like people whispered to him at the funeral. James found out that grief was volatile, just like the fleeting smell of roses in the summer back at the estate in the countryside. Sometimes, it hung over his head like a winter cloud, soaking through every bone in his body and pulling him down with a weight that he could not bear. Guilt crashed into grief, so abrupt that he did not even have time to think.

Such was what happened the night before. His mother had made a spectacle of his service at the dinner table with the Duke of Montmere and the rest of the guests, praising him like he had done such a priceless, great service. He wanted to tell them to instead praise those that died in those camps of illnesses, those who crawled in the mud and grime, their noses filled with gunpowder. And those who died in battle, their faces forever etched into his mind. But he kept mute, stomping his feet instead.

"Should I not have stomped it?" he asked himself quietly, his voice low enough that only he could hear it.

His eyes were tired now, drooping from the lack of sleep. James jerked his head up to face the sun so that the heat might rouse him from his dozing and it did. He was back to the world, suddenly grounded in reality that his teeth grated against one another.

"You have travelled such a great distance," he said to Deverel, his man of affairs.

Deverel was a stout man with a wisp of moustache that hung limply from the sides of his face. Like always, his spectacles were fogged over by his breath, and the limp in his step had improved.

He bowed, tiny wisps of hair curling on his balding head. "I have brought good news, my lord. The estate is in good order. Some more maids have been put in place to take charge of maintenance and I have also hired a gardener to take care of the vast lawn, hedges, and gardens."

James nodded with a smile, not paying as much attention as he should. His mind was somewhere far away, his thoughts slightly covered in grief. With the thought of his brother on his mind, James had avoided his mother all night. Not even once did he engage her in a conversation on their way back to the manor. When they got home, he stormed up the stairs to his room, bolting the door behind him. And then he felt a tear slip past his eye and drop to his cheek. The scarred one.

Deverel's words sank in. "You hired more maids?"

"With the amount of staff on the estate, maintaining it is not easy, and the housekeeper came to me about needing some more help. It is in your best interests that they were hired, my lord."

James let out a sigh and crumpled into the chair, fatigue sweeping through him. "What about the farm in Cornwall? I suppose you had a good look before coming to London."

Deverel nodded, removing his spectacles to reveal murky grey eyes. He cleaned it with a soft silk cloth and put it back on his nose. "Yes, my lord. In a few more months, the farm will be bursting with tea leaves! Planting and growing are right on schedule and the value just seems to be rising every day."

Finally, there was something worth truly smiling for. James recalled how his mother chastised him for closing the large farmland in the countryside that produced wheat and sold off the mills to a Duke who wanted to purchase it at a very exorbitant price. Even far more than it was worth. James had happily taken the fortune and bought land in Cornwall instead. His mother had complained endlessly about how the wheat farm was a family legacy and it was wrong of him to have let it go without telling her.

It had almost caused an argument, one that she would have lost but James quietly retreated to his study and drew plans for the new tea plantation. He was once tutored in the art of drawing plans when he was younger and the knowledge came in handy. Irrigation systems were soon laid out, and James used the remainder of the money to purchase the seeds and everything else needed to start.

"Before the Season ends," Deverel said, eyes squinting, "we would be the only producers of tea in London. All we need now are strong connections to push out the produced batches to all members of the ton. That way, we can sell for higher prices and make huge profits by the end of the year."

Deverel talked like he was yelling and it made James laugh at his enthusiasm. He was thankful that Ned had replaced the former man of affairs with Deverel. Not once since he returned did Deverel give him any bit of trouble. Even more, he proffered excellent advice.

"I am meeting the Duke and a few of his acquaintances for drinks soon," James said to Deverel. "Potential investors, you might say. They will be responsible for letting the rest of the ton know about our tea trade. I hope to make use of the women's talk to spread the news."

"A fine idea!" Deverel exclaimed. "If we make good business connections, we can maintain all the assets. Including the estate and the tea plantation."

James nodded in agreement with the ghost of a smile on his face. "Thank you for your time. You must have travelled all night. The guest room has been prepared down the hall. You may leave by high noon and return to the estate in time for dinner."

Deverel flashed him a toothy grin as he bowed. "Thank you, my lord."

James watched his man of affairs limp away from the drawing room with an accomplished look on his face. He felt the older man's happiness, the prospect of building something worthwhile that would be worth a huge fortune was enough of an accomplishment. But that did not take away the fatigue from his body. He needed a nap, and he shifted in his seat, angling his head away from the bright rays of sunlight streaming through the windows.

"James?" he heard his mother's voice call out to him from his sleep.

He groaned and turned away even more just as he had done when he was just a boy and his mother pulled his ear for ruining the rugs with his muddy feet. Only this time, he was unhappy with his mother. She had tricked him into going to the Arlington manor, promising that no other guests would arrive only for the Duke and the rest of his family to arrive. He knew that it was no mere coincidence, and he saw the slight smile on his mother's face when they walked in.

But he forgave her for that when the Duke began talking about business when they retired to the parlor. The unwanted attention that she attracted at the dinner table sat in his head nevertheless. He had seen the looks of dismay and light horror on their faces as he stomped his feet on the ground. If only his mother had not brought it up, the evening would have ended better than it did.

For some reason, James was also angry with the Duke's daughter. On their journey from the Arlington manor, the look of shock and disgust on her face when he greeted her remained on his mind. He was used to other people looking away from his face, but she stared at him long enough for him to notice and then her face crumpled afterwards when she saw the scar. For a long time now, he disliked superficial people. It was the reason why he hated balls and soirees and preferred the quiet of his own home. But he reminded himself that he was doing all of this for his sister, Alice. This Season could not end without him helping her to choose a virtuous gentleman as her husband.

"I know that you are not asleep," she said and took a seat on the plush sofa, her gown rustling. "Your tea remains untouched, and I know very well how much you like tea. Sometimes, I am baffled by your preference for tea over whiskey."

James liked the taste of whiskey: bitter, strong, and warm as it went down his throat. But he liked the sweetness of tea, the slightness of it as it reminded him of the time when Ned advised him to take it more.

"You were never like your father," she continued when he said nothing. "He always had a bottle of whiskey or rum wherever he went. Even in the study sometimes despite my rebuke."

He imagined the picture in his mind's eye: His mother screeching and grabbing the bottle, his father pouncing from his position on the chair and running after her. It made him smile, but he suppressed it and made his breathing even and deep - a way to avoid his mother.

"You cannot avoid me forever James," she said with an air of finality, tapping him. "Unlike Alice, you will remain in this house with me. I think it is best for us to settle our differences now."

James turned in the seat, pushing the words away. Throwing a tantrum was childish, but he wanted his mother to leave him alone. More than that, he craved the nothingness of sleep, the flippant dreams, and the feel of his sheets on his skin. He even tried to sleep as his mother talked, but her words kept him awake.

"You seem to forget that you have a duty to this household, James. You need to produce an heir for I will not watch some beastly cousin come from anywhere and take this title away from us. Not while I am still alive!"

It was an admonishment, a warning that James wished was not true. He understood how titles were passed from father to son, and a part of him craved companionship. True love that was deep, that searched beneath the surface. Past his scars and form and into his mind. But he could never have it.

James knew that his mother wanted him to get married and produce an heir. Even more than anything, she would want him to marry a lady of good standing in the society, someone with a sufficiently large dowry that would only add to their fortune. But James could not see himself with someone like that. Not with the horrid scar that marred his face forever.

He heard his mother's voice soften with emotion. "Even old men in their darker age, get married and bear heirs. You keep hiding behind your appearance, using that as an excuse to avoid your responsibility. But you cannot keep hiding forever, James.

"No one was even perturbed in the slightest by your appearance last night at the Arlington manor. Even the duchess received your greetings warmly with a smile on her face. I cannot keep chastising you forever, James. You need to take charge of this household."

His anger was brought to a boil by his mother's words as the Duke's daughter's face flashed in his mind. At that moment, her name came too - a sudden remembrance that was jarring and made his blood boil.

Lady Genevieve.

It was the name of the lady who looked at him like she had seen a ghost. Several people had looked at him that way over the months since his return, but he had not expected Lady Genevieve to sneer at him. The Arlingtons and Montmeres were a tightly knit family, a relationship waxed by years of friendship between the heads of both families. His family was also close with the Arlingtons and even though Lady Genevieve had not seen him before, she could have at least given him the courtesy of hiding her extreme shock and disappointment.

James turned around and his eyes fluttered open. Words played on his lips - words of his defence about his appearance. He wanted to tell his mother about the lady's stares, to inform her that he would never get married and he was contented with that.

"If you would not deem it fit to answer, I wanted to tell you that the Duke and Duchess of Montmere have sent us an invitation for their upcoming dinner ball," she said, her voice laced with happiness. "It is time you stopped hiding behind books and silence and started living. Being a recluse will do neither of us any good."

"Mother - he started but she swiftly interrupted him.

"Now, you want to complain?" she said sternly. "Do not dare bring Alice into this. She is a young lady and will get married soon. And once she does, you will have no more excuses! Alice will make a match this Season and there will be nowhere for you to hide anymore, James."

All the words he wanted to say died in his throat as surprise registered on his face.

"It is nearly time for the Kenford ball," she stated, glancing at the small clock near the porcelain vase. "We all should get ready."

And she left, her lurid skirts billowing behind her.

# Chapter 7

Genevieve watched her mother from the corner of her eyes, keeping her head down to stare at the open page on her lap. It was late afternoon now and Jenny was helping her get ready for their trip to the Kenford manor for the soiree. A part of her wanted to tell her mother that she was no longer interested in going after what happened in the music room and the thoughts that still pervaded her mind.

Knowing her mother, there was no way she would be allowed to stay at home and bury her nose in a book. Not when the finest gentlemen would be available and all the mamas would be trying to make matches for their daughters. Also, there was the juicy rumour going around that the most sought-after bachelor, the Earl of Kenford would be attending the soiree as well.

Her mind was still trying to choose whether or not to go when the lovely image of the earl of Kenford slithered into her mind. That day, she was walking through Hyde Park with Kitty and Elizabeth, all of them complaining about how the Season had been bad and they were going to end up without making a match for the second time.

Genevieve could still see the day like it was just yesterday, the memory clinging to her mind with a blinding luminosity. She was dressed in a lovely muted lavender, the latest dress from Madame Bellatrix. It hugged her body softly with its almost indecorous neckline, accentuating the slim curves of her femininity. Her mother had advised her that day to go to the park with Jenny and Lady Arlington as their chaperones to see if any eligible gentlemen would be wandering in search of their other half.

Kitty was lamenting when the horse shot past them, kicking up clumps of mud and grass. It was only midday, and she could see the lithe figure dressed in gold, arms spread out as if to invite the rays of the sun into his body. His sandy hair shone like a halo, hovering around him and the muted gold of his coat was dazzling. Everything about him reeked of elegance, boundless optimism, and propriety.

That day, Genevieve had been unable to get any sleep. All

she thought about was the earl in his shining clothes, his windswept hair and broad shoulders covered by the elegant clothes he wore. For weeks after, when Genevieve opened a book, he stayed in her mind.

Now, all she could see was the dazzling blue of the viscount's eyes, the softness of his face as he was eating, his mannerisms that contrasted with his roguish face, and his tight smile.

"You should stop reading that book, Genevieve," her mother called out in an irritated tone. "The countess will not expect you to bring a book to the soiree. No one does."

"I know, Mother," she replied, still reading the words on the page. It was poetry, and every time she read it, Genevieve found a new meaning to the lines. "Just a little more and I will return the book to the study."

Her mother sighed and took her seat on the bed. As always, Genevieve found that her mother was perfect. Her hair was done in a way that was elaborate but forced to look normal. A mother-of-pearl comb was in her hair and her eyes had a glow, one that Genevieve recognized. It was a great joy, one that came with assuredly flaunting herself at the soiree and hope to match Genevieve with a gentleman.

"My lady," Jenny said in a small voice. "Is this okay?"

A gasp of n astonishment left her lips as Genevieve stared in the mirror. Her face was a creamy white as usual, unmarred, soft, and supple. Jenny had done her face up with a little talc, and her lips shone from the homemade honey balm that Jenny did every fortnight. Her hair was bright gold, washed over and over, and combed through when she was in the bath. The smell of rosehip oil from the golden strands filled her nose, thick and inviting.

Somehow, Jenny made her eyes glitter - a vibrant blue-green hue, accented with thick golden lashes. Everything about her face was soft and beautiful. From the narrow arch of her brows to the full curve of her upper lip, combined to form a perfection that Genevieve had never thought she could attain.

Her mother's necklace sat at the base of her throat, a jade necklace that brought out the green in her eyes. Genevieve barely recognized her hair. It was in elaborate curls and twists, held together by a peridot comb and pearls. Even Genevieve knew that she was unabashedly beautiful.

A dimple creased her cheek as she smiled and dropped the book on the desk. Her dress was vibrant blue silk, part diaphanous, and made her look like a butterfly. The tulle accented the silk and satin so perfectly that Genevieve could not imagine anyone in the same dress as her. She twirled a little, letting the fabric swish around her and the curls that framed her face bobbed here and there.

"Perfect!" her mother exclaimed, covering her mouth with a gloved hand.

Jenny smiled at the compliment and dabbed at Genevieve's neck with a pad of cotton infused with perfume. A citrusy scent, bright and lush combined with the thick smell of rosehip and became even more wonderful, filling the room with a gentle and heady smell.

"You look beautiful," Jenny said calmly with a smile, fussing over the creases in the fabric that needed straightening.

Genevieve smiled, suddenly excited at the prospect of going to the Countess' soiree. She hoped to meet a gentleman and make her Season, to sway to the music and fill up her dance card before the night ended. Soon, all thought of worry was banished from her mind as she descended the stairs and made her way to the carriage.

*** 

The carriage was waiting just outside their residence when Genevieve got there, and her mother was fussing about how the horses' coats were not polished to perfection. The footman was shivering, his eyes fixated on the ground. Genevieve wanted to say something to save the footman from his fate but decided against it, knowing that her mother would just turn to her and look for any imperfections.

When the lashing ended, Genevieve sat beside her mother, shifting the folds of her dress. For the first time since the ball at Vauxhall, Genevieve felt absolutely beautiful. She looked in the mirror from time to time, observing how much of her mother's features she had. The blonde hair that formed a halo was from her mother; lush and golden locks that Genevieve had grown proud of as the years crawled by.

On her debut into society, most gentlemen complimented

her hair, but mostly, they talked about the peculiarity of her eyes. Of how they were rare, and Genevieve usually found herself blushing when they talked about her. But most of all, she was disappointed in the gentlemen she met last Season. While most of them had fortunes attached to their names and were from prestigious families, Genevieve did not envision herself in a marriage with most of them.

They only talked about how stunning she looked in dresses, and how beautifully she danced. But she expected them to say other things. To ask for her opinion on books, to speak with her about what she wanted. Elizabeth had told her that she should not just talk about books all night long, but Genevieve found herself not wanting to talk about anything else.

At the thought of enduring dances with boring gentlemen, her countenance fell. She turned towards the window, her mind focused on the soft breeze and the evening skies. And wonderful blue eyes. She shook herself from the thoughts of the viscount again, wondering why he kept appearing in her mind.

"You do not look happy," her mother said, breaking the silence with her high-pitched tone. "Surely, any lady would be happy to hear that the Earl of Kenford will be gracing this soiree with his presence."

Genevieve smiled, knowing that the earl's presence was the only reason why she agreed to go for the soiree in the first place. "I am happy. Just a little tired ,is all, mother."

"You should be prepared to dance today," her mother replied, the pearl comb shimmering in the late afternoon light. "If anyone can make a match with the earl, I am sure it will be you, Genevieve."

Genevieve could see that her mother agreed for her to make a match with the earl. She was reminded of her list under the inkwell again about the qualities she wanted in a gentleman. In her heart, she hoped that the earl's sandy-colored hair would be accompanied by dazzling blue eyes. One that was untainted by brown or green.

She noticed that her father had not said anything since the carriage rolled out of their estate and into the streets of London. It meant that he agreed with her mother's decision as well. Last Season, every gentleman she brought forward was not accepted and his silence meant that he held the earl in high esteem. He was of good standing in society and unlike most eligible bachelors, he was not in debt. And according to her mother's ridiculously high standards, the earl was perfect in their eyes.

More than anything else, Genevieve hoped that she would use the soiree as an opportunity to please her parents. Also, she hoped that he was not just perfect for her parents but for her as well. If he had all the qualities she wanted, Genevieve was sure that they would make a match before the Season even went into full swing.

Her thoughts were halted at the same time the carriage came to a stop. The footman announced that they were at Bastion - the Countess' residence. Genevieve's heart went aflutter as different thoughts serenaded her mind. Since that day at Hyde Park, she wanted to see the earl once more.

She was helped down by her mother and the butler soon came to lead them to the line of guests that were waiting to be received by the countess. There, they met the Duke of Suffolk with whom her father entered into a discussion about some tea trade. After Genevieve greeted him, they made their way to the ballroom.

Music floated in the air, and Genevieve was relieved to see Elizabeth and Kitty near the thick draperies in the ballroom. A smile curled on her lips as she excused herself from her mother and went to meet her friends.

"Surely, you have come here to make sure that every gentleman follows you back home with their calling cards," Kitty said lightly. "Madame Bellatrix never makes us any dresses like this."

"She wants to swoop in for the earl," Elizabeth said with a laugh. "As Kitty said, anyone would want to have a dance with you."

Genevieve felt her face heat up from the embarrassment of the compliments. "It is merely a dress. Also, it was not my intention to draw so much attention to myself."

Elizabeth guffawed. "Then you should not look like a lily in the midst of marigolds. Your mother must be pleased to see that you finally look perfect. Did she pick out the dress for you?"

They continued chatting, and for Genevieve, it was a welcome respite from her mother's almost constant nagging and telling her all about the Season's social events and how much responsibility was on her to make a match. When Genevieve was in the library or among her friends, she felt free of those burdens. And she hoped that the man she would marry would give her that same feeling. Like she was soaring through the clouds.

Silence filled the room quite suddenly, taking all of the noise away. Even the clinking of glasses could not be heard. It was so sudden that Genevieve whipped her head around to find the source of this change. But before she did, her heart was already racing at the thought that the silence might be a result of the earl's entry.

Only that when she turned, she peered into dark blue eyes.

***

James was rather tired from the carriage ride. He had been in the study all day, devising plans to expand the tree plantation past Cornwall and perhaps get a large acre in Malborough. He had received word earlier in the day from Lord Arlington that the Dukes of Richmond and Somerset were interested in the business and would like to be potential investors as well.

After the tongue-lashing from his mother, he was happy to receive the news. He sent word to Deverel immediately, telling him about the investment in the hopes that he would start preparing the workers. Also, he had received an invitation from Lord Arlington to come over to White's for drinks with some of his other friends. While James was quite skeptical about meeting all of these new people, the prospect of business took the anxiety away.

When his mother had come to tell him that they were running late for the soiree, James had been inclined to tell her that he would not be going. His mind was on something else entirely, and not some silly ball hosted by the countess so they could show off their wealth and make it an avenue for gossip. But he had no choice. Alice had to make her match this Season, and as his mother had said a few days prior, his sister was his responsibility.

Now, James felt like a mouse in a trap. Since he returned from the battlefield, he had not left the comfort of his home except when he visited the Arlingtons. Even that had been quite an ordeal for him because of the presence of the Duke of Montmere and his family. But the soiree was different. He knew how popular the countess' soirees were, and almost every member of the peerage would be seeking an invite.

James had attended once before he left for the battlefield, and for him, it was not enjoyable. He would have preferred a quiet spot in the park where he could read or banter with his friends. With the horrible scar on his cheek, James was sure that he looked even worse. Yet, his mother's words echoed in his mind. He could not keep using the scar as an excuse. If he wanted potential investors and help Alice to secure an eligible bachelor for a husband, he had to leave his house.

The instant he stepped into the ballroom, James wished that the earth would open up and swallow him. Everyone turned to him, and his fingers curled into his palms. He turned his face away, retreating to the far end of the ballroom with Alice's arm twined in his. James could tell that the sight of him was strange to them, and his scar tingled.

He kept his head down, reminding himself that his sole purpose for honoring the invitation to the soiree was because of Alice. James had a responsibility to fulfil and not even the astonished looks on everyone's faces could stop him from helping his sister.

James wiped the sweat on his face with a small silk cloth that Peter had slipped into his coat pocket before he left the house. Cotton irritated the scar and made it itch so much that it would ruin the rest of the evening. When Peter advised him to change to silk, James was more than grateful.

He smoothed his fawn-colored coat, already searching for ways he could slip away from the watchful eyes of the ton. And that was when he saw her standing in the darkness, her eyes focused on him.

Lady Genevieve.

She stood there in the darkness, her dress shimmering around her. Green and blue folds of fabric wove together around her, and James felt breathless for a moment. Her face was blank and bright, blue-green eyes staring at him. Her hair was unlike anything he had ever seen. Warped and twisted into elaborate holds, each part combed until it shone. From across the room, he suddenly had the strangest yearning to move closer and perhaps weave a finger through the golden locks.

He pulled himself away from the feeling, recalling the look on her face when she came by the Arlington Manor the day before. James saw the disgust in his mind's eye, but his gaze was still held with hers. He wished that she would squeeze her face again so that he could look away, but he stood there, entranced by the tranquility.

For a moment, everything seemed to fade away. His vision darkened and all James could see were the folds of silk and satin clinging to her body, her hair golden under the light from the chandeliers. The gentle curve of her face when she turned her head, her hair held in tight knots and twists, her slender neck as graceful as a swan's. And his breath caught in his throat once more.

James knew that he should look away as their gazes were so intense that it would be deemed scandalous. She was disgusted by the sight of him and he did not want to bring her into a wedding she would never want. Besides, she was superficial like the rest of the ton - a quality he never wanted to see in a lady even if he decided to marry.

He felt the rejection in her look there and then, deep in his bones. So much that a peculiar pain surged in his veins and made his blood boil. James quelled the rage by thinking of a happy memory, one where he did not have a scar and did the exact opposite of whatever his father wanted so that he could gain his attention.

"The Earl of Kenford," someone said from the doorway, and James forced himself to break the stare.

When he turned away, he brought the cloth to his face. James was grateful as he stepped back into the darkness for the arrival of the earl. More than anything, he wanted the people in the ballroom to take their attention away from the scar on his cheek. James did not need to be reminded that he would never be accepted by the ton because of something that was totally out of his control.

The earl's arrival took away the anxiety and pressure building in his veins, and James let out a sigh. One of relief as he melted away from the crowd.

# Chapter 8

"The Duke of York," Kitty was saying with gleaming eyes. "I heard he is quite the catch this Season. What does any of you think?"

Elizabeth snorted beside her. "I heard the Marquis of Briston earns twenty thousand a year. More than any marquis around."

But Genevieve was not listening. While her body was in the ballroom, her mind was far off, swimming in warm thoughts. Her eyes were on Viscount Hamilton - on his grey hair tickled with gold, his fawn-colored tailcoat, ivory shirt, and a cravat of the same brown. She watched him when he stepped into the courtroom with his sister, Alice, in his arm. They looked perfect, light and dark.

Alice was beautiful in her own way - with dark hair that was more black than ash. Her eyes were a startling peridot, pellucid pools of green. In that way, she looked like the viscount. But where her eyes were green, his were a vivid blue, dark and bright, shimmering as they walked to the far end of the courtroom.

"According to Lady Cumberland's sheets, the earl is supposed to be the catch of the Season," Kitty said, her voice laced with happiness. "I hope he attends this soiree."

"I heard that an invitation was sent to every house in London. Except he wishes not to attend, he will be here soon," Elizabeth replied, rolling her eyes as if she could not believe that her friend could talk about making a match with so much happiness in her eyes. "But I heard that his wife passed from influenza just last year. Do you think he will be ready to court just yet?"

Kitty snorted beside Genvieve, jolting her from her strange reverie. "That is entirely his opinion, Elizabeth. But his wife did not produce an heir. And that is what every man wants. Someone to carry his name."

Genevieve nodded listlessly, trying to hide the fact that she was not engaged in the conversation like her friends were. She said a few words from time to time, but she could almost not peel her eyes away from the viscount's face. Under the harsh glow of the chandeliers, the pink scar was an angry shade of red. It contorted the features of him that might have been otherwise great to look at.

She noticed that everyone also had their eyes on him since he stepped into the courtroom. The gossip sheets had spoken about him as an eligible bachelor, but Genevieve knew that most of the ladies would not even care to talk to him now. He had been away for so many years that none of them recalled what he looked like. Or better still, what he used to look like. Now, he had a horrible scar that tore his face in two and made him look less elegant than he would have been.

From where Genevieve stood, she could still feel the mystery around him, the darkness shrouding his frame. Her mind went back to the utter silence he displayed at the Arlington Manor, and she came to the conclusion that the viscount was a man who preferred his own company. Elizabeth had told her that he was a recluse, but Genevieve did not think that he would keep so much to himself. After the greeting, he barely said a word at dinner.

It struck her that the scar on his face could have been responsible for the change in his demeanor. He could have been an amiable person before the situation changed his life. And he could have been handsome as well. His defined jaw, broad shoulders, and aquiline nose told Genevieve that much.

She liked the mystery around him - it was something they shared. Genevieve preferred her own company as well, immersing herself in the pages of books in the library. More often than not, she wanted to sit in the house all day long and inhale the leathery scent of books and paper. But he was not someone that her parents or any member of the peerage would approve of.

"The Earl!" Kitty squealed, the shrill sound cutting through Genevieve's thoughts like a knife.

Her head whipped around at the entryway and a gasp left her lips. Genevieve had always thought that the earl might be just like any other eligible gentleman of the Season but never had she been so wrong. Her breath caught in her throat and it set her stomach aflutter.

The earl was led in by the Countess perched on his arm. She was in a high-collared dress, a deep emerald green dress that shifted in the light. There was a patriarchal air around her elegantly coiffed hair and bloodless elegance. The ruby on her neck pulsed as she walked, and the proud smile on her face said it all. She was a proud mama and was glad for the son she had. And Genevieve could see why.

"Earl of Kenford," Genevieve said under her breath, more like a gasp than words.

He was dressed in the darkest blue coat, and the silver buttons on the tailcoat shone in the light. His sandy-colored hair was light gold, curled and parted on his head. The earl had a pleasant smile on his face, one that melted the hold on Genevieve's heart. Everyone in the room was staring at him now, and none of them could pull their gaze away. He was the most handsome in the room by a long mile, even more than Lord Tompkins, who was adored by all the mamas and their daughters.

The Countess was introducing him to everyone in the room now, and the music continued, riding the air like a soft wave. All Genevieve could see was his tall and athletic form, the thick and curly blond locks that formed a halo on his head. She watched him bow to the Duchess of Gloucester, and she saw him smile. It was by far the most beautiful thing that Genevieve had ever seen.

His lips curled just slightly, pulling the defined lines of his face. From where she stood, she watched the softness in his smile, the fluidity in his gait and composure, the ladies blushing and swooning on all sides.

"Is he not the most good-looking gentleman you have ever set your eyes on?" Elizabeth drawled, clearly in a daze.

Kitty nodded. "I daresay that all the mamas and their fire-breathing daughters would want to have him to themselves. I mean, I want it too."

Genevieve smiled at her friend's words, knowing that every one of them was true. By many standards, he was London's most eligible and had resided abroad for almost six years. His presence was rare in the country as he usually came by dusk and left by dawn. And among the ton, the more a gentleman shies away from marriage, the more pleasing he is to the eyes. Genevieve had to say that the earl lived up to the expectations she had of him.

"Oh, look at how demurely Miss Devonshire is staring at the earl," Kitty gasped and Genevieve's eyes shuttered.

Genevieve could see what her friend was talking about. Miss Devonshire was the eldest daughter of the Duke of Devonshire. She just had her coming out into society and the Queen had named her the Season's incomparable. Even Genevieve knew that Miss Devonshire was well worthy of the title if only she could stop dressing in purple.

Miss Devonshire was looking away from the earl now, bringing her fan to her bosom. Her dress today was spectacular, a rosy color that made her complexion more beautiful than ever. She was blushing heavily and made no move to hide it. Even the Countess looked mildly irritated by her efforts but the earl did not show it. Instead, he presented her with his best smile yet - one that showed pearly white dentition that was unstained by tobacco.

Genevieve felt a twinge of jealousy strike at her heart. Her friends were still gushing about how the earl would make a great husband, and she could not agree less. She hoped fervently in her heart that he would meet up with the qualities she wanted in a future husband. Genevieve already knew that he was of good standing and from a prestigious family. Also, her mother had been talking about him all through their journey in the carriage. If her mother deemed him perfect, then Genevieve was sure that her family would accept him.

She watched the countess lead him away from Miss Devonshire with a forced smile on her face. Genevieve wanted to picture the earl's handsome face in her mind but all she could see were oddly intense icy blue eyes. Without a doubt, she knew they belonged to the man in the shadows who was doing everything possible to hide away from the ton. The man who wanted no attention at all but instead craved solitude. In her mind, Genevieve could envision the viscount's thick lashes covering his stark blue eyes.

"Stop it, Genevieve," she told herself. "Your parents will never accept a man like him."

Genevieve wanted to push the thoughts of the viscount away from her mind and instead fill the void up with the earl's handsome face and dazzling smile. She reminded herself more than once that her parents would never accept a man like the viscount. Not any family would accept a man like him. The mamas of the society were just like her mother. They wanted nothing less than perfect in all situations. Everyone wanted someone like the Earl of Kenford or Lord Tompkins or the Duke of Shrewsbury even though he was quite young. Not someone with a jagged scar marring his face.

She hoped to God in that courtroom that the earl would have all the qualities she desired. While she liked the viscount's penetrating gaze and the shroud of mystery he cloaked himself in, she knew he could never be a perfect fit for her. If there was ever anyone else, Genevieve was sure that it would never be Viscount Hamilton.

As the daughter of a duke, everyone expected her to marry well. Her potential husband must be debt-free and intelligent with a considerable earning per annum. Also, he had to be of good standing in society - a prestigious family with a title that might rival her father's. Genevieve knew that her mother wanted her to marry a duke, but she could settle for this beau before her.

"He has the most piercing gaze," Kitty groaned beside Genevieve. "And those hands of his even look softer than a lady's."

Elizabeth snickered. "Perhaps because he might spend his whole day at White's drinking brandy. Who really knows his story?"

"Now, you do not like him anymore?" Genevieve asked, looking pityingly at her friend. "You were going to fake a swoon, Lizzy."

Elizabeth shook her head one too many times. "I am merely contemplating his stature in society. Did you hear of what the Debrett's sheets say?"

"You read too much gossip, Elizabeth," Kitty crooned. "Maybe that is one of the reasons why you have still not made a match."

Genevieve stifled a smile and Elizabeth huffed. "He is only mysterious, is all. A little flamboyant you might add."

"Flamboyant? I have yet to see any trait that suggests vain glory," Genevieve said, turning away from the earl to face her friends. "Tell me, did you notice something out of the ordinary?"

"Ordinary?" Elizabeth shot back, her face red. "There is nothing ordinary about the earl. It is merely his entrance that suggests flamboyance. I heard whispers that he rode a white stallion to the very front door before the countess went to receive him."

"Stallion? Perhaps he went out for a ride before the soiree," Kitty defended. "I do not see that as flamboyance in any way. All the men ride horses, Elizabeth."

"Grand or not, I believe that -

The words caught in Genevieve's throat when she saw her father walking towards her. Earlier, he had disappeared with the older men, retreating to the parlor to talk about their real estate plans and accomplishments that happened since the end of the previous Season. Like with every other ball they attended last Season, she did not expect her father to meet up with her until after the soiree had officially ended.

But there he was, striding towards her. Within moments, he was pulling her away from her small circle of friends and speaking in hushed tones.

"I have been speaking with the earl before Lady Kenford came to pull him away," her father said brightly. "From what I observed, he is a good man."

"Father, where is this leading to? I believe that you have not just come to speak about the earl's goodwill all night."

He smiled. "Before Lady Kenford came to pull him away, I had spoken so much about you. And I believe that a marriage between the both of you will unite our families more than ever. Also, he is quite handsome and well brought up."

Genevieve could not believe her ears. Every lady in the ballroom - debutante or not - was waiting for a chance to speak with the earl and perhaps make him interested in them. She knew that sooner or later, she would have to speak to the earl but Genevieve did not think that it would be so soon. Anxiety bloomed in her heart, sending it into a race that reminded her of the clobbering hooves of horses on the track as the jockeys raced.

"Lady Kenford will be there as well, and will be pleased to make your acquaintance," her father said and without waiting for her reply led her away from her friends and down to the other side of the ballroom.

"Your Grace," he said, his voice smooth and deep as he spoke. "Meeting you twice in one night is not a mere coincidence."

Her father laughed - something that Genevieve knew was rare. "I am quite fortunate to listen to tales of your travels, but this is my daughter whom we talked about this evening."

"Oh," he said, his voice sending shivers down Genevieve's spine. She watched him take her gloved hand in his and kiss her hand ever so slightly that the pressure made her heart run wild. "You must be Lady Genevieve then. It is quite an honour for me to meet you."

Genevieve could not help the smiles that assailed her face. Lady Kenford was there too, her hand twined in her son's. She was smiling as well, soft ones that were accentuated by the ruby gleaming at the base of her throat.

"I wish you were around for the last Season, Henry," Lady Kenford said softly. "Lady Genevieve here was the Season's incomparable. The diamond of the first water."

"Ah," the earl muttered. "I am even more pleased to hear that. Surely, the Queen made a good choice."

Genevieve blushed. "It was merely a coincidence, my lord."

"Do not be so modest," Lady Kenford whispered proudly, high enough for Genevieve to hear. "She is a rare find, Henry. Now, we will leave you two to discuss."

Genevieve watched her father leave with a smile on his face and Lady Kenford went to join the circle of mamas near the tall tresses of flowers beside the entrance to the ballroom. Her heart was still racing, and she tilted her face ever so slightly to look at him.

The earl's face was the epitome of perfection, soft and hard in the right places. Golden tufts of hair curled slightly down his cheek, and up close, she could see the mane of thick curly hair. Her eyes traveled from his forehead to the first quality on her list. Blue eyes.

Or not.

His eyes were a light shade of brown, almost the same color as his hair but only a few shades darker. A bigger smile was plastered to his face, but Genevieve did not look further than that. She suddenly recalled the viscount's blue eyes and was disappointed by the earl's brown ones. They were soft nonetheless but held none of the intensity that the viscount's had.

Genevieve smiled, curling her fingers into a fist behind her and trying to hide the disappointment that threatened to show on her face. By the time she was able to will back the disappointment, her nails had dug little red crescents into her palm.

"Your dress is wonderful," he said. "I have been watching it since I stepped into the ballroom."

Genevieve mustered a blush. "Flattery seems to be your forte, my lord. I believe that other ladies have more magnificent dresses, but they decided not to wear them today."

The earl laughed lightly. "I must say that you are quite funny, Lady Genevieve."

The discordant orchestra sounds turned up, and the waltz began in full swing. Genevieve was almost tempted to visit the pianoforte and play it herself, to sway to the music and dance till her feet were sore.

"May I have the honour of your first dance tonight?" he asked, extending his hand.

At the thought of having the earl's first dance for the night, Genevieve felt a little elated. She hoped that even if he did not have the blue eyes she wanted, he might at least be a good dancer. From their small talk, she could tell that he was a kind person, and she was glad about that. It was on her list of qualities that she wanted in a future husband.

She held out her dance card, urging him to write his name down. He did with great aplomb, the ink pouring delicately on the card. Genevieve smiled several times in a bid to mask her disappointment at the color of his eyes, and she succeeded because she made herself blush when he was done filling the dance card.

Genevieve wrapped her hand in his and let the earl lead her to the dance floor. She could see Miss Devonshire glaring at her but it did not matter. She was glad that at least, it was an honor that every lady wanted. This was his first dance since he returned from his journey abroad. Secretly, she thanked her father for this opportunity and hoped that the evening would not be such a disappointment after all.

The earl held her like a fragile flower, and they started to dance. Soon, Genvieve let herself loose into the music, and the delicate dance steps that had been drilled into her mind from a young age came alive. The dress she wore was no hindrance at all, and the movements soon became fluid. Music filled her ears from all sides, and she twirled, smiling at the earl. He was smiling too, leading her along into the song. And that was when everything became a disaster.

The earl stepped on her feet.

At first, she took it as a mere distraction because he was smiling at her at the time. It broke Genevive's concentration but she regained it anyway, letting the music fill her veins. The coordinated movements came to a sudden jolt again when the earl stepped on her again.

"My apologies," he whispered. "I am quite clumsy these days."

Genevieve could see the other ladies staring at her now, wondering why they were stopping. She continued to dance again, leading him this time in the hopes that he might not tramp on her feet anymore. Easily, Genevieve was beginning to regret her decision of having her first dance set with him. The earl knew almost nothing about the dance, and soon, Genevieve wished that he was not so clumsy.

As the music came to an end, Genevieve forced herself to smile at him. He was happy even, smiling at her. Coupled with the lack of quality that she wanted, it was hard for Genevieve to restrain herself from storming away. But she held herself there and curtseyed. When her face was down, she frowned slightly but placed the smile back when she looked at him again.

She thanked him for the dance and he apologized for his clumsiness but it did nothing to take away the terrible first impression of him that was now on her mind. Slowly, she walked away to find a new dance partner, hoping that she might find someone that was not so terrible at waltzing.

# Chapter 9

James sipped the champagne, glad that there was at least some alcohol that might numb him to the hotchpotch of colors and voluminous folds of dresses around him. Alice was away now, dancing with some gentleman that James knew to be Lord Simmons.

From what James heard, he was a respectable young man - a little less than thirty - with substantial annual earnings. He was the earl of Scottsville, and the word was out that he had a kind and amiable demeanor. For James, he looked perfect for his sister. But while he wanted the best for Alice, he did not want to force her into a marriage that she did not want. He had seen a lot of loveless marriages and he would not have Alice be in one of them.

A sigh escaped his lips after the sip of champagne. James hoped that he would not be disturbed for the remainder of the evening. He was having a swell time being by himself and enjoying the soft music from the orchestra at the opposite end of the ballroom. For one, no one came close to him and he avoided everyone in the ballroom. He knew that the scar on his face was the reason why people thought he was the plague, but James could not care less.

Instead, he enjoyed the lack of attention that came from the Earl of Kenford's elaborate entry. And even James could not help but admit that his manners and ways were more gentlemanly than most.

The earl was dressed in a fabric of the darkest blue, one that was laden with silver buttons that shimmered when he bowed or moved. He had arrived on a white stallion, galloping through the grounds and letting the people outside stare at him with awe. For someone who was said to arrive in London by dusk and leave by dawn, he sure loved being the centre of attention.

But James was at least happy that it took all of the former attention away from him. He made no move to leave his position near the heavy draperies. It served as a cocoon where he could hide from the rest of the ton. But a part of him knew that soon, he would have to step into the light like the rest of the ton. There was the issue of marriage that his mother was always bringing up, and

James knew that there was no way avoiding it. But he had not seen any lady that even passed a second glance at him.

He still recalled the blank stare on Lady Genevieve's face, and at that moment, James wanted to walk up to her and ask her why she was staring. He felt like a flamboyant piece of clothing that she discarded and looked upon with something that was not quite disdainful.

James saw the Duke - Edmund - shuffle into the midst of some older men and there was a lot of boisterous laughter. He imagined and hoped that they were talking about investing in the tea trade because nothing could please him more. And there were plans on his mind to expand the trade past Cornwall and maybe into Malborough.

He looked away from them with an elated mind, watching the Countess parade her son like a trophy. It reminded James of the times when his father would take Ned around to meet his friends as a way to prepare him for taking over the position of viscount and head of the house.

"I think Lord Scottsville might make quite the match with Alice," his mother's soft tone said from the side and James jumped.

He groaned and almost turned away. Everywhere he went, it felt like his mother was always right on his tail. He had been avoiding her since the night before, and she made no effort to tune down her complaints about him not taking responsibility. But James felt quite the opposite. He had been working tirelessly since he arrived eighteen months ago to make sure that the house never ran out of money. For this season, they had spent a lot on new dresses and petticoats, on swathes of silk, satin, and lace, on corsets and parasols. That alone was a huge responsibility that crippled some men and why some kept running into debt.

"Mother you scared me," he whispered, keeping his voice to the barest minimum to avoid attracting unwanted attention. "But I have been watching Lord Scottsville all morning. He seems like he would make a great husband for Alice as well."

His mother harrumphed. "But while Lord Scottsville seems nice, there seem to be other gentlemen available at the ball. His Lordship earns too little to take care of Alice's needs."

"Mother, he earns 8,000 a year. That is quite substantial to carry them through the year and there will still be money left."

"Substantial?" she scoffed, sipping some lemonade from the ornate glass. "I do not want substantial for my only daughter. I want her to be well taken care of."

"Then perhaps I should leave you to find a match for Alice while I concentrate on keeping us alive," he joked but James saw the shift in his mother's posture and guessed that she did not take his words lightly.

"Do not try to avoid your duty, James. Alice needs you now more than ever," she said and turned to face the dance floor again. "Lord Lorwood has expressed an interest in Alice and they seemed to get along together. It might very well be a love match."

James was perturbed. Since he walked into the Kenford residence that evening, he had not heard of the name Lorwood. It felt rather strange hearing that someone had expressed interest in his sister without his knowledge.

"Lord Lorwood?" he asked. "And who might that be?"

His mother had a bemused smile on her face. "From what I have gathered, his father passed away a few months ago, and he just inherited the earldom. They have a country residence in Bath and he earns 12,000 a year from the investments his father left him. If only you were not trying to hide away, maybe you would be kept abreast of the situation at hand."

James could see that he was quite the catch for the Season. Any debutante in her right mind would snatch him for themselves. But then, he wanted Alice to be the only sole decision-maker for her future. While he wanted what was best for her, he also wanted to see her happy and content. Like his parents were. But he felt guilty as well. He was responsible for Alice and he was letting her down by hiding away from the rest of the ton when he should be mingling and getting to know eligible bachelors that might have Alice's best interests at heart.

"And where is this Lord Lorwood if I may ask?"

"Over there with Alice," she said with a smile tugging on the creased corners of her mouth.

James looked to the corner and searched for the familiar hair of his sister. And there she was with a young man, a lot younger than Lord Scottsville. She was laughing, enraptured by whatever discussion they were having. The smile on Alice's face was no longer mischief, but one he had seen in some ladies that evening. It was a smile that came with getting to know someone. Not out of courtesy, but from the freedom of your own heart. At the sight, he smiled as well.

"There are plenty of bachelors here, James. Some are even your age if you do not want to mingle with the men in their sixties. You should get to know them and find a husband for your sister. But even if you cannot do that, I will play my part as a mother and not leave your sister shaking in the wind."

James made no move to talk because he knew that his mother would just seize his words and turn them against him. So he just let her continue talking.

"I will go on to check for more eligible bachelors and perhaps introduce her to a few so that we might have some calling by dawn. But if anything, you must dance with Lady Genevieve tonight. One dance set at least."

James was mortified. From the first day he set his eyes on Lady Genevieve, he wanted to stay away from her for as long as he could. When Lord Arlington introduced him to the Duke as a potential business partner, James knew that he could only avoid her for so long. One way or the other, the Duke would invite him to their home. And there was no way he could look at her blank stares or contemptuous looks without uttering a word. He had kept his calm for a long time since he returned but his facade of tranquility was threatening to shatter under Lady Genevieve's gaze.

"What? Lady Genevieve? Why?" he asked frantically, the string of questions spilling out of him.

His mother watched him for a moment as if trying to bring the words in her mind into place. James could feel an onslaught coming, and he was sincerely astonished when she replied in an equally calm voice.

"Lady Genevieve is the Duke's daughter, James. And you want to be a business partner with him, I suppose? Do you recall that the Duke has good standing in the society?"

James shrugged, gingerly setting down his glass of champagne and reaching for another. "Mother, you always have ulterior motives. I am sure that you are driving towards a goal, but all I see is a preposterous rigmarole of words and gestures."

"Rigmarole?" she asked incredulously, eyes wide as she set

down the glass of lemonade on the stand beside a small ice sculpture. "I believe the right phrase was beating around the bush, but no less, I will make my point soon enough."

James smiled at the banter, knowing that talking to his mother like this only happened once in a lifetime. She was either nagging him to shoulder more responsibility or telling him how Alice failed to make a match in the previous Season and ought to make it before the end of this one.

"By birth, Lady Genevieve has good standing in society. Dancing with her will only increase your popularity among the ton."

James frowned. "I hope this is not one of your schemes to set me up with Lady Genevieve because I will not have it."

She arched her eyebrows. "This will only help your business, James. And that is all I want from you as of this moment."

Without any more to say, James watched his life temporarily crash before his eyes. For one, he was sure that Lady Genevieve disliked him. There was no way she would even accept his request for a dance. Most likely, asking her might cause a huge embarrassment for him. One that he was not prepared for. He had only seen her twice and both times, she either paid almost no attention to him, or was disgusted by him.

Only the elites attended the Countess' soiree. And none of them would want to be seen dancing with a man that had a horrible scar like he did. He felt his heart race as he looked at his mother's expectant gaze. He could sense some other motive going on, but he knew that everything his mother said was true.

For his business, he had to meet more people. And there was no other way than at soirees and balls where all the eligible bachelors and potential investors would be waiting. By dancing with Lady Genevieve, that might affiliate him with her father, the Duke of Montmere. From everything James heard from Lord Arlington, the Duke was trusted by all for his great business acumen. Dancing with her would only place him on a pedestal where other business investors might see him.

There was also the fact that he was partly affiliated with her father. He hoped that she would extend the same respect she had for her father's friends to him as well.

In the end, he swallowed his pride and turned to his mother.

"Since you have broached the subject, would you care to accompany me to Lady Genevieve?"

He let out a breath he did not know he was holding as a huge smile broke out on his mother's face.

"Come with me," was all she said and led him away from the darkness where he hid for the large portion of the evening.

Every step sent his heart racing even faster as the thought of embarrassment loomed ahead. James felt the scar warm up as they edged farther into the light from the chandelier. His mother just looked straight ahead, smiling widely. James' feelings crashed into one another, encompassing his entire body in the fear of humiliation. But still, his legs managed to move.

He could see her golden hair now, the strands shimmering like silk and his heart dropped to his stomach. But James knew that coming this close to a woman was not as scary as seeing your life flash before your eyes on the battlefield. With that thought in mind, he mustered courage and walked faster. Enough to earn a look of surprise from his mother which was promptly followed by a smile.

The countess' perfume assailed his nostrils when they arrived at Lady Genevieve's position. The Duchess - Lady Genevieve's mother - was there too, and she was doing most of the talking. From the snippets of conversation that James could hear, it was mostly about the earl.

"Lady Genevieve," James called out after clearing his throat silently.

It felt like his voice echoed through the whole ballroom because a certain odd silence stuck to him after he spoke. The Duchess was frozen mid-speech, astonishment written all over her face. The Countess looked confused as well, her mind working on reasons why James might be calling Lady Genevieve.

The silence lengthened uncomfortably and James cleared his throat once more and took a bow before the women. "Pardon me for the intrusion I have caused."

No one spoke. Not even Lady Genevieve. This urged James to speak even more despite his voice crackling with the fear of being humiliated before all and sundry.

So when he spoke to her again, he smiled. "Lady Genevieve, I was hoping I could have the honour of sharing your next dance set."

He raised his head a little, waiting for Lady Genevieve's answer but by no means did he miss the look of anger and contempt on the Duchess' face. All her elegant features were marred for the tiniest of a minute, but it was enough to let James know that he was not welcome to intrude on their conversation. Now that he was used to the feeling of being frowned upon, seeing her face contort in anger, James did not let the duchess' feelings get to him. Instead, he wore a smile on his face, expectant for an answer.

"Gladly," answered Lady Genevieve when the first chord of music was struck again.

# Chapter 10

Genevieve smiled as the viscount led her away from where she was. She had been looking for an excuse all night to leave her mother's side and go back to her friends. She knew that they would be thrilled that she had her first dance set with the infamous earl of Kenford. As dashing as he might be to other ladies and their audacious mamas, Genevieve was very disappointed by the earl.

His dance steps were notoriously inane, almost like a sacrilege to the slow tempo ritual of a waltz. While she had been let down by his light brown eyes, the earl kept stepping on her feet and apologizing intermittently, and that did not blossom into a conversation. Genevieve did not even want it to. All she wanted was to get away from him and douse her parched throat with a glass of cold lemonade before she began to wilt.

Her mother had led her to the countess afterward and they began to talk of the earl's travels to Messina and beyond, voyages past the open seas. All that time, Genevieve thought of the ocean. Of the water meeting the skies, washing the world in a blue so brilliant that it lit up the world. And those thoughts directed her to the viscount.

Viscount Hamilton.

His name was on her lips all through the night and she secretly searched for him when she was dancing. When she twirled, her eyes looked to every nook and cranny; to reach out to see his strange hair and bright eyes. But everywhere she looked, Genevieve's eyes were met with darkness and emptiness.

She had seen the viscount approach them from the corner of her eye when she stopped listening to the discussion between her mother and the countess. Genevieve kept her glances down, hoping that he would not break away and leave. She could almost not keep the excitement from her eyes when he asked her to dance. A part of her hoped that the dance would take longer than usual so that she might have the chance to get through the shroud of mystery that wrapped around him. Also, Genevieve already had an idea that the viscount knew more than he was letting on. His eyes were brimming with knowledge, and his silence only made it more pronounced. As someone who spent most of her time reading books, Genevieve was excited to let the viscount lead her away from the dour conversation she was stuck in earlier.

The music was instantly concordant, and Genevieve looked at the viscount's face. His disposition was sullen, which made her only more excited at the prospect of learning the intricacies of his mind. And she hoped that he would not disappoint her as the earl did. He bowed slowly - a fluid and genteel motion that made Genevieve's heart jump. She pushed down the feeling when she curtseyed, not taking her eyes away from his face.

The orchestra began with a slow tune, and she laced her finger with his. Through the gloves, they were quite soft - unlike the rough hands of the earl. Despite his demeanor, he looked quite graceful. They started swaying softly at first, slow movements that Genvieve was used to. Soon, she settled into the dance, her shifts becoming less jerky and more fluid.

He was silent, and Genevieve felt the need to initiate the conversation. At first, she wanted to ask him about his life on the battlefield but before the words left her mouth, she suddenly recalled how he acted when her father talked about the war.

"This is a rather eventful evening, do you not think, my lord?" she asked, almost stumbling over her words.

They turned together, a maneuver that the earl would have never gotten. The viscount was light on his feet, stepping back and forth soundlessly on the parquetry. For the first time, his eyes were aglow with a hint of excitement, his blue eyes turning a shade brighter.

"I suppose it is," he mumbled, turning slightly and edging closer to the centre of the ballroom.

Other people were dancing as well, and the ballroom became a swirl of color. Bright greens and dark blues, lavender and moss, satin and lace, silk and cotton. More than anything else, Genevieve was starting to get lost in the music.

She was thrust back to when she was just a few months over nine years old and the governess made her dance till her feet hurt. Genevieve used to hate the older woman, wanting to escape from the house and run to the shrubberies at the back of the estate. At the time, Genevieve did not know the importance of dance until she entered society. Only then did she begin to immerse herself into the sounds of music, the intricate steps and turns, the movements and slight thrusts. Soon, Genevieve began to see dance as something beautiful, ornate even.

And now, she was beginning to have the best night of her life. The viscount's steps were polished, better than any gentleman that had gotten the opportunity to share a dance with her. Swift and slow at the same time, graceful and intent. She spun around and he acted as her anchor, pulling her back ever so softly that their bodies grazed each other.

But more than the dance, she yearned to speak with him. Genevieve wanted to let herself into his mind, to see the way he worked. She'd heard some things about him from her father, and one of them was that he was a successful businessman with a mind that had never been seen in all of London. That alone prompted her to speak more than she usually did.

"How is the weather, my lord?" Genevieve asked softly this time, her voice tinged with sarcasm.

Most gentlemen liked for ladies to stroke their egos with their words, and she hoped that it would work on the viscount as well. As they continued to dance, she was unable to take her eyes from his, the stark blue coruscating in the dark - a contrast of blue and gold.

"I would rather we talked about something more than the weather," he said softly with a small smile and the deep baritone of his voice sent tingles down Genevieve's spine.

"And what would that be, my lord? Surely, you must have a subject in mind that you wish to discuss."

Genevieve was looking at the scar now, the crater of pink skin that tore the viscount's face in half. It was horrible, stark against his face, and made the other side of his face droop as if every muscle in there was tired. She knew that without the scar, he would have been a catch like the earl. Someone that society's mothers would want for their daughters. They would chase him throughout London, breathing fire.

"James," he said slowly, every letter enunciated as it rolled off his tongue. "Call me James. That should be a start."

Genevieve shook her head. "I could not do that, my lord. But I will have it in mind."

His smile grew wider for a while, the scar creasing in a way that made his face seem a lot gentler than ever.

"Not many people want to talk about what I want," he said. "Instead, I try to hear what they want to talk about. Then, we can find common ground. But really, talk about the weather takes the depth out of any conversation."

Genevieve smiled wider than ever, her heart fluttering. "Perhaps we should implement a change. Maybe this time, we talk about something that you find interesting, my lord."

His face was thoughtful for a moment, blue eyes glazing over. They turned lightly, surrounded by ball gowns and tailcoats. And then he smiled.

"Do you like literature then? And I do not mean the gossip sheets of Lady Penelope or some other thing like that," he asked.

"I hear that Lady Penelope is quite savvy with her words," Genevieve replied as a joke. "But yes, my lord, I am quite interested in literature."

"I would have never pegged you for someone who reads nothing more than Almack's journals and gossip sheets. Like the rest of the ton."

Genevive sliced her hand through the air in a bid to look mortified. "I can assure you that I do not spend my pennies on gossip sheets, my lord. I see most of them as aspersions."

He turned to face her again. "Brutally honest, I see. But if you have read some literature, perhaps you could enlighten me a little."

"It has been mostly poems. They seem to have different meanings whenever I read them. Better than most."

She was glad that he looked rather astonished but continued either way. "Then you must have read the work of John Milton. Paradise Lost maybe?"

Genevieve felt her cheeks heat up. She had picked up the book a week ago from her father's study and had read through it. For a long moment, she had not understood the book. But when she came back with biscuits and tea, the words felt simpler. In a few minutes, she was fully enthralled by the verses.

"Innocence once lost, can never be regained..." she trailed off.

"And darkness when gazed upon can never be lost," he completed with a bemused smile on his face.

"Maybe you know more than you let on," he said, more

excited than Genevieve had ever seen him.

Their dance came to a rather abrupt end and Genevieve wished that the music would play until dawn. Not only was the viscount a good dancer, but he loved what she had interests in. From the little conversation they had during the dance, she could tell that he was an intelligent person - someone who reveled in discussions that could bring solid change instead of virtually meaningless talk like the condition of the weather.

"I am very sorry that our little conversation has to come to an end before we even began," she said, smiling as they stepped away from the dance floor.

"I wish - he started, but they were interrupted by a flurry of activity. In the tumult, Genvieve heard the butler announce that all the gentlemen at the soiree were invited to join the earl in the parlor. Before she could whisper her goodbyes, the viscount was lost in the crowd of eligible bachelors.

With a sadness that weighed on her heart, Genevieve retired to the drawing room to meet the rest of the ladies. She could see Elizabeth, Kitty, and Alice talking excitedly with gestures that felt rather too loud.

"His hair was like melted gold," Alice said, fanning herself a little too hard. "I heard that he is a consummate sportsman as well. Someone who knows his horses."

"I cannot wait for Lady Penelope's next gossip sheet. I cannot wait for what she has to say about the earl!" Elizabeth squealed. "I wager she will say something about his bone structure."

"Or his charisma," Alice cooed. "Every mama in the room wanted him for their daughters."

Kitty hissed. "They had better keep their hands off him. But I heard that he once had no intentions to enter society."

Genevieve took her seat on the brocade sofa, giddy with excitement. She wanted to tell her friends about the viscount. But they were so intent on their conversation about the earl that they almost did not notice when she took her seat beside them.

"I think the Countess told him to enter society. He is the only son and needs to produce an heir as soon as possible. What better time to enter society than now?" Elizabeth said, reclining on the sofa and crossing her hands on her bosom.

"Even if he does not want to enter society, I am sure that the mamas would never allow that. It would be such a waste to keep him buried under all the finery in this house," Kitty said.

"And he only had one dance tonight," Elizabeth stated, joining the conversation again and looking at Genevieve.

Kitty smiled. "The only dance he had tonight was with Genevieve. I tell you, she is the most fortunate of us all."

They all turned to look at her as if expecting her to recount the night's events. None of them had mothers or fathers that were as close to the countess as she did, but the opportunity she got was not worthwhile. She could still feel her feet hurt from all the times the earl stepped on them, but she was glad that dancing with the viscount was able to take away all of the heartfelt disappointment.

"Tell us how it was," Kitty squealed. "It must have been the best dance of your life!"

Genevieve was about to speak of her long list of bad attitudes that the earl possessed when Alice shot to her feet. She excused herself, taking her lace-trimmed fan with her. Her mother was motioning for her to come, and from the corner of her eye, Genevieve saw Viscount Hamilton but her heart fell when she saw that he paid no attention to her.

Once Alice was gone, Elizabeth let out a loud sigh - something she only did when something was bothering her.

Genevieve arched her eyebrows. "Elizabeth, whatever is on your mind will give you wrinkles and make you look like an old maid in a matter of days."

Kitty laughed. "You only sigh when something is evidently wrong. Attention-seeking as it might seem, we are always happy to help."

Elizabeth frowned. "This is not about me, Kitty. It is about Alice. My concerns for her only grows as the days slither by."

"Concerns?" Genevieve asked. "And what might they be?"

"Alice entered society a year earlier than we did," Elizabeth stated. "And she is still attending balls and soirees with us. This is her third Season and she is yet to be married. I fear that she might wilt with every Season."

"I have thought about it too," Kitty said sadly. "She seems like a nice person."

"But she has difficulty fitting into society," Elizabeth intoned. "Her father passed away and shortly after, her brother did too. It must have been very hard on her. She has been a close friend of mine for a while now."

Genevieve spoke now, understanding what was going on. She knew of a lady that used to be in Alice's situation. Now, she was living in the country by herself because she was already well into her spinster years. If Alice did not get a match by the end of the Season, it might as well almost be over.

"What do we do to help?" Genevieve asked. "Anything at all?"

"My family will be having a picnic at the Thames tomorrow," Elizabeth said, "and I hope that the both of you will be there. Alice will be attending as well, so this will be an opportunity for her to make some friends."

"I will tell my father about it," Genevieve said. "But it is almost certain that I will be in attendance. Your kitchen maids make the best biscuits."

Kitty laughed. "I will be attending as well. For Alice."

"For Alice," Genevieve repeated.

# Chapter 11

James had been unable to sleep for a few hours. He had been rolling through the soft cotton sheets for a while now, looking out the window at the twilight skies. He had arrived back home from the soiree, exhausted but excited. It had been eerily wonderful, and he was pretty glad that he had decided to go after all.

When the butler called all the men to the parlor, James had almost been the centre of attention. Most people knew nothing about him except the word of mouth in the gossip sheets, and a few were vaguely terrified about the scar on his face. But he made the most of his attendance by telling almost everyone about the perpetual success of his business.

And since he danced with Lady Genevieve, the Duke backed up his business proposals. All night, he explained how the tea trade was going in Cornwall and how the tea leaves would be ready for harvest and distribution in a few months. With the Duke's approval, almost all of the men believed that he was a good person and most of them left him calling cards to talk more about the trade and possibly invest at a later time.

But that was not what kept James awake. It was the dance with Lady Genevieve that consumed him like wildfire through the night. For the first time in his life, he enjoyed dancing. Usually, he was a man who spent most of his time with brandy at White's or on horseback. Never once did James dance of his own volition except for one time when he was a lot younger and Ned asked him to.

Last night, James did not even want the dance to end. At first, he thought that she might decline his offer to dance. But when she turned the string on her wrist for him to write his name on her dance card, it felt all too surreal. Even though she agreed, he could not bring himself to forget the look on her mother's face when he interrupted their discussion.

He had seen the Duchess first at the Arlington manor, and she smiled at him when he bowed before her. She said little during dinner except when the subject of gossip started. James never thought of her as someone who could have a look of utter disgust and disapproval on her face. Her features were contorted, her lips turned up and her nostrils flaring. He knew that most people did not want to associate with him because of his looks, but for the duchess to sneer and hiss, it was new.

But none of that mattered when James stepped onto the dance floor with Lady Genevieve. He had watched her from where he stood beside the draperies, seeing how she danced with the earl and he could tell without a doubt that she was a very good dancer. When his mother asked him to share a dance with her, James had been devastated. It felt like someone dropped a rock onto his head and made everything inside him run wild.

The moment the music started, he forgot all about how he felt. Lady Genevieve was not only beautiful but also graceful on the parquetry. Every movement was coordinated - swift flicks and turns, genteel steps, and meandering twists. He wanted to compliment her at first, but he kept his lips sealed because he thought that she might say something out of turn that might further irritate him.

Lady Genevieve had spoken first. Her voice was smooth like a stone run over forever by cascading waters. In his mind, he knew that the analogy was wrong, but that was the only statement that he could think of. Now that he was staring out at the bespangled starry skies, a million words formed in his mind. James felt like he could have talked to her more, initiated a conversation, and made the dance an event that would be almost unforgettable.

The words that came out of her mouth were full of intelligence, so much that they dwarfed many by comparison. He had always thought that she would be someone who could not converse about anything other than the weather or about conversations that were talked about at the park. In his mind, Lady Genevieve was someone who was wholly superficial, who received ribbons and flowers on a daily basis and received vouchers.

She surpassed all of his expectations. Most ladies of the ton could not understand sarcasm, but Lady Genevieve was proficient at it. Every word dripped with common sense, and when she talked about literature, it came with a fervor that he could not believe still existed. Her mind was a treasure trove, one that a man could mine around forever.

James would have liked it if he could enjoy her company

once more. To talk about their common interests, to talk about the interpretation of poems, and laugh at the silliness that might come up during conversations like that. Not even gentlemen wanted to talk about literature. Lady Genevieve was the only person he had seen in all of London that also cared about what he liked.

He rolled to the edge of the bed, watching the sky turn from black to blue and finally to russet and orange. It was a new day - one that he needed to himself to rest and work on the final plans for expanding the trade. Also, it was a time to remind himself that he could not let himself be moved by Lady Genevieve.

From where he stood with a glass of champagne in hand, he could see her face when the earl came into the ballroom. The look on her face was one of awe - a young woman who was smitten by him. Just like most of the ladies in the room were. Even James acknowledged that the earl was almost perfect with his sandy hair streaked with gold and his bright eyes and manners. Even when they danced, Lady Genevieve still had that look on her face. She was enraptured by him, all of her enthralled by the man before her. More than anything, he was sure that Lady Genevieve would prefer the earl's company than his own.

When James came to that conclusion, he heaved a sigh. It was finally time to rouse himself from his reverie and wake up to the harsh reality of the world he lived in. He would forever live on his own as the rest of the world tumbled past him. And he would be happy with that. At least, he hoped.

***

"Yessssss," James heard his mother's voice drawl out when he stepped into the elegant drawing room for breakfast.

Alice was eating already and mumbled her greetings while wiping her mouth with a napkin. James greeted his mother and she just mumbled a reply before going back to the sheet before her. From the back and the delicate print, he could tell that she was reading a gossip sheet. James was wondering how much their household had spent on five Seasons on just gossip sheets. Judging by the number of papers in the spare room beside the study, he could tell that it was quite a fortune.

James knew that every member of the ton feasted on the juicy gossip just as much as his mother did. It was all they lived for. In the scandal and news of the events, the authors did a good job of recounting every event in such an articulate manner without sparing any detail. Sometimes, James wondered who was writing those sheets and the fortune they must have made from them. Somewhere in London, a lady was getting enriched with the ton's money.

He had barely sat down when his mother's voice resounded in his ears like a jolt.

"Your name has made it to the gossip sheets yet again," she said with a mischievous smile on her face. "I hope you can see now that I have made a good decision by telling you to dance with Lady Genevieve."

James was taken aback by those words. In one swift move, he took the sheet from his mother and read it aloud.

"*Lord H only shared one dance set with Lady Genevieve at the Countess of Kenford's soiree. Could it be that Lord H is looking for a future viscountess? He will have to watch out as the Earl of Kenford with his dashingly good looks and charm will be hard to live up to!*"

James crumpled the paper into a ball and curled his fists. Enraged, he hurled it across the drawing room. He could see that his mother was clearly waiting for him to say something, and he did after a heavy sigh.

"It was a mistake to have danced with Lady Genevieve," he said, shoving his fists behind him. "Being the topic of discussion in a gossip sheet is not the kind of reputation I am hoping to build. Everything this author said about me is dubious, to say the least!"

"Dubious? All this fervor about matrimony is because the Season is just starting. But it was not a mistake to dance with Lady Genevieve. If more than anything, it would help your reputation. It would have been a mistake if you had not asked her and just stood there in the darkness like some hooligan."

"All this gossip would do no one any good," James replied, taking his seat at the table. "If more than anything, it will only deceive them."

His mother sneered. "I am quite sure that this author's column about you will not hurt your business chances. It seems that is everything you care about now."

James sighed, knowing that his mother always brought everything back to the business and that he was seemingly neglecting everything else. "The business is keeping us afloat, Mother. I would rather do that than enter into a sanctimonious relationship with any lady of the ton."

"I am sure that the gossip will die down soon anyway. The ton will chew at this for only a little while and leave it soon enough when there is another juicy gossip for them to sink their teeth into," his mother said, turning around with a smile on her face.

James ate in silence for a while, wondering how his name entered the gossip sheets in the first place. He knew that he would have had an uneventful evening if he had just stayed where he was and not brought himself into the open. The duchess' face flashed into his mind and his eyebrows creased. He wondered what she would be saying to Lady Genevieve when the gossip sheet reached their home.

"Alice has been invited for a picnic by the Arlingtons," his mother said, changing the topic and James saw his sister's head perk up. "According to the invitation, it is scheduled to hold by the Thames at high noon."

He looked at his sister's eyes, searching before he spoke. "I am finally glad that Alice is fitting back into society. This will be a chance for her to meet more people."

His mother - Marcia - nodded. "I thought so as well. But unfortunately, the Marquess of Brentwood has invited me over for tea and I cannot turn down the invitation. Would you help me to chaperone her?"

James knew that he could not refuse. For a long time now, Alice has had trouble entering society. At first, it was the fainting spell on her debut before the Queen. Their father passed away shortly after and it had been devastating for the whole family. Afterwards, Ned passed away from an illness and Alice broke down completely. It had been hard for her since then and she spent most of the previous Season indoors.

More than anything, he loved seeing Alice leave the house and do something that interested her. No matter how annoyed he was about the gossip sheet, he was happy that Alice has a good time. She kept all of the details to herself, but he could tell that she was content with the soiree. And this was another opportunity for her to leave the house and meet new people - potential husbands. He would have decided not to leave the house, but he would do anything to make his sister happy. Even to his detriment.

"Of course," he said with a smile. "I will be happy to chaperone. This will be a good time for me to relax as well before I start smelling like an old man."

They all laughed, and the tension at the table returned to normalcy. He hoped that it would remain normal for a long time. At least, till Alice was married.

# Chapter 12

The early light of dawn turned the skies to russet and gold, and Genevieve watched as the light streamed in past the heavy draperies that hung over the large windows in her room. The candlelight was still burning, wax pouring down onto the stand. She inhaled the heavy scent of honeysuckle from the candle, reminded of the events that had happened from the beginning of the Season.

Slowly, she reclined on the chair and almost let it topple. Genevieve struggled to find balance for a moment before resting on two legs. The list she had written was still in her hand, heavier because of the thoughts that weighed on her mind. She had been staring for hours at the list, trying to find correlations between the Earl of Kenford and all of the qualities she wanted in a gentleman. Every time she tried to find something nice about him, the situation became almost too messy that Genevieve could almost not make any sense of it.

For one, the earl was the worst dancer she had ever met. Last Season, she met a marquess at a ball in the Malborough residence and Genevieve had claimed that he was the worst dancer of all time. But the earl set an all-time low standard for her that irritated her whenever she thought about it. He was jerky and uncoordinated - every step mixing and stopping even before he took the next one. All evening, she wanted to tell Elizabeth and Kitty about him after Alice had left, but they gave her no opportunity to do so.

Everyone was talking about how fortunate she was to dance with the earl. His only dance of the evening was with her and he retired with the other gentlemen to the parlor where they spent the rest of the evening. But Genevieve did not feel fortunate at all. He spent all of the time they danced with apologies, muttering and mumbling under his breath. In the end, she was the one directing his steps - a feat that would be impossible for any other lady.

She sighed heavily before blowing out the bright flame of the candle and brought the chair to rest on all of its legs. Her mind was still fluttering from the events of the night before, between disdain and discomfort. After the soiree, she had been so tired that she could not even ask for Jenny to help her massage her toes. They still hurt from all the places the earl stepped on her feet with his heavy Hessians. She made a note to ask her lady's maid to massage her hands with her homemade oils.

Apart from the fact that the earl was the least graceful of dancers, his eyes were not a quality she wanted in a gentleman. Genevieve wanted blue eyes - a trait that was as rare as it was beautiful. Brown eyes were common among the peerage, and in the earl's case, it was rather shocking. The countess' eyes were a strange grey. One that reminded Genevieve of her father's gun. She hoped that he might have grey or his eyes might be blue and match the bright sandy color of his hair.

But the color of honey, light, and dark at the same time was most disappointing. All night, Genevieve kept her eyes away from his and it was made easier because she had to watch his steps and hope that he would not step on her yet again. Since they talked about almost nothing, Genevieve did not know his interests, and neither could she talk about hers. A part of her knew that the earl must be one of those gentlemen who were verbose - always speaking about tales of his travels to fascinate the ladies. But she knew people that travelled regularly, so she knew that it was not a topic that would be intriguing. Already, she was getting tired of the unwanted attraction she was getting because she had danced with him.

Just as she dropped the paper on the mahogany desk, a startling image filtered into her mind. It was a child with pudgy hands and bright blue eyes. He looked like an angel with a shock of wooly blonde hair like hers in little tufts on his head. Blood rushed to her cheeks, filling her face with heat. She smiled while covering her face with her hands because she knew in her heart that she had seen that blue eyes so many times not to recognize them.

It was the Viscount's or rather, James'. Thinking about his name felt all wrong, like they had been friends for a long time even though the most conversation they had ever had was at the soiree. All the time, Genevieve used to think that the viscount was an arrogant man, someone who wanted to keep to himself at all costs. It only made her more inquisitive about him and it took everything from her not to ask Elizabeth questions.

Already, she was frightened that her friend might have

already noticed that she and the viscount shared a look that would be considered scandalous. Even at the soiree, Genevieve was watching and waiting for Elizabeth to bring up the matter. But Kitty and Elizabeth were so enamoured by the earl that they talked about nothing else. It made Genevieve relieved, but also irritated that there was nothing more to talk about.

She could still see the viscount's blue eyes in her mind - stark and beautiful. Not only was he so mannered and an elegant dancer, but he was also great at speaking. The way he said her name was different from the other people. Even her parents. Each syllable was enunciated, spoken with a softness that she could not quite place. And when he spoke about literature, it was with a certain fondness as if he had once lost himself in an array of books just glazing through the pages. For the first time, she found a mind like hers. One filled with knowledge and the hunger to know more. She wished that the conversation could have lasted the whole night. Genevieve knew that she would have certainly known more about him.

"Put an end to these thoughts," she berated herself loudly, recalling the horrid and sagging scar that marred the other side of his face.

Genevieve knew that getting close to the viscount will only spur her mother's anger. Even when he asked to dance with them, she had seen the look on her face. It was one of pure contempt - the same way some people looked at dogs and other irritating animals that were slobbering at the mouth. From when her father asked her mother to send an invite to the viscount, Genevieve had seen her mother's evident dislike for him. Even though she acted like she was comfortable with him at the Arlington Manor, her mother bore hatred for the viscount. And Genevieve could tell that it was because of the scar on his face.

In their house, there were certain unspoken expectations. To her mother, the viscount was less than perfect. First, there was the issue of his title. She was the daughter of a duke and no matter the fortune attached to his family name, her parents would want her to get married to someone of high ranking in society as well. Perhaps a duke or a marquess. The least was an earl. Anything after that would be considered impossible.

Also, there was the awful scar that tore his face in two.

When looked at from the side, Genevieve could tell that the viscount was once a handsome gentleman. He was tall and broad-shouldered with a smile that was slight but no less beautiful. Ash blond hair crowned his head in soft locks, curling delicately around his ears. The scar was an imperfection, one that Genevieve wished she could erase. An imperfection that her mother would swoop down on and be sure to point out.

Her lips curled downwards in a frown as she folded the piece of paper into a perfect square. The knock on the door prompted her to slip the square under the inkwell once more where it would not be discovered.

"Who is at the door?" Genevieve asked, curling back under the sheets and pretending like she did not spend most of the night in deep thought.

"It is only me, my lady," Jenny said from behind the door in a slightly jovial tone, one that meant that she was in a great mood.

The door opened shortly after and Jenny slid into the room. "You should not be in bed for too long, my lady. Too much sleep can cause wrinkles. Look at the case of Lady Moffat."

Genevieve smiled. "How did you know that? Lady Moffat rarely shows her face at balls and soirees."

"Maids talk," was all Jenny said, and helped her out of bed.

It would soon be time for breakfast, and she had to be in the dining room for it. Missing it would only incur her mother's wrath and Genevieve hoped that she would not have to talk about how her dance with the earl was for she might not be able to control herself from speaking about her displeasure of the earl.

***

Genevieve entered the drawing room, her stomach grumbling at the sight of food laid out on perfect ceramic plates. Usually, she was not always hungry when it was time for breakfast so she kept her eye on other things like the atmosphere of the dining room. Sometimes, her parents would be arguing about how much expenses were being incurred every month of the Season and how the old dresses would have to be shoved away or given out to the maids who wanted them.

That morning, it was awfully quiet and that in itself was unusual. Genevieve eyed her father but he paid no attention to her. Instead, he helped himself to generous servings of food with gusto, smiling as he ate. He was usually her saving grace in tense atmospheres like this one.

She took her seat beside him, trying to avoid making contact with her mother's eyes which were feasting on the words of the small pamphlet before her. From the slight lavender curlicues drawn on the front and the delicate script on the white sheet, Genvieve immediately knew that her mother was reading her regular gossip sheet which came every week. It was now six pennies and the increment was because the author's gossip was the best in London.

Wisely, Genevieve continued to avoid her mother's eyes even though she watched her closely. In the house, it was always wise to make no comments or conversation at times like this. When her mother was with a gossip sheet was one of the only times when she made use of the large library because there would be nothing there to disturb her. Any disturbance was met with screeches and apologies from whoever was the encumbrance.

She continued to eat, not minding that her mother was looking at her with disdain. Genevieve knew that starting the conversation would have disastrous consequences that she would rather avoid. She was still in a good mood and would be going for a picnic at the Thames by noon.

"Will you not talk to your daughter?" her mother wailed all of a sudden, slicing her hand through the air.

Her father shrugged, not saying a word. Talking would only invoke her mother's wrath and it was best for everyone to stay silent.

"Genevieve, your name has graced the gossip sheets," her mother said finally, fuming so much that she threw the paper across the table. "Read how much your name has been maligned! The last time your name was in these sheets, the Queen had named you diamond of the first water! And look at how much you have fallen since then!"

Genevieve snatched the paper from the air, eyebrows furrowed. She could not believe her ears at first. Her name had not graced the gossip sheets in quite a while and she never wanted the attention either way. When her eyes glazed over the sheets, she was horrified.

*"Lord H only shared one dance set with Lady Genevieve at*

94

the Countess of Kenford's soiree. Could it be that Lord H is looking for a future viscountess? He will have to watch out as the Earl of Kenford with his dashingly good looks and charm will be hard to live up to!"

She felt her stomach tighten into knots as the words resounded in her mind. The world seemed to fade away for a brief moment as Genevieve tried to make sense of the words.

"You should never have danced with him!" her mother continued to screech. "I wanted to pull you back but you had already slithered away. Even the countess agreed that it was most undignified! Of all people to dance with? Lord Hamilton?"

"Mother -

Genevieve was swiftly interrupted. "Nothing you say will ever change this! All of London will remember you as the woman who danced with that Hamilton man!"

"Sybil," Genevieve heard her father speak for the first time since she stepped into the dining room. "Do you not think that you are reading into this a little more than you should? It is only just gossip."

"In London, gossip can either make or destroy your chances of a good match. I do not want our daughter to end up with the Hamiltons! Do you not see everything that is wrong here?"

"The viscount is a good man, and I have no issue with him except business. As I have said, he will bring us a fortune with his tea trade. More than anything, I want to do business with him!"

Genevieve watched the back and forth between her parents. Her mother let out a heavy sigh. "Do not just speak so nonchalantly, Edmund! How would you feel if your daughter was married to such a horrid individual?"

Her father smiled at her. "Genevieve knows what kind of match she is expected to make. And that is all that matters."

The dining room slowly relapsed into an uncomfortable silence with Genevieve at the center of it all.

# Chapter 13

Staring out the window, James saw the London streets roll before his eyes. The carriage bumped from time to time, coming with jolts that sent tingles up his face. He struggled to keep himself aright, trying to remind himself that he did not make a completely bad decision by going with his mother's decision to chaperone Alice for the picnic.

A few hours ago, James thought that maybe being out in the sun might be good for him. He had been spending most of his time away from people, stalking in the dark corners of ballrooms and locking himself up in the study. It was a habit that he had grown used to over the months even though he knew that one day, he would have to come out of his shell. But he never thought that day would come so soon.

But the time had come for Alice to make a match and it was his duty to help her choose between the gentlemen of the peerage so that his sister could live happily. For one, he would have to assess every gentleman and get information about each one. Their earnings and fortunes, their behavior in clubs and towards their maids as that would tell heavily on how one might treat his wife. While he wanted the best for his sister, James also wanted her to have a love match. It was one thing to be married to someone and another to marry someone that you were interested in.

James knew the difference between the two scenarios and while he would guide Alice to make the right match, he also wanted it to be her decision. At least, it was what he had wanted for himself as well even though he now knew that it might never happen.

A part of him wondered whether true marriages still existed among the ton or if everything was just meant to keep up appearances. Behind every lavish ball and lurid dress, James knew that there was an almost unhappy woman who just wanted to let everyone know that she was comfortable while lying to them, or rather, make them believe that she was happy.

James knew that his father would have helped Alice make the right match. And he was doubting himself at the moment. Even though his father never had the time for him, James knew that his father always made the right decisions for the household. Even when the wheat business did not flourish that well, money was still kept aside for the family's upkeep. And usually, it was always more than enough. He wished that he could be like his father. A man who was well capable of taking care of his family.

He continued to look out the window every night and then, his mind drifting back and forth. For minutes now, it was all he could do. James turned his direction away from the window to look at his sister. Now that he sat in the carriage with his legs crossed, he could only think about his sister, Alice.

She looked resplendent in her green dress covered with lace of a slightly brighter color. The lady's maid - Francine - had made a good choice of the color as it brought out his sister's piercing gaze. Lately, James noticed that Alice was different. After the death of their brother, Ned, almost all of the family relapsed into a deep and dark time that took almost forever. Mourning and grief ate deep into their bones, and James slowly watched his sister get leeched of life.

On most days, she lay in bed and watched the rain sluice on the glass panels in her room. He would bring hot broth to her and take the plate of uneaten food, asking her to eat for her own sake. Sometimes, Alice would be unable to stand because she was so weak that her skin was sagging on her frame. She barely left the room for weeks on end, and even after some time, James had to force her to leave the bed and come with him when he came to clear his head on horseback.

It felt like aeons ago when they would ride into the sunrise and he would keep Alice under his watchful gaze so that she would not fall off the horse. But her grip was usually steady despite her weakness and slowly, he watched life come back to her. Alice was healthier now with plump cheeks and a round face. When Ned passed away, she lost all her baby fat and grew into a beautiful young woman who looked so much like their mother.

But where their mother's interest was in gossip, Alice loved art with the same passion with which he loved books. More often than not, James made it a priority to take her to the art gallery in London, travelling way from the countryside just to see the paintings. At some point, he even took her to the Art Academy on Piccadilly and he smiled when he saw her face light up in appreciation.

Alice was no longer as fervent with art as before, but James still saw the marvel on her face when they walked into the countess' residence the day before. Numerous art pieces hung on the walls in the drawing room that fascinated even him. There was a particular still life that caught his eye and he imagined how it would be to wake up every morning to see the composition of light and dark.

"You have been staring for quite a while brother," Alice said, breaking the silence. "Is there anything on your mind?"

James shook his head even though he was eager to make a conversation with his sister. "Not really. I just have a lot on my mind for now."

"I doubt that the matrimonial fervor of the ton is finally getting to you. You are not one to be troubled by that. Except it is this morning's gossip you are thinking about."

James waved his head as if to dismiss Alice's words. "Not even a word on that gossip sheet drips with the truth. The ton tells themselves what they want to just to make themselves feel better. It is only a matter of time till it all dies down."

"That is true. But do you not think that you have a chance with Lady Genevieve? I mean, even if she is not the diamond of the first water anymore, she is still quite a catch this Season."

"Diamond or not, it does not matter, Alice. None of it does anymore. Not with everything that is going on. Why do we not talk about you?"

Alice smiled, fanning herself tersely. "All of this talk about matrimony will soon end, brother. And then you will have to find a wife for yourself. At least, to produce an heir that will carry your name."

"None of this talk about matches would have ever come up if you did not come along," James said. "I would have only thought to deal with the hassle when I am nothing less than two and fifty," he said with a sigh.

They both started laughing - something that had not happened in a long time. It was relaxing to see Alice smile and chortle, with her eyes beaming with life.

"Nevertheless, mother would bother you till the ends of the earth unless you make up your mind to make a match. By next

Season, Mother would have made a list of potential brides in London and start setting you up for promenades."

James smiled. He knew that his mother was capable of being like every other ambitious mama of the ton. Sometimes, she could be calm and relaxed while other times, all she talked about was getting her children married. When they were little, James wondered how Ned must have felt with all of the responsibility weighing down on him at such a young age. It was his turn, and he was trying to shy away from it.

"Mother can do such," he said, smiling. "But then, I might be able to escape after all. Who knows?"

"It is more unlikely. And it would be nice if you think about it well."

He was itching to change the topic now, no longer wanting to talk about how his mother might treat him if he did not get married. Not like he was planning to anyway. But the thought of the future was sometimes nauseating and troubling.

"Perhaps we should talk about you now," James intoned. "Mother told me all about Lord Lorwood."

Alice blushed so much that her face turned a brilliant shade of red. "Lord Lorwood? What about him?"

James knew that his sister was trying to play ignorant so that they might evade the conversation. Alice was usually not much of a speaker and even when she was a child, she kept to herself. Seeing her blush prompted James to tease her a little more.

"I saw you speaking with him after the dance," James whispered. "I watched the subtle laughs and eye flutters. Were you trying to get him to notice you?"

Alice hit him on the hand so hard that James flinched a little and her voice came out in a screech. "I would not! Lord Lorwood is not a man who would have even noticed something so suggestive."

"Then you already know what kind of man he is. How magnificent! And to think that all of this happened in one evening."

"If you do not stop teasing me this much, then you will end up learning nothing," she threatened playfully.

"Alright," James replied, suppressing a smile. "But you know that by threatening me like this, you would need to give as much information as possible."

Alice pursed her lips. "I will only say what I want to. But you need to stop interrupting me!"

"Have the floor, Your Grace," James mocked and received another hit on the arm.

He settled in his chair and listened to Alice. Her voice was tinged with happiness when she spoke, and there was more of a glint in her eyes.

"We mostly talked about art," she said. "The pieces in the countess' residence were almost priceless from what I heard. And he has quite the collection himself! I was so overjoyed when I learned that he shared a mutual interest in art! No one else in London pays attention to these beautiful pieces that it has gotten so lonely all by myself."

"I hope he did not just leave. Did he say when he might call on you? Something for us to be sure that he is interested in making a match with you?"

"I never said that!" Alice screeched, burying her red face in her palms. "But he promised to call on me so that we could talk more about our interests."

"It is settled then," he replied. "I should invite him to our little meeting in White's. He is a man of interest, I take it. Perhaps he might also be interested in making a fortune from tea."

"I will talk to him about it -

"I am not asking you to talk to Lord Lorwood about my business, Alice. While that would be admirable, it is my duty. And I will carry it out myself."

"He is a kind man if you must know. More than anyone, Robert is the kindest there is in all of London. He is also good at dancing and -

James interrupted her. "Robert? On a given-name basis now? Mother would be perpetually grateful and perhaps, she might even get off me."

Alice blushed again. "It is merely introductions, brother. But enough about me. Let us talk about something else."

But Alice's voice already faded into the background. James was thinking of how much his sister had grown. He was glad to hear about Lord Lorwood and he hoped that the baron would not dash her hopes against the rocks. He made a note to find out more about him before they started going on promenades in Hyde Park. James just hoped that Lord Lorwood's interest in Alice would not be deterred by the latest gossip in the scandal sheets about his family. The author had cast aspersions on their family name, but there was nothing he could do about it. He prayed that the ton would soon find another topic to chew on and enjoy.

"I just think that you and Genevieve would make a fine couple regardless of what the gossip sheets say."

James sputtered, his train of thought completely shattered by the words. Alice had never been so outspoken before. Usually, she suggested what she wanted to talk about and this stark bravery completely astonished him.

"What?" he sputtered.

" I know that you have been quite troubled about marriage, brother, but not everyone out there cares about appearances. What truly matters is what is in your heart. Appearances will fade with time, but the heart will withstand the test of time."

He was out of words and Alice continued to speak. "You have a good heart, James. And it will be foolish for any lady to overlook that."

The carriage came to a sudden halt, saving James from the distress of having to speak about his feelings. They were a part of him that was better bottled up. Also, he did not want to talk about the possibility of finding a lady who might accept him even with his scars. But even as he alighted the carriage, he started to question the possibility of Lady Genevieve accepting him even with his scars. He thought about it for a while as he led Alice down the cobblestone path and down to the shore. James soon let go of the thoughts as he got to the Thames Shore where Elizabeth and the rest of the Arlingtons were waiting.

He extended his greeting to them, smiling as he did so.

"So, when will the others arrive?" Alice asked.

"Others?" James questioned, arching his eyebrows. "Which others?"

Elizabeth smiled, setting down a wicker basket. "Genevieve and Kitty should be arriving any minute."

James felt a shiver go through his body despite the heat of the London afternoon.

***

Genevieve had left the house almost immediately after the slight altercation with her mother about the gossip sheets and how much she had lowered her chances of making a good match. Her father did not object because he had high expectations of her, but Genevieve just wanted to be normal.

Among the ton, most marriages were not born out of love but responsibility. Genevieve felt like she had only read about true love all her life but had never felt it. She wanted to feel it twist her heart, to wreck her mind with various thoughts of a faceless beloved. But all she could feel in her heart was a pit of darkness so vast that it was unquantifiable.

Jenny had been happy to let her leave the house with a cloak because Genevieve did not want their fingers pointing at her as she moved along. She never found the dance with the viscount as humiliating as her mother made it out to be. She wanted to say that it was enjoyable but after living in that home for as long as she could remember, Genevieve knew that keeping her lips sealed would only keep the peace. And that was what she craved the most now. Some tranquility and maybe a book or two so she could read.

The picnic was scheduled for noon by the Thames and Genevieve had already packed a book along with her that she could read to pass the time. It was one by Shakespeare about a merchant who wanted his pound of flesh because the other person bound by the contract could not pay his debt. Genevieve found the book intriguing, and the passages were more soothing than laborious. She just hoped that no one would bother her while she was reading.

Genevieve was relieved to be away from home and her overbearing mother. Being perfect for an evening was one thing but Genevieve had been perfect all her own life. Kids her age had played in the rain till they caught colds and were nursed back to health, they danced in the mud and dirtied their fingers and dresses, played with dolls, and set imaginary tea meetings. But Genevieve did not have that childhood.

She was brought up strutting around the drawing room with a pile of books atop her head to help her build good posture, playing the pianoforte until her fingers were numb, dancing till her feet hurt and she never went to bed without a massage. It was arduous keeping up with her mother. Sometimes Genevieve wondered how her mother managed to keep every step perfect and elaborate.

Taking the thought away from her mind, Genevieve tried to concentrate on the evening ahead. She knew that Elizabeth would be at the Thames by now, arranging the baskets of baked goodies on a blanket and preparing for their visit. So, she told her mother the night before that she would be attending with Kitty and her older brother, Charles as their chaperone. Also, since her family was close with the Arlingtons, her father just dismissed her with a wave of his hand.

"We have been waiting for you all morning," Kitty's voice drawled in a monotonous way, just like it did when she was angry. "Where have you been?"

Genevieve climbed into the carriage and greeted Charles briefly before turning back to Kitty. "Did you not see the gossip sheets this morning? My mother was panicking so much that I thought she would start screeching. In fact, she did!"

Kitty's face fell. "I saw the sheets, Genny. I am so sorry about that."

"It is all just baseless conjecture," Charles said softly, his deep voice gliding into their conversation. "All these authors use the same pattern if you have not noticed. First, they bring up a scenario and then try to instigate a scandal. Did any of you not know what happened with Lady Jessamine last Season?"

"Lady Jessamine?" Kitty repeated. "And who is that, brother? You seem to know everyone in London."

Charles rolled his eyes a bit too dramatically. "The daughter of the Duke of Sussex. She danced with Lord Eversleigh first and then, they were caught in the orangery in such a scandalous position that they had to get married. Now, they reside in the countryside, and away from the prying eyes of the ton."

"Lord Eversleigh? The one with the crooked nose?" Kitty asked.

Charles nodded. Everyone in London except Kitty knew about Lady Jessamine and the scandal surrounding their marriage. The gossip was on everyone's lips for months, and it all started with a tiny gossip just like Charles described. But Genevieve knew that Lord Eversleigh had always wanted Lady Jessamine for himself but everyone knew that she did not return his affections.

Once, he even bought a rare variety of flowers for Lady

Jessamine, arranging it from her doorstep and all the way to the ball that would take place at his abbey. At first, the gossip sheet came out and Lord Eversleigh read a different meaning to it. What he saw was that the poor woman was his, and he accosted her in the orangery where they were caught. Without even thinking about it, Genevieve already knew that Lord Hamilton would not read anything into the gossip. In fact, she thought that he would even recluse himself further, staying within the confines of his home until the news died down.

"We have arrived," the footman announced shortly after they took a bend and the door opened.

Charles was the first to get down and helped Kitty. Then, he reached out for Genevieve and she took his hand. When she stepped out with the book under her arm, she was glad that she decided to leave her house and not let her mother's complaints weigh her down. The sun was bright and the weather was fair, maybe a tad too hot. The blue-grey water of the Thames was cresting softly on the grassy shore, sparkling under the sun and the breeze was cool on her skin. It was a good day for her to relax and be out in the world instead of sulking in her room and seeing the world from the windows of her bedchamber.

The second carriage carrying their - hers and Kitty's - lady's maids came to halt as well and the two women - Jenny and Maria - stepped out. They all walked down to the large tree by the shore where they could see Elizabeth setting baskets. She hurried to them once she caught sight of them and led them over.

"You are early Genevieve!" Elizabeth moaned. "This is a first!"

Genevieve laughed. "I thought I should make a change for once. At least, so that you will not pull my hair out and I will not miss those biscuits."

"I had the maids make more than we planned. It is going to be a rather great day!"

Genevieve felt even cooler under the shade and was about to take her seat on the soft picnic blanket when she saw that unmistakable frame. He was tall and broad-shouldered, eyes squinting in the sun and the scar on his face was almost a flaming red. He was dressed in a dark blue tailcoat and a grey shirt that matched his ivory inexpressibles. Beside him, Alice was walking towards them in a moss green dress that was embroidered with gold.

Her heart raced in her chest and her temples throbbed from the rush of anxiety brewing in her throat. Their eyes met for a moment, and Genevieve's mind was spinning. She expected Alice, but not the viscount. His image was intimidating yet relaxing. Genevieve was so enraptured with her thoughts that she did not hear him speak.

"Good afternoon, Lady Genevieve," he said with a bow, ash blonde hair tickling the sides of his face.

"My lord," she reeled her mind back instantly, dipping a curtsy.

Genevieve looked up to see his eyes on hers again, and this time, she hoped that her face had masked the surprise she had from seeing him once more.

# Chapter 14

James just stood there watching, unable to take his eyes off Lady Genevieve. Not in his wildest dreams did he ever expect that she would also attend the Arlington picnic. As he maintained his position under the quaint lemon tree, he wondered if leaving the house was a good idea after all. After what had happened that morning with the gossip sheet, James did not even think that Lady Genevieve would take to any outing.

He was desperately trying to hide the astonishment from his face and he was glad that Alice took all the attention that should have been directed at him. But James did not miss the look of surprise on her face when she extended her greetings. It was slight, just like the look of disdain on her face when they first met but it was there. Even as he shifted his weight from foot to foot, he could not help but think so much of the look that marred her face just a few seconds ago.

"I am thrilled that you could make it here," Lord Arlington said, extending his hand toward James. "I did not know you would come after the stress of the soiree yesternight."

James took his hand. "It is merely an indulgence. I would do anything to be in this serenity and have this quietude. Rather pleasing is it not?"

A girl he recognized as Kitty nodded with a polite smile. James turned to face Lady Genevieve but her eyes were averted as she was gazing at the blue-grey waters of the Thames. He did not find that disturbing in the least, but he could not take his mind away from the impression on her face earlier.

Having served as a soldier for years, James had learned quickly to be keen on details. It had saved him a lot over the years and the one time he threw all caution to the wind and just go with his gut, the scar on his face happened. On some nights, James wished he could go back to that day and pay attention to the details. After his recovery, every little detail was not spared. It made him able to read people's feelings based on the look on their faces, to determine ways to speak to them without inciting them and to get them to trust him. Just like he did to the other bachelors and gentlemen and the soiree to get potential investors into his trade.

Lady Genevieve was neutral now, shifting into a more comfortable position which made the folds of her dress rustle. He stared at her face, trying to decipher what was going on in her mind. And for the first time, he could almost not tell. From what he had seen earlier, James had concluded that she was probably harboring resentment toward him. While it was not a definite conclusion, he was slightly sure that the gossip sheets had a toll on her. And for that, James wanted to tell her how extremely sorry he was for putting her in such a difficult situation.

James loathed the gossip sheets, and he hoped the authors would stop spreading such aspersions and baseless accusations. They were the most infuriating set of people, hiding behind covered faces and inkwells, using people's personal lives to make money. But James did not blame them. Instead, he blamed the ton for paying for those sheets. Once he'd heard that the Queen was even an avid reader of the gossip.

Last Season, James spent most of his time in the study and away from the outside world. And from time to time, his mother sent a maid to place a gossip sheet when he rang for tea and biscuits. Most times, he neglected them but the few times he brought himself to read the words, all he heard was about the famous diamond of the first water and how many proposals she had rejected. About how many gentlemen were vying for her hand.

And that diamond was none other than Lady Genevieve.

Even now that she was no longer the diamond, James could still tell that most gentlemen wanted her attention. And yet, he had easily taken a dance with her. To his surprise, she had accepted his offer of a dance. A part of him felt it was out of pity and because she did not want him to be humiliated. But more than anything in that soiree, the dance with Lady Genevieve filled him with so much joy.

Conversing with her came fluidly unlike with other people. They spoke little, but those minutes were the absolute best. James wondered if she had a great time, but she had already drifted away after the dance and he did not get the opportunity to ask her if she enjoyed his company just as much as he enjoyed hers.

It was now glaring that she did not. Lady Genevieve did not even meet his eyes, and there had been resentment on her face.

'Does she resent me for what happened in the scandal sheets?' he asked himself, wondering what could have happened.

James immediately recalled that the Duchess did not approve of his time with Lady Genevieve in the ballroom. He wondered if the gossip sheets might have angered her further and prompted some response that might have resulted in Lady Genevieve's resentment. The huge lack of information made James curious.

'Perhaps the gossip sheets might have been misinterpreted? Or does she dislike being the center of attention?'

The questions were still filtering through his mind, each one giving rise to another and there was no answer in sight.

"Let us take our seats and have a great time," Lord Arlington's boisterous voice rang through the clearing and broke through James' thoughts.

Like all the other people present, James took his seat on the warm blanket. The scar on his face warmed from the heat, sending a pleasant feeling through his body. At this point, he thought that perhaps being outside the manor might be good for him even with Lady Genevieve avoiding him at every turn. And for that, he blamed his mother.

James would have never danced with Lady Genevieve if not that his mother was the very person suggesting it. Even with his reluctance, his mother's overbearing attitude pushed him to ignore the Duchess' contemptuous look and take Lady Genevieve to dance. While it was pleasing, they were now the topic of the week. James could tell that his mother was secretly happy with the words from the gossip sheets. Like always, there was an ulterior motive that bothered on responsibility. And he always hated that most times, his mother was right.

"A wonderful day is it not?" Kitty's breathy voice soared through the silence, soft and feathery and there were mutters and groans of agreement from the settling bodies.

"This is a wonderful punch, Lord Arlington, I suppose you should not know how it was prepared," a man James recognized as Charles -Kitty's older brother - concluded as he sipped the dark liquid from the ornate glass.

"But of course, he would not, which gentleman ever has an idea about the intricacies involved in running a household?" Lady

Arlington chuckled softly, covering her lips with a fan.

Lord Arlington let out a huff. "I beg to differ, ladies but I am well versed in the workings of my manor. After all, it is a man's responsibility to look after the management of his home."

Miss Elizabeth bellowed out a burst of unladylike laughter and the crowd's response to her zealous display was soft snickers covered with even softer coughs. No one wanted to deny the marquess' statement as they were not as confident and gutsy as Miss Elizabeth was.

"Come now, Elizabeth, your father does more than either of us give him credit for," Lady Arlington said quickly in her husband's defense.

"Well, I should agree with Lady Arlington. I read the latest column of the paper and the author says that men are getting more and more involved in the running of their manors," Charles said.

"Are you?" Kitty asked with a playful grin on her lips. "Lord Hamilton?"

Feeling ambushed, James' eyes scanned the entire party and settled on Lady Genevieve sitting on the other end, as though she chose where she sat just to be far from him. "I am unfortunately not one of the better men, Lady Kitty," he responded much to her chagrin. "But usually, I manage what a man is supposed to. Earnings and paying for dresses and everything else."

"I do have to admire you, Lord Hamilton," Elizabeth said. "Father always says honesty makes a man, and it is a virtue, to be honest."

"Are you saying that your dear papa is not honest, Elizabeth?" Lord Arlington asked with a hand over his heart in mock terror.

Elizabeth's lips parted slightly, and she looked around the room with a dramatic pause before she spoke. "I said nothing about you, papa."

"I shall rather like to hear about your time during the war," Charles said. "I have heard quite an earful from Kitty and I must say that I have been very curious."

James almost let out a groan of displeasure. But he was simply thankful that he caught himself before he gives the gossip column even more information to work with. He was sure that whatever they discussed would not go out to the public, but no one knew how the author got their information. In London, if they did not discuss the words in the manor, there was every probability that it would be in the next column of the gossip sheet.

"Why would you suggest such a gruesome topic?" Lady Arlington cried. "I am sure that the viscount would rather not talk about such tales."

'Gruesome?' James thought ruefully. It was quite the endeavor to survive the pressure involving war and having to come back and have society trivialize and humble all the things he achieved.

"I would much rather talk about Lady Charlotte's dreadful gown at the ball last night. How could she possibly think that awful orange would look good on her pale skin?" Lady Arlington spoke, trying to dismiss Charles' topic.

"Mama, you do not have to be mean!" Elizabeth scolded her mother.

"I should rather agree Miss Elizabeth. Lady Charlotte has beautiful skin and quite the complexion if I might add. But I also have to admit should her mother keep putting her in those off-putting colors she would have a tumultuous time finding a husband." Kitty replied.

"With a fortune as heavy as hers? I do not think so," Charles put in, smiling in the corner.

Seeing as they both disagreed, they sought a neutral party to quell the argument. They turned to the one person with enough influence to settle the matter once and for all.

"Lady Genevieve, do you believe a woman's desirability rests within her looks or her fortune?" Kitty asked.

Genevieve looked up and her eyes met James' for a split second before she faced Kitty once more. Confusing the rattled man even further, she met his eyes. A lot of things were on James' mind when his eyes met hers.

'Did that mean she glanced at me?' he asked himself, steadying himself on the blanket and trying not to spill the punch.

James only paid attention to what they talked about when his name was mentioned, Lady Genevieve's expression held the rest of his interest that lovely afternoon.

'But why would she look at him before she spoke?'

Shaking off the thought James diverted his thoughts to another matter - Genevieve's answer.

"Should that question not be posed to the party doing the desiring?" Genevieve replied.

"How boring," Kitty sighed and gave up.

But not Elizabeth who was set out to prove a point that Lady Charlotte would be married, dreadful frocks or not.

"But in your point of view, you were the diamond after all. What about you did you think men were after?"

Genevieve's breathing hitched as she regarded the surrounding silence. Everyone was waiting for her response and James could see the hesitation in her eyes. Yet, she only really cared what one person might think.

"I do not know for a certain what men think, but I know what we should desire from a marriageable woman. She should be knowledgeable, delicate, and kind. She should add rather than subtract from her husband and she should know how to raise good children and run a household properly for money does not make one happy and looks shall fade."

"Well said, Lady Genevieve," Charles said. "Just as one would expect from the most knowledgeable person in the group."

Kitty and Elizabeth scoffed, eliciting laughs from the rest of everyone. James felt rather glad that everything they talked about did not coincidentally include the horrid words of the latest gossip sheets or the war that he never wanted to talk about.

Taking himself away from the hubbub of voices, he turned to face the Thames shoreline. In that slight moment, James let all the tension from overthinking flow out of his body and escape into the warm afternoon air. A strange feeling of tiredness overwhelmed him, and soon, he lapsed into a state of calm. One where he could just relax and lose himself in whatever was on his mind. This time, it was about the tea trade.

"Lord Hamilton, do you care for more punch?" Lady Arlington asked James after a pat on his shoulder, breaking him from the daze he was in.

He turned to her with a smile. "Yes, please. It is quite a delight."

As Lady Arlington poured more of the savory liquid into his glass, James turned to Lady Genevieve's position. She was talking excitedly with Alice and soon they were both smiling. For that, James hoped things might eventually turn out well for his sister. At least, he owed her that.

***

Genevieve was glad that the viscount did not notice the surprise on her face. Or at least that was what she thought. Lord Hamilton was not a man of many emotions, and the most she had seen on his face was a crooked smile that felt more forced than real. But that was enough for her because Genevieve did not know what she would have done if he had said something out of turn.

When the conversation about the Season started and about men being more involved in the affairs of their residences, Genevieve wished that Lord Hamilton would have said something. She wanted his opinions on more than just literature, and her thoughts about what he might think of life plagued her mind. More than just being kind, Genevieve wanted to marry a gentleman who understood the workings and intricacies of the world. Someone who could provide solutions to problems and not just indulge himself with brandy and champagne.

So far, Lord Hamilton just listened through the conversation. On some occasions, he offered slight laughs that lit up his face and made him slightly handsome. Genevieve had the faintest feeling that he wanted to say something but kept holding his opinions to himself. So when a question was directed at him, Genevieve was glad.

"I am unfortunately not one of the better men, Lady Kitty," he responded softly, the deep baritone of his voice ringing through her mind. "But usually, I manage what a man is supposed to. Earnings and paying for dresses and everything else."

Just like the time they spoke at the soiree, Lord Hamilton said little even though his face reflected something else entirely. He was not a man of many words, and Genevieve concluded it must be because of the events that befell him. When she first heard about Lord Hamilton from Elizabeth, Genevieve got the information that he was a recluse. A man who stayed out of the way of other people and locked himself in the darkest alcoves of his manor.

To see him at the Thames, closing his eyes under the sun and letting the rays bathe his face was a little disconcerting for Genevieve. Even at the ball, she noticed that he kept to the farthest sides of the room like an insipid wallflower, sipping glasses of champagne and observing the events around him. His eyes glowed now, the stark blue brighter under the light from the sun. They seemed to draw Genevieve's attention away from everyone else as if the waves of the Thames were calling out to her.

"Genevieve," a soft voice called out to her, bringing her thoughts to a halt. "I could not help but notice you looking at the painting on the mantelpiece the night before."

Genevieve turned to face curious green eyes on a small face. It was Alice, Lord Hamilton's sister. In more ways than one, they were opposites of one another. Where the viscount had a large frame and towered above most people, Alice was slight and looked almost as fragile as a lily. Her face was pale - like she had not been in the sun for too long, and her round face was delicate. But where they were similar were their eyes. Even though both of them had different colors, they were vivid and verdant, piercing Genevieve's soul.

She collected herself. "That painting? It has been a favourite of mine for a while. Why do you ask?"

Alice smiled and dropped her fan. "Painting is merely an interest of mine. Colours have always been so fascinating."

Genevieve's eyes widened. "Do you really mean that because you like paintings? Or because women are meant to admire them?"

"Of course not. I have always admired a painting because most of them tell silent stories that come from the artist's mind. I mean, there is one painting that has stuck in my mind for a while now and it reminds me of the winter. Cold and darkness, but with soft lights without heat."

"Wow!" Genevieve exclaimed.

Most ladies in London had interests in the arts because the men admired them as well. They visited galleries because they went with the men and dabbled in watercolors because society wanted them to. Most ladies had other interests, but they were not inclined to show them.

Genevieve had been an avid admirer of the arts since she

stumbled on a painting in her father's study. She had been no less than thirteen, and the paintings told her a certain story and that began her fascination with the arts. But at the soiree, she was merely looking at the painting like everyone else, trying not to gawk in admiration for it would boost the Countess' ego. In fact, she was trying not to be caught staring at Lord Hamilton. But now that Alice talked about it, the painting sprang into her mind.

Alice blushed, picking up her fan. "I have just always loved the art. Paintings, drawings, and even sculptures. If it were up to me, I would have been in the academy. But alas, ladies are not allowed that kind of education."

"Maybe that is because most ladies are inclined to have other interests. I mean, rarely do you see a lady gawking at paintings. Most are preparing for either hosting or attending balls."

Alice groaned. "Balls have always made me wilt. It is a wonder that many ladies fancy it so much. If I had my way, I would spend all of my days just watching pictures and reading books."

"You seem so sure about that," Genevieve said with a smile, seeing how Alice's face lit up when she talked about spending the remaining of her days before paintings.

"Perhaps, more than anything else in the world. After marriage that is," Alice replied.

"Marriage comes first for every lady, does it not?" Genevieve asked with a small smile on her face. "I thought it might be different for someone of your demeanour."

She had not failed to notice Alice's introverted nature throughout the time they were seated by the Thames. Even at the soiree, Alice spent most of her time in a corner, just like her brother. But in the end, Genevieve saw her dance with Lord Lorwood. And it brought a smile to her face, just like talking about art did.

"Mother expects me to make a match this Season of course for fear that I might be called an old maid by the next and I must say that I understand her fears. But that does not take away my interest in painting, does it?"

"Painting?" Genevieve asked. "Do you paint by yourself as well?"

Alice nodded. "I have hung a few around the manor. Perhaps when you come to visit, you might get to see a few of them."

Genevieve flushed, her face heating up for a moment. She had never once thought of visiting the Hamilton residence. Even the conversation she was trying to have with Alice was partly because she was trying to avoid thoughts of Lord Hamilton, his dark blue eyes, love for books, and amiable personality. She looked up and immediately wished that she had not.

His eyes were on hers at once and Genevieve felt a rush run through her body from the intensity in his eyes. They were dark, masked by thick and dark lashes. She tried to smile, but her body would not respond. In the end, she settled for dipping her head slightly.

"I will be going to the Pall Mall galleries in two days' time. Would you like to join me?" Alice asked.

"I would love to," she replied with little thought.

Genevieve would have done anything to escape her mother's watchful gaze. And visiting the galleries with Alice felt like the right opportunity. Also, Genevieve felt like going with her might help improve her standing and increase her chances of making a match this Season.

Lord Arlington's words interrupted their conversation. "Now that we have almost exhausted the food, perhaps we should all take a walk along the shoreline and feel the wind in our faces?"

Everyone mumbled in agreement, and they set off in pairs. Lord and Lady Arlington were the first to set out and Genevieve's heart jumped when Lord Hamilton extended his hand toward her.

"Would you like to go on a stroll with me?" he asked, his deep voice resonating through her mind.

Genevieve felt the world stop for a moment and she could only feel the slight thud of her heart. There was a small expectant smile on his face, and when she gazed at him, all she could think about was the dance they shared. Genevieve saw this as an opportunity to further gain entry into his mind.

With a smile, she replied. "I would love to."

# Chapter 15

James was striding down the shoreline, gazing at the enormous expanse of water as it flowed on its merry way. One would think that he was deep in thought about the world or something along that line of cogitations. But James was thinking about Lady Genevieve's slim hand wrapped around his own.

Her touch was delicate and soft, just like at the ball. The silk glove on her hand grazed his skin, and he felt a sudden cold rush over him. They had been walking for a while now and none of them had said a word. James had a lot of things on his mind that he would like to speak about to someone of like mind, but the perfume that danced from her skin was altering every thought he had.

The others in attendance were walking in pairs just before them, and James wished that one of them were close just to stir a conversation. At least, it might help to break the endless drone of silence and the squawking of birds as they flitted around the shoreline. He turned to look at her but she was staring straight ahead, at the small apple orchard in the distance.

He turned around for a slight moment to see Jenny, Lady Genevieve's lady's maid gently trailing behind them. She was smiling slightly, attempting to hide her expression whenever James looked at her. He thought it was strange that with everything going on, Lady Genevieve's lady's maid was having a great time. But James had concluded that different people had separate priorities. Whatever was happening in the gossip sheets would be none of Jenny's business.

He let out a small sigh, trying to find a comfortable position that might not make Lady Genevieve agitated. She had said almost nothing throughout the conversation unless she was talking with Alice. Even, James could see on her face that she was distracted by something. But that was the end of his deduction. Whatever was on her mind was closed off from him and that troubled James.

And then their eyes met.

James saw the world stop, all the conversation around him straying into a void of silence. All he saw was Lady Genevieve's pale face, the blonde tresses that fell across her back in luscious waves, her pearly blue-green eyes that reminded James of the ocean and where it met the skies in perfect tandem, a slender neck that was just as graceful as she was. And the slight curve of her lips, full and soft when she smiled.

For a full minute, James was fighting the urge to keep staring at her. A cold sweat broke out on his back and he was happy that his valet had picked out a dark color that would help to mask the perspiration. Tingles ran through his veins, and the world became a hodgepodge of nothingness.

"Might something be wrong?" Lady Genevieve said finally, her soft voice breaking through the heavy silence.

James' breath caught in his throat. "Nothing is wrong. Just some minor inconveniences springing up from time to time. But be rest assured, it will be well taken care of."

She smiled - a sly one. "Do these inconveniences include the affairs of your house? Or maybe of your trade?"

James stopped his face from smiling just in time. "I am sorry if this conversation started on the wrong foot, Lady Genevieve."

"And what would you mean by that, my lord? We started quite nicely if you ask me."

"I have wronged you, Lady Genevieve," he started, his voice quivering. "And I ought to apologise for my misgivings as I am the cause of the aspersions on your name. I should never have asked to share a dance with you for it would bring you into the spotlight and give you an unwanted and the wrong kind of attention."

When he was done, James felt like a tremendous weight was just lifted off his chest. He breathed better, the air suddenly sweeter and cleaner. The silence that entrenched them a few moments ago was back now, heavier than before. When she did not speak, James knew it was his cue to say more. So, he did.

"I would have never consciously caused you or your family any scandal. And if I did, I must express how sorry I am for any misinformation and thoughts that might have been misconstrued as a result. Once again, I am truly sorry for putting you in the spotlight at the Kenford soiree because of the dance."

He expected her to say something, to quell his troubled heart. James turned to face her and her expression was one of someone who was deep in thought. As if trying to reach a decision to accept his apology or not. It made James want to reach into her mind and bring forth an answer. But he could not read her actions or thoughts.

It then occurred to James that Lady Genevieve might have read the gossip sheets as well. And that meant that the Duchess would have set her eyes on them too. Just like every member of the peerage. James was even more conscious now, knowing that he was treading on slippery ground. For one, Lady Genevieve might just be taking a stroll with him out of politeness and obligation and not because she wanted to do it. In fact, she might even detest him because of those sheets.

"You do not need to apologise, my lord," Lady Genevieve spoke finally, her voice halting all of James' thoughts. "You did nothing wrong as far as I can see."

"Nothing wrong?" he repeated, clearly astonished.

"Yes, my lord. Only when someone has done wrong, do they need to give an apology to whom it is due. And nothing of the such has happened."

James felt relief flood his body when he heard those words. In his heart, he thought he placed Lady Genevieve into an uncomfortable position that no member of the ton would want to find themselves.

"If you are worried about the dance, my lord, be rest assured that I quite enjoyed it. I was taken by your gentle dance steps and slight movements."

James grinned. "Might you be saying it because you are just trying to be polite?"

"Polite?" she laughed airily, the melody floating on the slight breeze. "Most occasions do not require me to be polite. And if I tell you this secret, you must keep it close to your heart."

"Secret?" James asked, enthralled. "Of course, I am a big keeper of secrets. Not like I talk to people, anyway."

"If you will keep it, then you must know that the earl of Kenford is not a brilliant dancer. Had you not asked me to dance, the rest of the evening would have been dreadful."

James smiled. "Thank you. I did not notice that I was good on my feet."

"There was also the short but interesting discussion we had, my lord. It was the best I have had in quite a long time."

James was completely stunned. He had not expected such

words from Lady Genevieve. Instead, he hoped that the hurtful words she might say would not have an effect on him. Seeing her smile at him sent his heart into a frenzy.

"The soiree was great because of you, my lord. I should be thanking you," she said with a smile.

This time, James could see the details in her eyes. Lady Genevieve's words were full of sincerity and it made his heart skip a beat. He wondered whether she was not bothered by the scar that tore his face into two halves.

"I - he started but was swiftly interrupted by the appearance of Alice, Elizabeth, Lady Kitty, and Lord Devon - Lady Kitty's older brother. The ladies had apparent joy on their faces and it sparked his curiosity.

"Lord Devon was just asking us if we would like to attend the theaters this coming week!" Elizabeth exclaimed, her eyes shining. "I was just about to ask Genevieve if she would like to come with us."

James could see that Alice was eager to go with them. He was grateful that at least, she wanted to go out more often now and that would increase her chances of making a match. As always, he wanted to make her happy.

"I would love to come," James and Lady Genevieve said at the same time and she laughed.

James cleared his throat. "Alice and I will come together. But we would be taking our leave now. There is a lot to be attended to before the day ends."

In a few minutes, their carriage was rolling down the streets of London and back to their residence.

"It was a rather nice outing, was it not?" Alice asked. "I am glad that you decided to accompany me. Mother would have been completely overbearing."

James laughed, trying to picture the image in his mind. But all he could think about was seeing Lady Genevieve again. Their conversation was short once again, but he enjoyed it and wished that they could have stayed more. While a part of him started to think about what they would say when they met at the theatre, another part of James - the part he had been living with for a long time now - told him that if things continued like this, it would end as a disaster.

One that he would not be able to control.

# Chapter 16

These days, sitting behind the pianoforte and looking at the black and white keys was getting tedious for Genevieve. To her, it had been a long time since she stopped playing the pianoforte for herself. These days, she practiced the pianoforte under her mother's supervision and no matter how perfectly she played, her mother still somehow found a fault. Sometimes, it was that Genevieve got the note wrong even though the music was sounding just exactly right. On other days, Genevieve was so carried away by fear of doing the music imperfectly that her fingers slipped and went out of tune.

Just the day before had been one of the best days of Genevieve's life for the Season. She knew that the days of freedom were about to end when the matrimonial fervor was in full swing and the ladies were escorted by their mamas to prospective husbands on the marriage mart. They had spent so much time near the Thames yesterday and it felt like Genevieve had done nothing at all.

She wished that she could have talked to Lord Hamilton sooner and engaged him in conversation. But he did not speak unless spoken to and getting him to talk was one of the hardest things that ever existed. At least, that was the conclusion she came to after seeing him a few times. Genevieve just had to wait for him to speak and she was quite surprised when he expressed his heartfelt apology about the gossip sheet.

Genevieve was taken aback by the sudden expression of apology and she would have never expected Lord Hamilton to feast his eyes on the words of a gossip sheet. She deduced that his mother must have told him about the sheet and one way or the other, he must have learned about it. And he expressed his words with sincerity and hope that she might forgive him when in fact, Genevieve was delighted about dancing with him.

"Genevieve, you seem rather lost in your thoughts," she heard her mother's voice say. "You cannot keep on working one note all day long."

Genevieve sighed, taking her hands off the pianoforte for a second, and looked around the drawing room. Her fingers were slightly numb from playing for too long and she needed a break. But her mother's watchful eyes were on hers. In a way, she was grateful that her father was sitting in the room and reading the papers as well. It seemed to alleviate some of the tension in the room, but she knew that in a few minutes, her father would leave for the study.

"Can we get on with it? We do not have all day," the Duchess said, fanning her bosom tersely.

"Alright Mother," Genevieve grumbled and struck the keys again.

The discordant music filtered out as she concentrated on the notes in her mind. She had played the music over a million times and it was already ingrained into her mind. Her music teacher was one of the most influential in all of London and her father went to great lengths to hire him when he was working for the Queen regent.

She focused on the dust motes, letting her mind swing away from the world. Slowly, Genevieve dissolved into the music, her fingers working on their own accord. She continued playing softly, the music entering her soul. It brought her alive and memories rushed and collided in her mind. Soon, she was a wildfire, the music her lodestone.

To her, the music was different this time. It sounded more beautiful, the sound richer and fuller to her ears. At some point, Genevieve started to hum in rhythm to the song she was playing. Behind closed eyes, her thoughts were a piece of driftwood, just sailing away from the shore into a vast water of calm.

In her mind's eye, she envisioned Lord Hamilton before her, his blue eyes dark with delight as she played. His broad figure slouched on the velvet sofa, a book open in his lap, but his attention was drawn away from what he was reading because of her music. He appeared in her thoughts more often than not like a taunt, pulling her heart towards him at all times. She saw the scar on his face, the gruesome pinkish skin that covered almost all of his face. To other people, it might be an aberration, a sort of mark that told him apart from the rest of the world.

But to Genevieve, it was a certain kind of vulnerability. What most men hid behind well-tailored coats and polished Hessians, Lord Hamilton carried on his face. He was a recluse, staying away from the rest of London when in fact, he was supposed to be out there with his fiercely intelligent mind, educating all the gentlemen that came to London for the Season.

Soon, the thoughts clouded her mind. Blue eyes shone before hers, all layers of reality falling apart and tearing apart the seams. The world became a vast layer of color, twisting and roiling powerfully in her mind. Lord Hamilton was cutting through her thoughts, and Genevieve suddenly recalled the piece of paper under her inkwell.

Softly, she recounted all of the qualities in her mind, spinning them and ticking off those she had experienced. His blue eyes were the first thing that drew her to him but there was also the soft part of him. Seeing him apologize cracked something inside of Genevieve's heart. Also, there was the intelligent side of him; the avid reader that piqued her interest, and the mysterious side that left her curious and wanting to find more of him.

The music was coming to a slow now, the last of the notes serenading the room. She played the last of it with everything in her heart, pouring all of her emotions into it. The feeling of anger at her mother's attitude, the fear of the gossip sheets, and her dislike for the earl. All of the swirling agonies dissolve through her and into the song. When the last of the notes left her fingers, Genevieve felt a deep relief within her soul.

"That," her mother trailed off, dabbing at her face with a soft embroidered cloth. "That was the most beautiful thing you have ever played."

Genevieve let her lips curl into a smile. "Thank you, Mother."

"I want you to play this song for our dinner ball. The guests will fall head over heels for it. Even the Countess will give words of appreciation. Perhaps, the earl might even be in attendance."

"And what does the earl have to do with this, Mother?" Genevieve asked, wringing her hands.

"His attendance will bring all of the gentlemen in London," the Duchess replied. "And praising you before everyone will only improve your status in society."

Genevieve stared on incredulously. "Status? I do not think -

She was interrupted by the arrival of the butler into the drawing room. Genevieve was glad that she would at least avoid her mother again for the greater part of the day if there was a visitor at the door.

"Your Grace," the butler said. "Lady Genevieve has a caller."

Genevieve was astonished. Joy bloomed in her heart at the thought of having a caller. She thought that perhaps Lord Hamilton sent his footman with a calling card after they arrived from the picnic.

"A caller? Who might that be? There were no callings slated for the morning," the Duchess asked.

"The earl of Kenford, Your Grace. He sent a calling card the day before on your outing with Lady Redwyn," the butler said. "Should I send him in?"

All the happiness seeped out of Genevieve's mind just like the music drained all of the energy inside of her. She was suddenly thrust back into the ballroom, the earl's heavy feet tramping on her own. So far, the earl had ticked none of the qualities on her list, and just seeing him would make her miserable.

"Send him in, Perceval," the Duchess said. "On your way out, send the maids for biscuits and tea for our guest."

Genevieve wanted the earth to open up and swallow her. Her mind swelled with disappointment as she tapped her hands fervently on her lap. The earl was not a good match for Genevieve and she knew it. But her mother had already taken such a liking to him that she was even allowing him in without seeing his calling card.

She was barely done gathering her thoughts when the earl stepped into the drawing room. Like every gentleman, he was fastidiously neat. His hair was swept back in sandy waves, close-cropped and dazzling as always. When he came in, he stood just beside the window, auspicious with his golden hair and honey-colored eyes. His taste in finery was top-notch from what Genevieve could see, and any lady in her right mind would want to make a match with him. But alas, Genevieve wanted someone entirely different from the earl.

"Good day, Your Grace," he said to the Duchess and turned to her. "And to you, Lady Genevieve, I have brought these."

In his hands was a bouquet of white lilies, each one beautiful and eye-catching. Coupled with the lilies was a part bouquet of moon        flowers,        white        and        shimmering. "I thought to bring something as fair as you are," he said sweetly, his smile widening with every word. "But even these flowers will not do enough justice to how beautiful you are, Lady Genevieve."

In the corner, Genevieve saw her mother smile her widest. There was a look of contentment on her face, and she almost cringed. It was enough pain for her to think about the night at the ballroom. There was no way Genevieve would spend the rest of her life with the earl. He was the most auspicious person that existed - the light of the room and every ball and outing. The exact opposite of Lord Hamilton's darkness, charisma, and mysterious personality.

"But I - Genevieve started but her mother beat her to it.

"This is just beautiful. You must have spent quite the fortune on this, I suppose," her mother said, reaching to get the flowers from the earl.

"I had to look through every florist in London, Your Grace," he replied. "And when I finally found one in Piccadilly, I bought the entire store."

The Duchess exclaimed. "You should not have, Lord Kenford."

"I would do anything to impress Lady Genevieve. Even if it means spending quite a fortune on flowers."

Genevieve could only pull up a small smile that she prayed did not look awkward so that her mother would not complain. All her life, she always hated flowers because they attracted bees. One time, a bee stung her elbow when she was younger and it had been very painful. Instead, she would have preferred books. At least something that could spend the whole day without wilting.

"Please, have a seat, my lord," Genevieve said at her mother's behest. "I will have a maid take these flowers and store them in our finest vase."

He smiled and passed the flowers to her. Their fingers brushed slightly and it sent a shudder through Genevieve. It felt like she was wading through oil in her finest dress. She pulled back almost immediately, dropping the flowers on the newly polished rug.

"I am sorry, my lord," she muttered. "I have only just finished playing the pianoforte and it has taken quite a lot from me this morning."

"I must tell you that I am quite taken with the pianoforte," he replied. "Just as much as I love riding."

A maid rushed in, balancing a tray in her hands. Genevieve could already smell the biscuits and she wished that the earl were not present so that she could eat as much as she wanted without being embarrassed.

"Lord Kenford, I have come to wonder why you have not called before the Season started fully," the Duchess said. "And I was informed that you called just the day before."

The earl bowed slightly, expressing his apologies. "I am sorry, Your Grace. I have been quite busy with business that it has held me from fulfilling my duties. I would have liked to call on Lady Genevieve even before my mother's ball but I have been constrained by many activities."

"Men and their businesses," Genevieve heard her mother say with pride. "But you need not apologise. The Countess has talked to me about the business constraints. While business is a good thing, this is the Season to make a match."

"I understand," he stated. "I will try my best to be available now that the Season is in full swing. I can assure you that I will be more present at your residence than mine."

Her mother laughed, and Genevieve had to force a laugh as well. She was already regretting the future ahead now that the earl would be more available.

"I heard that the opera will be putting on some amazing performances," he said once he turned back to her. "The Dance of the Night has been on for quite a few days. For someone who plays the pianoforte, I am sure that you will be taken by it."

Genevieve shook her head lightly, knowing that she would never want to go to the opera with the earl. She had already agreed to go with Lord Devon - Kitty's older brother - and Lord Hamilton.

"I will -

Once again, her mother interrupted her. "She will be delighted to accompany you. Genevieve has no other outings scheduled for the week."

"I will be looking forward to seeing you at the dinner ball by the morrow," he said with a bow. "I will be taking my leave now for I have a few things to check up on before I retire for the evening."

Genevieve watched him leave, his tailcoat billowing behind

him. Her mother watched him with happiness in her eyes as he left, and it only irritated Genevieve further. She had an outing to the theatre with her friends, and her mother canceled all of it without blinking an eye. While her friends might be comfortable with the earl's company, Genevieve knew that only misery would come of this new plan.

"Is he not such a good man?" her mother said, dropping the fan. "The perfect example of a gentleman!"

Genevieve sighed. "I think not, Mother. While he might be a catch to other ladies, he is not the same to me."

"He bought out a florist for you, Genevieve. The least you can do is be a bit appreciative."

"Mother, when have I ever loved flowers? I detest them!"

The Duchess held her hand over her heart in mock terror. "You always have your nose in books all the time! How then will you know if you appreciate flowers? Have you never seen how beautiful our ballroom is?"

Genevieve guffawed. "Books are the most beautiful things in the world, Mother. I cannot have bees sting me to death as they did to Lady Edmund."

"Lady Edmund was bitten by a snake, Genevieve. But that is entirely different!"

Arguing with her mother was futile and she knew it by now. "I need to rest, Mother. I have to get some rest before I meet father in the study."

"Do not take too long," her mother said. "Lady Surrey has invited us for tea by high noon."

Genevieve just mumbled her reply and escaped, wanting to be alone with her thoughts.

# Chapter 17

Having sat in his study for quite a long time, James' thoughts were starting to drift away. The papers before him were blurring into a mess of ink and white sheets and no matter how much he tried to bring himself back to his responsibilities, he kept moving even further away.

At last, he stopped trying and straightened in the chair, pressing down on the armrests to support his weight. From the start of the Season, James had been up to his neck with appending signatures to ledgers and looking over account books. It took a lot from him, but he liked it anyway. It was his way of dissociating from the world, leaving the flamboyant courtesies of the ton behind and immersing himself in a world of numbers.

But that afternoon, he had other thoughts weighing on his mind. Much more than anything, he wanted to look over the ledgers and make sure that the family was well taken care of. Since they were no longer in the wheat business, it had been a little tougher to get around but James was sure that his new tea trade would bode well, and soon, the family would thank him for it. They were purchasing a lot now, and the proper grooming of the house for the Season was a lot to consider.

He rested his back on the velvet, wondering whether to put his ink-stained hands on the leather cover of one of the literature books posing like sentinels on the oak shelf. Shaking his head slightly, he turned to face the window. His body felt sore from sitting for too long and he poured himself a small amount of brandy from the glass decanter. It would be enough to soothe his woes, but definitely not too much to impair his proper functioning.

James took a swig of the warm liquid, letting the heat run all the way to his belly. A hoarse cough found its way from his mouth, and he smiled. He was suddenly thrust back to the days when he was only twelve and had his first taste of the brandy in their father's study. At the time, James wanted nothing to do with alcohol because he had seen how their father squeezed his face when the golden brown liquid touched his lips.

But Ned was persuasive. James could still see the expectancy in his eyes as he pulled him along to the study, their feet echoing through the silence in the house. It was past midnight and James wanted a glass of milk and some biscuits from the kitchen but Ned had other plans. They got to the study with as much stealth as possible, crouching down when they reached a window and making sure to walk slightly so as not to allow the floorboards to creak.

The study was empty by that time and their father had retired to his chambers for the night. Ned tilted the contents of the decanter into the glass, a mischievous smile on his face. It was the most mischief Ned had ever committed, but at the time, James was glad that he was not being the black sheep as always. Ned had a taste and wrinkled his face in disgust.

As James closed his eyes, he was thrust well to that night. The sputter and coughs from Ned, how his face reddened so bad that anyone in the dark would have mistaken him for a very ripe tomato. James howled with laughter when Ned complained about how adults drank brandy like it was water.

He took the glass from Ned and drained the contents, immediately regretting his actions. At the time, James was sure that he would die. His throat shot up, filled with heat and liquor. His eyes swam with tears and Ned burst into laughter. His nose watered from the heat and he coughed so hard that they did not hear their father walk in.

At the memory, James thundered with laughter. He really wished Ned were here now, to pull him away from this life and run around the house like they did when they were children. But Ned was gone now, lost forever in the family's catacombs. As much as James wanted him to be here, he knew that it was a lost cause.

James gingerly set the half-empty glass of brandy on the table and tapped his fingers on the desk. The scent of pine and roses wafted in from the open window, serenading him with a wave of nostalgia. For a moment, James was lost in time as his mind traveled, trying to find where he had picked up the scent. It was light and intoxicating at the same time, spicy and soft so much that he wanted to hold onto the smell.

At once, he recalled where he had smelled the perfume. James had never really noticed but the softy scent had been around him since he stepped foot into the Arlington Manor earlier in the Season. His mind recalled every encounter, and each encounter was filled with the image of one person.

Lady Genevieve.

James pushed his hands into the plush armrest and reclined his head toward the window. The perfume continued to pour over him, a mix of the pines in the distance and the rose garden just by the side of the study. He was soon reminded of the dance they had at the Kenford soiree, the walk they had by the shore of the Thames. Soon, his mind was consumed wholly.

He could see Lady Genevieve's slim face and the slight pout of her lips that reminded James of himself when he was only a few years old. While his pout was that of a petulant child, Lady Genevieve's had a certain grace that he had not seen on anyone. With his eyes closed, James could see the vivid blue-green of her eyes that once reminded him of his voyage across the calm seas. The colors crashed into one another powerfully, yet they had a certain softness that James had come to love.

As they walked the Thames the day before, her hair was fluttering behind her and James could almost not resist running his hands through them. But that would be deemed scandalous. In his mind's eye, James could still see the locks of blonde, dancing around her face like a halo. Spun god met the rays of the sun in a blinding manner, so much so that James smiled under his breath.

If more than anything, Lady Genevieve was beautiful. James knew that much already. She was intelligent as well, versed in literature and he was sure that her knowledge of running a household could not be lacking as well. He enjoyed her company more than he deigned to believe, and he hoped to see her again.

He brought a hand to his face, his fingers crossing over the scar on his face. James was reminded again that he did not fit into the crowd of the aristocracy. Lady Genevieve was the belle of the Season and he was nothing more than the viscount who lingered in the shadows for he wanted no one to see how bad he –

"His Lordship, Lord Lorwood has arrived," his butler's voice said from the door, interrupting James' line of thought.

He safely tucked his cogitations away, his wan smile creasing together into a neutral face. Lord Lorwood was the only gentleman that Alice seemed to be interested in at the Kenford soiree, and he hoped that the baron felt the same way about her.

"My Lord," the baron, Lord Lorwood bowed slightly, his dark hair falling across his face. "Pardon my intrusion at this time."

"Intrusion? Of course not," James replied curtly, yielding a smile. "But I wish that you sent a calling card beforehand so that I might have welcomed you more hospitably."

Lord Lorwood nodded. "I wanted to make some certain things known before I sent a card, my lord. I believe that there must be an order to things and I am sorry if my unexpected arrival has stirred up some inconveniences."

James smiled, surprised by the baron's kind apologies and courtesies. "Please, have a seat. I cannot keep you standing for too long."

"No need for the formalities, my lord. You can call me Robert," Lord Lorwood intoned and perched on the seat close to the window.

"Only if you will call me James as well," he replied, taking another glass from the shelf. "Brandy?"

Robert nodded slightly, feasting his eyes on the spines of books on the mahogany shelf. "You have quite the collection of books. My assumption was correct after all."

James' eyebrows perked up questioningly as he poured the brandy from the decanter. "Assumptions? May I ask what these assumptions are?"

"I have not been honored to speak to you like this before, but I can tell that you are a very intelligent man, my lord. Keeping to the farthest ends of the ballroom, always in your thoughts. Your advancements with the tea trade have spread through the minds of every gentleman in London, and I can say that White's has had a lot of people who would want to be investors."

James was appalled. It had never occurred to him that people noticed him as much as he thought. He was used to people moving away from him because of the scarring on his face but he never had the idea that he was being talked about by almost everybody.

He passed the drink to Robert, trying to hide an accomplished smile. "I only read a lot of books, Robert. I do not think that qualifies for the compliments you have showered me with."

"Only an intelligent person would diversify from the usual

into a more profitable business. The wheat trade is not as flourishing because of the large producers and I admire your courage for delving into something unconventional."

James reclined in his seat and adjusted the lapels of his double-breasted coat. His veins thrummed with pride at Robert's words, and he found himself smiling. Albeit a small one, it carried through the room. He sipped a little of the brandy afterward, letting it warm his belly before he spoke.

"Enough about business," he said slightly. "I do not want us to be carried away for I know that you did not come here to merely talk about the tea trade."

Robert nodded. "We will get to talk about business in the nearest future, my lord - James - I mean. I am hoping to invest a certain fortune that I have just stumbled upon instead of letting it sit and rot away. But you are correct when you said that I did not come for business."

"So, what have you come here to inform me of in the heat of the afternoon, Robert?" James spoke after a swig of brandy. "It must be quite important for you to be here without calling first."

Robert smiled. "I have merely come to ask for permission to court Lady Alice, my lord. Since our first encounter at the Kenford soiree, I have been unable to take my mind away from her. This morning, I was pushed so much that I had to rush down here to speak with you."

The words were a tumble, rolling and slurring into one another. James smiled at the rush and the slight reddening of the baron's face. He could also see beads of sweat sluicing down his skin despite the cold breeze that wafted into the study. Another smile crossed James' lips and he rose to his feet.

At first, James was unsure of what to say. He had never been in a situation where he had to decide for someone else before. Before his father's passing, he did not even make his own decisions. Seeing a grown man asking for his permission to court Alice was mind-numbing. But more than anything, there was a certainty in the baron's eyes. They were expectant - a mix of joy and happiness. It reminded James of when his father and mother would sit in the gazebo on the wide field, watching the setting sun and talking.

He could tell that Robert held deep feelings for Alice. Also,

James had noticed that the baron and Alice shared some kinship for the same things. They talked about art with such fervor, even more than James spoke about books and horses to other people. When they spoke, James saw the happiness in Robert's eyes and it was the same in Alice's.

For the first time after a long time, Alice's peridot eyes were lucent with happiness. When she spoke to him about the baron, she smiled so hard that James sometimes wondered whether her cheeks might fall off from excitement.

His decision was sealed with the conversation they had just a few minutes ago. The baron was an honorable man, someone who did not flatter and was also intelligent. Those were the qualities that James wanted to see. Not someone who was so frivolous and extravagant that they wanted to be the soul of every outing. He wanted for Alice, someone like herself. Quiet, industrious, reserved, intelligent, and good at managing the affairs of his house. Also, he wanted Alice to love.

If not for himself, James wanted his sister to know what true love meant. To be vulnerable for someone because they did the same for you. He wanted her to be happy and safe.

"I give you my permission, Robert," James said finally. "But if you even dare to hurt my sister in any way, you will have to answer to me."

A smile burst on the baron's face. "You have my word, James. I will never do anything to hurt her."

They talked some more about his prospects before Robert stood to leave. Time had flown by so fast that it was evening when Lord Lorwood rose to take his leave. Just when the baron left to attend to something, James saw his mother come in. A groan escaped his lips as he thought of what she might say. Since they returned, he was at least glad that she was in a great mood. The invitation to tea seemed to lift her spirits.

James poured himself another glass from the decanter and took his seat on the sofa. "Mother, I was just about to come for dinner. I hope this is not another one of your talks about my duty to our house."

"While I want to talk about that, it is not the reason I have come. You have been held up in the study for quite a while and I wanted to know whether you were fine."

"I was in the middle of something important, and I come bearing good news. One that you are most surely interested in."

"You are definitely not a carrier of gossip, so I assume that this has to do with Lord Lorwood's visit to our manor today?"

James gave his mother a warm smile. "I do not want to be hasty, but I think that Alice might have made her match this Season. Lord Lorwood just came to ask my permission to court her."

He watched a huge smile form on his mother's face and it evoked one from him as well.

"At least, I have one less thing to worry about," his mother said. "All that is left is for you to make a match."

Swiftly, he evaded another bout of nagging by setting the half-empty glass on the desk with a soft thud and turned to his mother. "I am rather famished this evening. Dinner would not be such a bad idea right about now."

He moved briskly out of the study, down the flight of marble staircases and elegant balustrades into the dining room down the rug-covered corridor. Alice was sitting there already, waiting for them.

James took his seat at the edge of the table and waited for his mother to say a small prayer. In a few minutes, James was lifting forkfuls of peas into his mouth and piling some more chicken into his plate.

"Alice, I have given Lord Lorwood permission to court you," he said after clearing his throat. "I believe it is the best course of action."

James watched his sister's eyes widen with excitement and her face turned a shade of red so dark that it almost matched the color of her dress. From the look on her face, he could tell that he made the right decision by giving the baron his permission.

"Brother," she said with a hint of gratitude seeping into her voice. "I wanted to ask if you could accompany me to the Pall Mall Galleries tomorrow. Kitty and Elizabeth are coming for it as well and I do not want Mother to keep nagging at me."

James and Alice shared a laugh as he nodded and their mother fumed furiously.

"While you will be my chaperone, it will be a great opportunity for you to further familiarize yourself with Lord

Lorwood. It seems you have taken quite a liking to him."

James thought about it for a moment, wishing he did not have to go out anymore. But this was necessary. He was doing it for his sister.

"I will be honoured," he replied and watched her eyes erupt with happiness.

# Chapter 18

Genevieve did not have any rest almost through the night. Even as she gazed out the window with her list in hand, it was still hard for her to keep her mind in one place. She was sitting on the chair now after spending a few minutes to stretch and reorient herself.

So far, Genevieve knew that her mother was responsible for the unrest. Their duchy was considered one of the largest and it was her mother's idea that they throw a ball every Season. Since Genevieve had been old enough not to run around during balls, her mother made her invested in the preparations. It was arduous work, but her mother loved doing it for she made plans for it at the end of every Season when they retired to the countryside.

From where Genevieve stood, she could see her mother's starched skirts rustling in the morning breeze by the open window, the ivory folds crashing into one another and reminding her of the times when she used to sit in the gazebo and watch the clouds drift softly with a book in her hand. Genevieve missed those days when she had a break from needlework and the pianoforte. When she could get away with reading all she wanted until the start of the next Season.

She slipped into her lilac dress without her lady maid's help, making sure that she would be able to leave the house when she wanted. Placing the paper that contained her list of qualities she wanted in a gentleman under the inkwell, Genevieve wiped her hands down with a soft cloth. A letter had arrived from Kitty the night before, telling her how important it was for them to get away from the bustle of the Season.

In her heart, Genevieve had promised her friends that she would be at the Pall Mal Galleries that morning. She made sure to inform her father that she was to leave the house when he was busy and his grunt of an answer was the only permission she needed. But they were in London and not the countryside. Not even she could get away with her father's grunt of approval. As always, her mother was the only person standing in her way.

"I must leave," she muttered, patting down the lacy folds of her dress. "If not, Kitty and Elizabeth will marry me off to one of those gentlemen that no one wants to associate with."

She ended her soliloquy with a small smile and descended the flight of stairs to the dining room for breakfast.

As always with the ball, they were eating in the smaller antechamber in the dining room while some maids were adding fresh flowers to large vases. Chrysanthemums and Sweet Williams dotted the dining room and added splashes of color to the otherwise dour atmosphere. Genevieve was glad that she could finally see some hues apart from the dull blue tapestry that covered the windows and its silver tassels.

"I expect that the preparation for the ball is going smoothly," her father asked, not taking his eyes off the morning papers. "After all, you have been the most involved."

"I have been the only one involved," Genevieve heard her mother reply a little too softly. "And no one else in this house takes it upon themselves to help."

The Duke raised his head with a small smirk of satisfaction on his face. "Every penny that goes into the preparations goes through me. There is still a lot of work in my study that I must attend to before the day runs out. Perhaps you could ask Genevieve for help."

Genevieve was aghast. And so was her mother.

"Genevieve?" Sybil groaned in vexation and turned to her. "I hope you have your pianoforte polished to the finest. Guests will be arriving -

She was cut short. "Florence! The tapestries still have to be taken down and changed. I cannot have dust motes near the lemonade!"

Genevieve sneered at her father but he was so invested in the paper that he did not seem to take notice. She wondered why her father decided to put her in trouble that morning. She had gone to great lengths to find ways to slip out of the house.

"Bridget, put the porcelain close to the harp so that no one plucks the strings in a bid to show their mastery. No one is taking the spotlight from Genevieve."

"Yes ma'am," the maid replied, bobbing her head several times before disappearing with the flowers.

Genevieve watched her mother's face relax as soon as the maid turned round the corner. "They never seem to do anything perfectly!"

"Hope you have tended to your fingers, Genevieve? I will take no mistakes. This ball is centering around you and we must get you a husband before the Season runs out."

Genevieve groaned slightly, not loud enough to receive some tongue-lashing from her mother.

"I heard the Prince is coming," Sybil said in a high-pitched voice, so much that it was almost a squeal of delight. "He just returned from a journey and wants to rest in London."

"London?" The Duke asked warily. "If he is not here to seek a bride, then he should retire to Bath."

Sybil would have none of it. "Prince Frederich is here to visit his aunt and we will treat him like royalty. Genevieve, I just want you to have options. The earl is still available and has shown great interest in you."

Genevieve scoffed but her mother was too focused on telling the housekeeper to fetch more flowers from the florist across town.

"Take out the dead flowers, Bridget. Ask Agatha what appetizers are going to be served! The guests have to know that this is the best ball of the Season."

"Mother," Genevieve said softly, her voice barely a whisper. "I am visiting the Pall Mall Galleries with some friends."

"Florence, tell Noah to bring in the new tapestries. The ones along the hall to the study need to be changed as well."

"Mother," she called out again, sincerely hoping that her mother was distracted. And thankfully, she was.

"Don't be late," her mother said. "And you will practice the Dance of Winter on the pianoforte when you arrive by late noon."

Genevieve nodded softly and cleaned the sides of her mouth with the linen napkin. Without further talk, she left her mother to make sure that the ball was perfect while she slipped out of the house.

***

It did not take long for Genevieve to pull Jenny away from the house and the carriage was happily rolling down the cobblestone streets. She was happy to leave the hustle and bustle behind and when she slipped back to the window in the carriage, the nearby scent of oranges invigorated her mind.

"You are itching to say something," Genevieve said, watching Jenny pick at the thread in the fabric of her woolen skirt. "If you want to, just say it. We have known each other long enough to be frightened."

"If I may, my lady," Jenny said with a smile. "His Lordship, the Earl of Kenford sent flowers in the morning. The finest bouquet of white carnations and tulips I have ever set my eyes on."

Genevieve was not moved. "Tulips?"

"Never in my life have I ever seen flowers arranged so wonderfully, my lady," Jenny replied with a dreamy smile on her oval face. "So much thought must have been put into it by the earl himself."

She groaned and looked out the window, tired of listening to Jenny's ramblings about the earl. For one, he fitted into none of the qualities she wanted. His eyes were a murky brown in the dark and honeyed in the light. Also, he was sheepish like every gentleman she met last Season. They were so quick to show their affectation and none of them even asked her what she wanted. All they did was send flowers. It angered her that the same thing was happening this Season as well.

"If I had known that you will sing praises of the earl, perhaps I would have let you stay at home with Mother. The floors need to be polished once more and the vases cleaned out for the morrow."

Jenny sniffed and shrank back. "If you do not want to speak of him, my lady, then I will not. I was merely trying to get you to smile."

Genevieve was dreading the day that the earl would come knocking with the tickets to the opera in hand. Knowing him, he would choose the best seats in the house, but Genevieve had watched performances so much as a child that the mere thought of it made her weak.

She wanted none of the noise and high-pitched voices, the dances, and false silk dresses. Instead, she wanted to lose herself in poetry and art, to whirl around on her feet and forget about needlework. More than anything, she wanted to rest. With a cup of warm ginger tea beside her and a pile of books that she would read until exhaustion claimed her.

A knock on the carriage jolted Genevieve from her reverie and the footman's gruff voice roused through the mid-morning air.

"We are here, my lady."

Softly parting the heavy tapestry in the carriage, Genevieve looked outside the window. She had only been to the gallery a few years ago before her introduction into society. Her father took her whenever he had the time, and the memories came soaring back into her mind. It had been so long, and a wave of nostalgia hit her as she stared at the ivory building.

Columns held up the elaborate roof, each carefully sculpted with lines and swirls. As a child, Genevieve had run her hands along the columns, feeling every indentation under her palm. They were past Trafalgar Square now, and Genevieve could still recall the streets like it was yesterday.

"The day waits for none, my lady," Jenny whispered softly, urging her to step outside. "Her Grace expects us in a few hours."

Just as Genevieve was getting down, two other carriages came to a halt before theirs. She let go of the pale folds of her lilac dress, letting the lace float softly to the ground. Jenny was beside her now, fussing with her reticule. Genevieve straightened, her mother's teaching coming alive in her mind.

But everything fell apart when she turned. Out of the carriage layered in oak, he stepped out. He was climbing out of the carriage, his fawn-colored coat almost shimmering under the glare of the sun. His height still bemused Genevieve, but he made up for it with how graceful he was on his feet.

Their eyes met and Genevieve felt her heart race. It was sudden, like when Jenny added some oil to the lamp and the flickering flame burst to life. Her cheeks warmed at the sight of his dark blue eyes - a roaring of dark and light that never ceased to take her breath away.

Genevieve was suddenly thrust back to the parquetry floor at the Countess' soiree, being led by him around and back. It was a pleasant feeling, one that Genevieve would never forget for as long as she lived. His skin was darker now as if he had spent so much time horse-riding in the sun. Curly hair was swept back in arcs, more delicate than the sculpted columns yet rough and without form. The recklessness and appearance brought Genevieve to a sudden stop.

"My lady," Jenny nudged her and her mind came floating back.

She blushed so much, covering her face with the fan as she turned away. It only felt like a fraction of time, but Genevieve could see it in Jenny's eyes. She had looked too long at the viscount that if anyone saw her, a scandal would erupt.

"My lady, you were staring," Jenny said pointedly and heat rushed towards Genevieve's face.

"Mother would swoon if she were here," she admitted, murmuring under her breath before straightening. "And I was not staring, Jenny. I was merely observing."

Her lady's maid only nodded sullenly and Genevieve flushed again. Everything Jenny said was true. She had been staring at the viscount, but it was not without reason. His eyes never stopped to captivate her, but Genevieve knew that she should have had more restraint. It was the most unladylike thing to stare at a man so much that people began to notice. Huffing, she turned around.

"Genevieve!" A squeal came from the distance and Genevieve saw Alice in a pale blue dress that brought out the green in her eyes. "I cannot believe that you made it!"

She smirked. "Alice, it is so great to see you too."

"Lady Genevieve," the viscount's rumbling baritone shook through Genevieve as he bowed. "We seem to have arrived at the same time."

"Indeed," she replied curtly. "And who might this be?"

Another man was standing behind the viscount. He looked quite familiar but Genevieve could not recall where they had met.

"Good day, Lady Genevieve," he said, bowing. "I believe we have not met. I am Lord Lorwood. But everyone calls me Robert."

"Ah!" Genevieve exclaimed. "Now I remember. Lord Lorwood, the baron. Pleased to make your acquaintance."

A gentle smile played on his face as he held out his arm for Alice. "May we?"

"Gladly," Alice replied, her eyes twinkling brightly like never before.

Together, they walked through the vaulted arch at the entrance and into the gallery.

# Chapter 19

James had not known that he would meet Lady Genevieve at the gallery, and he had no idea it would happen this way. He had been so invested in his work at the study pending the upcoming preparations of the mid-Season's purchases that he had forgotten her acceptance of the invitation at the picnic they had on the shore of the Thames. Usually, before he went out, James planned every event that would happen. The bows, polite greetings, averted faces, the careful silence punctuated by nods and short answers. But somehow, Lady Genevieve always caught him by surprise.

First, it was the dance at the Kenford soiree. James had been there at his mother's behest and much to his chagrin, she urged him to dance with the Duke's daughter. For one, it was rude to just walk up to her and since it was never in his plan for the night to have a dance, James wanted to slink even further into the dark and enjoy his brandy on ice with his thought frolicking through his mind.

But his mother's voice kept nagging at him, pushing him to do the unthinkable. It was not tough for James to summon courage. What was difficult was breaking his stream of plans for the evening which included a few more drinks, some greetings if allowed, and a long ride back home on the plush cushions of the new carriage.

In the end, James ended up breaking his plans and asked her to dance. After, he started trying to find ways to regret it but he just could not. Lady Genevieve was more than polite and more knowledgeable than most of the ladies of the ton who knew only how to sip tea and make fancy needlework. She knew much more than that and was rather interested in literature which came as a shock to him. He half-expected her to ask about his estate and lodgings, about what kind of family he would want to have. At least, those were the questions the ladies used to ask Ned.

Watching Alice walk in with Robert, James turned to Lady Genevieve. Her blue-green eyes were twinkling, like the starry night in the countryside. They were rather close now, and James could smell her perfume drifting softly on the breeze. Spiceflower and lemons and sea salt - a scent that reminded him so much of his time in Eton when he would go running in the yard and climbing to the rooftops so that he could watch the school sprawl under him.

He got reprimanded by their father almost every time and once, his mother even called him a squirrel and Ned teased him with that for years. Standing beside Lady Genevieve brought back years of memories. The times when he used to shinny up the lemon tree so that he could sneak in some corn for the sparrows nesting in loose stones on the roof.

James jolted himself back to the present as he felt Lady Genevieve's lady maid's - Jenny - eyes on him. There was no other courteous thing to do than lead Lady Genevieve in. James wanted to do it of his own accord. The last time they met and had that walk by the Thames had been phenomenal. And he could almost not wait.

"May I escort you?" he asked simply with a small smile on his face that he hoped would not make the scar look worse.

She nodded softly, wisps of golden hair spilling from their prisons of jade pins and combs. They fell around her face, shimmering like molten gold. James wanted to reach out and push them back, but he restrained himself. More than anyone, he did not want to be attached to a scandal.

He felt her arm slide through his and his heart skipped a beat. Her perfume was overpowering yet soft that it was almost too much for him to bear. James kept his breathing steady despite his erratic heartbeats and hoped that he managed to hide his surprise well.

When he left the house with Alice, all she could talk about was her excitement at seeing the work of famous artists and how it might help improve her skills as well. Like their father, Alice was an excellent painter and he hoped that one day, society would become lax on its rules and allow ladies into art academies. While Alice talked about everything she wanted to and also spoke out her excitement when Lord Lorwood sent a letter to honor her invitation, she failed to remind him that Lady Genevieve was coming.

James blamed himself for not recalling and also blamed his sister as well. If she had told him even before they left the house, he could have dressed in more formal clothes. A sigh escaped his lips at the thought of her seeing him in a brown cashmere coat. But he was here and she had seen it. There was nothing he could do about it now.

"Are you alright, my lord?" her gentle voice brought him back from the edge of his thoughts. "You seem rather tense."

James smiled forcefully. "Tense? Of course not, Lady Genevieve. I was merely excited about how much artwork is in there to peruse."

"Then we do not have to spend all day out here in excitement, do we?" she replied, her voice carrying smoothly. "If we keep thinking, we will never act."

Without further ado, James led her into the gallery while her lady's maid followed carefully behind as her chaperone.

For someone who had almost no interest in a gallery like this, James was bewildered. High vaulted ceilings formed filigreed domes above them. Chandeliers hung from the ceiling and cast soft bronze light on every piece of art in the room. Suddenly, James wondered how Alice must have felt when she stepped into the gallery. She came with her father on many occasions, but the pieces were changed almost every month as the Academy of the Arts sent forth astonishing new pieces.

Marble statues stood on glass pedestals, bathed in bronze. Paintings were framed and hung on walls, their colors pulling James in every direction. Like a bee to a flower, James felt himself pulled to the furthest part of the gallery. Vivid portraits hung on the walls, picturesque and wholly mesmerizing.

Arms still intertwined, he brought them to a stop before a huge painting. It was an oil on canvas that depicted a woman in a silver dress. Her hair was thrown back, hands lifted towards the ceiling. Her hair was the same shade as Lady Genevieve's, so gold that it was almost unnatural. When James closed his eyes, he could feel the softness of the fabric between his fingers. Her unshod feet were cracked and peeling - a tale of endless suffering and prayer.

"Beautiful, is it not?" Lady Genevieve asked, her voice tinged with awe. "Whoever painted this must have felt such a deep and emotional connection."

"I believe so," James whispered back, not wanting to break the silence between them and the painting. "Such a mastery over colours. I wonder how the silver was just the right shade. Black and white will not cut it?"

She shook her head. "Black and white will never form a sheen as vivid as this. Perhaps, a kind of dye?"

"I highly doubt the efficacy of dyes. And this is oil on canvas. Whoever painted this piece must have been an expert."

"How so?" Lady Genevieve asked.

He smiled. "I fear that if we go into details, we might miss the entire point of coming to see this entire collection. Perhaps some other day."

They walked down the aisle, arms still locked. In the warm air, James felt even warmer. It was a huge task to keep his body from trembling and he did not want her to notice anything was wrong.

After seeing three sculptures and a few more paintings, James stopped before a landscape painting. It was not signed, but the painting felt unreal. Like the colors were stripped from the world and placed on paper. It was so vivid and bright despite the darkness of the room.

Verdant grass grew in a field overlooking a waterfall. The grasses were dotted with flowers in all colors. Pink, purple, white, yellow, and even fuschia with their petals singing towards the skies. Trees covered the sides of the field, twisted branches reaching deep into the soil. Much more than anything, it was beautiful. James imagined himself with Lady Genevieve in that field, dancing and blowing away the dandelions and chrysanthemums. In his mind, he could already feel the music playing from a violin, rising above the thunderous echo of the waterfall.

"Absolutely beautiful for there are no other words to describe this," Lady Genevieve gasped. "I am pulled so much towards this."

"So am I," James replied. "I have never seen an artist that manages to find a way to funnel all of my thoughts into their work."

"Exactly what I wanted to say! I have been an ardent lover of art for quite a long time, but this is my best one yet!"

"Evoking brilliance and perfection! I never thought such a painting existed," he said and turned to Lady Genevieve. "What kind of art interests you, my lady?"

She blushed slightly, averting her face for a second. "If you must know, my lord, I am very fond of landscape paintings. I just wonder how someone can capture the world with the strokes of their brush. Magnificent really."

James smiled, his eyes glazing over. "It was exactly what Alice said when she was a child and just learned to mix paints. Since she was a little girl, Alice was either painting or drawing landscapes. I can still recall when she had my father make an easel for her in the gazebo so she could paint the stars."

At once, James was thrown back into his memories. He was sitting on a tree in the countryside, trying to hide from Ned. He watched Alice paint, staring intently at the paper and smiling, each brush stroke bringing joy and happiness to her eyes. It had been her very first painting, and their father hung it over the mantelpiece in his study. Not only was it beautiful, but also mind-blowing. Over the years, James formed a connection with that painting every time he walked into the study in their home in the countryside.

Smiling, he could not believe that he recalled such a memory. After everything he had been through after conscripting and coming back home to meet the news of his brother's death, James could not believe that a memory so beautiful could still remain in his mind. He had not thought of their childhood together in such a long time since Ned passed. Now that they kept coming, the ice in his heart started to thaw.

Just then, he turned round to see Lady Genevieve looking at him intently. Her blue-green eyes were filled with so much warmth that they threatened to melt his heart.

"It is lovely that you have such a close bond with your sister," she said with a dazed smile on her face. "I know plenty of siblings who have turned on one another, and just seeing you talk about your sister was on a whole new plane of affection."

He smiled. "She is an excellent painter nevertheless. I should show you her own makeshift gallery."

"I would very much love to see it," she replied. "From the way you talked about it, she sounds magnificent."

"Of course, she is."

"I have always wondered what having a sibling would be like. Born alone with no one to chase around has been quite rough," Lady Genevieve spoke in the most hushed tone James had ever heard from her.

"I - he started, but Robert and Alice appeared just then, laughing and talking about the paintings they had seen.

"Really, my lord," Alice said daintily. "I can only dream of the time when I will be as great as these artists."

"You are already great," Robert answered swiftly. "You explained composition and saturation schemes, forms, and style. Who better an art connoisseur than you?"

James watched his sister blush heavily at the compliment and hoped to help her escape from her shyness.

"We should see the other end of the gallery together," he said. "There is still a lot to be seen."

They continued checking around for the next half hour, exclaiming at the beauty of sculptures and paintings. James could see that Alice was really enjoying herself and that was what mattered. Lady Genevieve and Alice talked at length about hues and tones in landscapes to which he and Robert just watched their banter. James was really starting to enjoy himself.

Almost done with the tour, they stumbled upon a painting that made everyone come to a halt. A man and woman stood under a moonlight night by a free-flowing stream, their faces obscured by the darkness. The stars shone bright, illuminating their bodies and James could vaguely see their expressions. Their eyes were filled with an emotion that James had seen too many times before.

It was love. They were lovers that seemed like they could not get enough of themselves.

# Chapter 20

Genevieve continued to stare at the painting, her eyes trailing over every detail. The canvas was stretched in the frame, supple as sin. Greys mulled over the painting like smoke and mist, clinging to the very picture as if trying to hide the focus.

The picture was as clear as the London afternoon, but in her eyes, they were hazy. She gasped with subtle delight, the picture coming alive in her mind. The woman was dressed in black silk, hidden under the starry sky. There was an urgency in the way she stood as if she were rushing back home to help her mother prepare dinner. Flowers danced at her feet, burnished gold flecks that leaped at Genevieve's mind.

Her face was obscured by the darkness, but Genevieve could feel the painting in her mind. Whoever did it had definitely not created such a masterpiece from a place of imagination. Instead, it had come from a place of longing and love. And those emotions were captured on the canvas for all to see.

The man was obscured by the shadows as well, his clothes drifting behind him like smoke. But he was tall, unreasonably so. The darkness clinging to him reminded Genevieve of the Kenford soiree when the viscount retired to his spot beside the tapestries with a drink in hand, ready to delve into the shadows.

In the painting, the man's eyes were a deep ultramarine. Only flecks of paint to anyone else, but Genevieve could only see Lord Hamilton. There was a small smile on his face now, and she wanted it to stay there forever; brightening up his eyes and making them sparkle in the fading afternoon light.

Her thoughts crashed into one another at the sight of the painting and the only thing that remained on Genevieve's mind was her list that was carefully tucked under the inkwell on her desk. The qualities came rushing back, and like a deer caught in a trap, Genevieve was trapped by the Viscount.

Every quality on the list started matching up in her mind and slowly, Genevieve came to a foregone conclusion. Everything she wanted in a gentleman, the viscount had them all. He was tall and broad, yet graceful and light on his feet. When they danced, Genevieve became the wind - soaring as high as she could with excitement thrumming through her veins. It was a powerful sensation, a dazzling contrast to the anger she felt when the earl asked her for a dance.

Not only was Lord Hamilton a good dancer, but he was also a good listener. He waited for her to speak first whenever they were together, focusing on her as if the world would tilt out of balance if he did not. At some point, Genevieve could not have cared if she were important to anyone except her parents. But the picnic at the Thames changed her perspective of everything. He apologized with so much relish, the words tumbling out of him as if he could not stop them.

Also, he was interested in literature as well as art - the same things she loved. Genevieve knew that if given the chance, he could talk all day about literature and poetry and never get tired. The viscount also had a close bond with his sister and his kind heart shined forth in their conversations. Beneath the scarred exterior, there was an honorable man.

She turned her head to the side, looking at his face. Turning this way and that, she tried to find the scar on his face. But when Genevieve looked at him now, there was no scar. Only a man who wanted to see the world. His face was turned away from her now and she reached out her fingers to tap the taut muscle of his back.

According to everything on Genevieve's list, the viscount was more than qualified and she could feel her heart thud in her chest at the thought. But her mother's high-pitched tone shattered Genevieve's thoughts like glass. Her parents' expectations rang too close in her mind and she knew at once that her mother would never approve of the viscount for he was far too imperfect. At least, that was what her mother would say.

The tour finally came to an end before a marble bust, and Genevieve let out a sigh of contentment as the viscount led her out of the gallery and into the busy streets.

"While we wait for our carriages," Alice said sheepishly, "I wanted to thank you, Lady Genevieve. For gracing us with your presence here today."

Her face pulled into an easy smile. "I should be thanking you, Alice, for inviting me. You saved me from my mother's torment and I will be eternally grateful that you have helped me this way."

"I did not know if art was your forte. But everyone seems to

149

love it either way," Alice replied.

"Unlike other people," Genevieve spoke and shifted her reticule properly to her wrist. "I am an art enthusiast. Also, I would like to see your own paintings someday, Alice. His Lordship told me everything about them."

Alice was beaming with pride. "Of course. And I am glad you enjoyed the outing. I will be seeing you later at the ball tonight?"

She nodded curtly. "If I skip it, Mother will send me to a finishing school or let me freeze out in the winter with a needle between my fingers for embroidery. And I do not think I can take any more patchwork making. So yes, Alice, you will be seeing me tonight."

"Goodbye, Lady Genevieve," Lord Lorwood said and began to escort Alice to her carriage.

The silence was heavy and dark after Lord Lorwood escorted Alice to the carriage. Genevieve stood there watching, her heart thudding. Jenny was in the carriage already, waiting for her arrival. But Genevieve did not want to leave. She wished the day could last some more so that she could spend some time with the viscount.

He broke the silence with a soft smile, one that turned the edges of his lips. "Lady Genevieve, I am rather glad that I was able to come here today. More than anything for a long time, I enjoyed my time with you."

Her face gave way to a smile as bright as the pastel carnations sitting in the vase back at home.

***

"If I had known that you were interested in the arts, maybe I would have frequented the gallery a lot more," Lady Genevieve said with a smile on her face.

James felt a rush of heat to his face and was thankful for the cast of the dipping sun on his face. In the setting sun, Lady Genevieve's hair caught fire - auburn, and gold rushing together into a conflagration that he never could have imagined.

Suddenly, he wanted to write. To capture this very moment on paper so that he would never forget it. He wanted the world to stop for just a moment, to bask in the known silence between them.

"I was never interested in going out," he replied. "And no one ever thought to ask."

Lady Genevieve laughed now - a soft airy sound that send pulses through James' mind. "I enjoyed our time together as well, my lord. It has been a rather eventful day. One that I might never forget."

He felt his heart thud in his chest at those words. For the first time, James did not feel the need to guard himself. He wanted to be left open, to smile as much as he wanted to, and let the world know that he was not as bad as they thought him to be.

"Your ball is this evening, correct?" he asked.

She nodded, the sun catching her hair and setting off strange sparks of orange and gold. "Yes, my lord. An invitation has been sent to your residence if I can recall. But I doubt you will honour the invitation for you seem to be a busy man."

James smiled. "Of course, I will honour the invitation, my lady."

"If you will, then I will be looking forward to having your name on my dance card this evening."

He had never imagined Lady Genevieve to make a comment so bold. The suddenness of it made him speechless and before he could respond, her carriage was rolling away into Trafalgar Square.

James was lightheaded as he sauntered back to the carriage and rested on the feathery pillows. The thought of dancing with Lady Genevieve again brought him some sort of consolation. He hoped to talk to her again, and perhaps they might lose themselves in the music and art of dancing. Just like they did at the gallery.

"Alice, I have taken offense to your behaviour," James said suddenly, even startling himself. "Why in the heavens did you not inform me that Lady Genevieve was coming as well? You invited her without telling me?"

"It must have skipped my mind, dear brother," she replied with a sly smile crossing her petite face. "But I am quite sure that informing you might have further lessened your chances of you accompanying me. And I did not want mother coming to fawn over Lord Lorwood. It would have been completely embarrassing."

James sat forward, propping his chin with his hand. "There is something strange about you, Alice. By any chance, are you trying to play matchmaker like all those other ambitious mamas?"

He saw Alice avert her eyes and smile and he knew then that something was up. "And I thought our mother was bad."

At that, they both erupted into laughter until their bellies ached.

# Chapter 21

The last slivers of the sun were receding when Genevieve turned towards the large mirror just behind the fir closet and took a look at herself. She was still playing the day's events in her mind, running over everything she had done during the day. The paintings were still in her mind, and she smiled whenever she remembered the way the viscount spoke about the paintings or the way he talked about his sister. From their encounter, Genevieve could see that they were a closely-knit family and it was everything she wanted.

She brought her mind back to the event at hand, trying to prepare her mind for the event that evening. It was going to be a long one like always and she hoped that her mother would not be as overbearing as she was at the Kenford soiree. For the first time in a while, Genevieve wanted to enjoy a ball and it was secretly because she knew that the viscount would be in attendance.

"Is the corset tight enough?" Jenny asked softly, her hands loosening on the cords of the whalebone. "Or do I need to loosen it some more?"

Genevieve sighed - one of relief from the extreme tightness that she could not almost feel her legs anymore. "If you tighten it so much, how might you expect me to dance?"

Jenny smiled and straightened her petticoats. "Dancing is easier when your corset is tighter, my lady. It helps to better your movements."

"Loosen it a bit more. I do not want to swoon in the middle of a dance. It would be most embarrassing," Genevieve spoke softly, patting down the cream petticoats.

Once they were done with the corset, Jenny laid out the dress that she was supposed to wear for the night. Her mother had picked it out at the modiste - a simple but beautiful design of silk and lace that draped beautifully over the wooden mannequin. Her mother was talking about the dress all day, but Genevieve had never really gotten to see it.

Now that the dress was on her body, Genevieve's mouth opened in awe. It was made from lilac silk so diaphanous that it shimmered. It clung to her body just right, emphasizing the length of her arms and the dark color of her eyes. She ran her hands over it and the fabric slipped through her fingers like running water. Smoky lavender grey lace covered the almost decadently low neckline and tickled her skin. Like the silk, it was soft and comfortable, much more than any of the dresses her mother had ever picked out for her.

The sleeves were puffed low and exposed the graceful curves of her neck and shoulders. It was then Genevieve knew that Jenny was right. Because of the corset, the dress was beautifully cinched at the waist and it disillusioned even her. She twirled before the mirror, a small smile on her face as numerous thoughts came to her mind. At the forefront was the look on Lord Hamilton's face when he saw her like that.

"The modiste really did a splendid job on this dress. One would have thought His Grace had it shipped from some distant country. Perhaps the borders of Messina."

Genevieve ran slim fingers over the silk once again and the translucent fabric shone under the light from the chandeliers. "Mother has really outdone herself."

Twirling once more, she said to Jenny, "You have done splendidly as well."

Truly, Genevieve's lady's maid did a great job every time there was a function. Even now, Genevieve was sure that she would be the center of attention at the ball. Just like her mother wanted.

Before she put on the dress, Jenny helped her into a tub of scalding hot water. Genevieve liked the heat, and she stayed in there for as long as she could. Raw, Jenny lathered her body with scented cream and rose oil and in minutes, the light floral scent permeated the entire room.

Usually, Jenny made her hair into a pile atop her head with pins and combs but tonight, she brushed it so much that it gleamed like molten gold. At intervals, she massaged grapeseed oil into her hair and instead of holding it up, Jenny decided that letting it fall in waves was better. And she was right.

Genevieve looked magnificent with lightly rouged cheeks and bright eyes. She knew now that there was no way she could avoid being the center of attraction when she was literally glowing. She just hoped that Lord Kenford would honor himself and not come close to asking her for a dance.

"You may go now," she said to Jenny and the maid bowed before leaving.

Alone, Genevieve pulled the gloves from her hands and reached under the inkwell for her list. Carefully, she wrote Lord Hamilton's name on the paper with a smile on her face. He was the only gentleman that had all of the qualities she wanted. The other gentlemen she danced with at the Kenford ball had their names in some qualities, but the viscount's was in all of the qualities.

Genevieve jumped from the chair when the door opened and she turned to see her mother staring at her.

"Do you know what time it is, Genevieve? The ball will soon begin and you are not even ready?"

"I was merely finishing up, Mother. All that is left is to put on my gloves and dab some perfume on my wrists," Genevieve replied, holding the gloves.

"Stand up then. Let me get a good look at you."

Genevieve stood up and the list on her lap fluttered listlessly to the floor but she paid it no attention. Her mother wanted perfection tonight and that was what she would give. Anything less and the night might not be as enjoyable as she had planned.

Her mother stood there and watched her quietly as Genevieve spread out her arms. Just like her, her mother was dressed for the occasion as well in an ivory dress that flared out magnificently at the waist. It was grand and trimmed with gold thread, the neckline adorned with gold embroidery and pearls. The pearls caught the light when she turned and Genevieve smiled knowing that the modiste must have gone through a lot of trouble to make sure that the dress was beyond perfect.

"Jenny really did great work on you," she said, a small smile appearing on her face. "Just the way I wanted."

Genevieve nodded. "You look ravishing as always, Mother. Without so much effort."

"Thank you, but know that your flattery has no effect on me. You are still playing the pianoforte tonight and there must be no mistakes. People have heard the Dance of Winter so many times at the opera that they will notice even the slightest tune out of key."

Genevieve groaned. "I know, Mother. I practiced it throughout the week. It will be great."

"It had better be," she said and her tone softened a bit. "Your hair looks marvelous as well. It will surely make an impression on Lord Kenford."

At the name, Genevieve wanted to groan. But she knew that her mother's mood might turn up at any moment if she dared say a word out of turn at the earl. Her mother and the countess were close friends, and the talk of a betrothal had always been in the air but she never believed such a thing would happen.

She had not known the earl a lot, but from the little time she had spent with him, Genevieve learned that he was lavish and pompous, a little extravagant because of the large bouquet she came home to meet when she returned from the Pall Mall gallery with Jenny. Not only was he not a good dancer, but his eyes were a plain brown. And in more ways than one, he did not fit into almost any of the qualities she wanted. But she could not deny that he was handsome. Every mama knew that and wanted him for their daughters.

"Lord Kenford will be in attendance? Why was I not informed of this earlier?" Genevieve asked, trying to keep her irritation under control.

"You need not be informed of every working of the house, Genevieve. Your father is waiting in the hallway and if I must say, he seems quite morose."

"Morose? Why?"

"Because he feels that the ball is rather unnecessary. But it is necessary now more than ever. Perhaps you can cheer him up before we start receiving our guests for the wonderful evening we have prepared."

Genevieve huffed. "I will see what I can do about Father. But I do not think he will listen to me. When he has his mind set on something, it is hard to relieve him of those thoughts."

"Just be ready to receive the guests as they will be arriving soon."

"Are you not going to come with us?" she asked.

"Go on ahead," her mother replied. "I still have some matters to oversee."

With that, Genevieve nodded and left the room.

Once her daughter was out, Sybil reached for the paper on the floor. Her curiosity got the better of her and she unfolded it slowly to avoid ruining her gloves with ink. At the sight of the paper, her mouth opened in dismay.

The paper contained a list of qualities that Genevieve wanted in a gentleman. It seemed like a plan to help her make a good choice, but Sybil was convinced otherwise. The list had names of potential suitors that appeared a number of times and she smiled when she saw the earl's name on it. But what was more appalling was that the scarred viscount's name - Lord Hamilton - appeared on the list more times than the earl's. With every quality, his name appeared and the more Sybil read the list, the angrier she became.

"I will not allow my daughter to be associated with such a man," she said under her breath, fuming. "Such a scandal will not be attached to this house! I will do everything I can to make sure that this does not happen!"

With that, she stormed out of the room while trying to keep her emotions in check.

Genevieve stood in the hallway with her father, and the moment he saw her, a smile burst onto his face like a ray of sunlight on a cloudy day.

"You look beautiful," he said. "I am sure that your dance card will be filled within the first hour of the evening."

She blushed. "I do not think I can take so many dances within that short time. Only if it is a quadrille."

Her father's boisterous laugh filled the room afterward. "Witty and funny! That's my daughter!"

They laughed together and were soon joined by the duchess. Her face was hard and unflinching, just like at the start of any ball. Genevieve was sure that her mother was only trying to prepare herself for the receiving process at the door.

Together, they walked down the flight of stairs and towards the door to receive their guest.

# Chapter 22

"Hmph," Alice expressed disdain and turned to look out the slightly open window of the carriage as they traveled to the Montmere manor.

James could tell that his sister was actively trying to look away from their mother. All through the evening, they had taken to a conversation about Lord Lorwood and his incredulous graces at the Pall Mall galleries. James was filled with fascination at Alice's shyness for it was something he had never seen before.

Even though Alice was reserved, she was outspoken when she wanted to be. And it was one thing James was envious of. Her heart was curious and free, her mouth spewing words with confidence. Never did Alice express such shyness at the mention of a gentleman's name. Perhaps some things did change after all.

"You need not be in a snit just because I spoke about him," the Dowager viscountess - Marcia - replied with a sly smile on her face. "I think you both look great together."

"Mother, you never apologise, even when you are at fault. Remember the incident with Lord Cumberbatch?"

"That was two seasons ago, Alice. Do you mean to tell me that you did not forget that?"

"How could I forget, Mother?" Alice groaned and fanned herself tersely. "The gossip column spoke about you the entire week. Even Lord Cumberbatch had to leave London."

James was intrigued. "What is this business about gossip columns and Lord Cumberbatch?"

Alice was about to talk but their mother stepped in just at that moment. "You need not worry, James dear. All you need to focus on is this ball we are heading to."

Then she turned back to Alice. "Lord Lorwood will be in attendance, correct?"

Alice's lips were in a pout. "Of course. An invite was sent to his family. And as everyone knows, this is the best ball of the Season, not even falling short of Vauxhall."

"Since when did you care about balls, Alice?" James asked, surprised at the turn of events. Never in this life did he think his sister would care about such frivolities. But here she was, excited at the prospects of dances and gentlemen. Or a gentleman in particular.

"Mother brought me up to speed about everything to know, James. I must say that I am quite taken by this Season's festivities."

James groaned. It was better when there were two bad eggs. Now, Alice was on his mother's side and she even tried her hand at matchmaking. On her first try, she excelled much more than their mother ever did with her insufferable nagging. But James was also happy for Alice. That she found love with someone honorable who loved her back. He had seen true love, and he concluded that this was it.

"Festivities? Where did you keep my sister, you stranger?" he bellowed and they all burst into laughter.

"But really, you should stop giggling like a madwoman. Love is not just simpering after the gentleman," James said and turned away.

Alice wanted to blurt something out, but James was saved by their mother. He turned away from the giggling ladies and let his mind take flight. Tonight, there was a lot on his mind, and the greater part of that was the ball they were heading to. He relaxed on the plush pillows and straightened his back, anxious to get to their destination.

James wanted to smile and giggle, but he knew that his mother would only ask questions and he did not want her to pursue her motivations even further. As much as he tried to hide it, a wan smile crossed his face and when he still heard the duo chattering about the baron, he turned the other way to stare at the fleur-de-lis patterned wallpaper that covered most of the carriage's interior.

James' eyes swept over the interior decor and damask chairs, glazing over in a short time as his mind was once more consumed with thoughts of the fair Lady Genevieve. In his mind, he could still see her as bright as day. The soft smile that turned her face brilliant, the way she accentuated her words so that every one of them sounded important and stuck to his mind.

He could no longer deny that he did not enjoy her company. A few weeks ago, James might have berated himself for this line of thought. For a long time, he had not thought of a woman. At least, not this way. Some time ago, James had been one of the most popular rakes at Oxford and even the gossip columns chattered about, naming him a reprehensible rogue. But a lot of years had passed since those days and James was now nine and twenty.

His mother was right to put pressure on him to settle down and bear children that might inherit the viscountcy. Marcia had married when she was just eighteen - on her debut - and their father was just one and twenty. They were quite young in their years, and they loved each other very much. He had seen the way his parents looked at one another when he was younger, and he believed it was the same thing he felt when he looked at Lady Genevieve.

The day was more memorable after they walked out of the gallery with content on their faces. Lady Genevieve's hair had caught the rays of the setting sun, turning ablaze in the summer heat. After Robert left, it had been a bit awkward just being there with her. James' tongue was scraping the insides of his mouth as he searched for the right words to say.

And then she had hinted at them dancing again. The first time had been short but very well worth it. She had taken him by surprise when she fumbled for her dance card and presented it to him. The Duchess was frowning so much that James thought she might be set alight by the fury.

As he led her to the dance floor, his heart thudded so much that James thought he might shatter. She was a ravishing beauty, and not like all the other well-born ladies of London. Most people would consider her bookish, but James could only see perfection. She was fiendishly entertaining with her words, and her knowledge of literature was almost boundless. And there were her soulful eyes. Shimmering this way and that with the light, verdant and blue, mesmerizing enough to keep him tongue-tied. James leaned on the heavy oak wood, letting his mind travel to his very first dance of the Season. The dance with Lady Genevieve.

She had her hand on his, warm to the touch. The scent of grapes was in her hair and it hit him powerfully with every turn of the dance. Lady Genevieve was simple yet intoxicating, so vibrant that she set his world into a bright light that never went off. But that dance had put James' name in the gossip columns.

A dance was harmless in the eyes of the ton, but James could see that the author of the gossip column was joyfully deviating away from the dance itself. Suggestive comments filled the column, and James knew for certain that it would send the lovestruck men that followed Lady Genevieve like a puppy into a crazed frenzy.

When she hinted at them taking to the dance floor once more, it came as a huge surprise to James. The first time was met with such gossip, and he wondered what would happen if he reserved one of her dances that evening. From the conversation they had during the picnic at the shores of the Thames, James could tell that Lady Genevieve was not worried about the gossip at all. Even if she were, she did not show it at all.

James could not help but wonder if there was truly hope for him after all. The scarring on his face made all the ladies evade him but somehow, it only pulled Lady Genevieve closer. He kept wondering if perhaps, she could be the only lady to look past society's standards for good looks and see him for who he was despite the terrible scar that marred his face. If she was really not bothered, it would make James happier. More than anyone else in the world.

Alice sent a mischievous smile his way. "Whatever could you be in so much thought about?"

James sneered, his smile curdling like sour milk. "Perhaps Lord Lorwood might be able to answer that question for you. Seeing as you have decided to make my ears bleed by calling his name so much."

Their mother laughed and Alice's cheeks turned a flaming red. "Pay no attention to your brother, Alice. He is merely miserable because of his loneliness."

The subtle insult hit James between the ribs but he laughed either way. "But you must agree with me that you have grown rather weary of Alice calling his name all day. Be scrupulously honest here, Alice, you have grown fond of this gentleman."

She turned away with a wry smile on her face. James went back to his thoughts as though nothing happened. It was only when he decided to think once more about Lady Genevieve that he heard the footman's voice announce that they were at the Montmere Manor.

"Good heavens," Marcia exclaimed as they stepped out of the carriage. "Surely, the duchess let loose of every penny."

James could see what his mother was talking about. The steps that led up to the manor were wreathed in light and covered with a soft rug. Hedges were ornately trimmed and the scent of their perfume was in the air. People were coming in, starched clothes and other accouterments shimmering in the golden light from the chandelier in the doorway.

The guests that came for the ball were received by the Duke, Duchess, and finally, Lady Genevieve. And James felt his breath wrenched away from him when he got to the door.

Lady Genevieve was dressed magnificently in lilac silk, and her hair cascaded down her back in soft waves, combed and oiled until they gleamed. She was smiling softly, hand outstretched to welcome him. James urged himself to move, but he was stunned by the graceful line of her neck, the tenderness of her shoulders, and the rouge that played on it. Her eyes were brighter than ever and the loose gown of silk and lace clung to her body like a spiderweb.

"You look stunning," he wanted to say but his throat would not let the words out and all James could do was stare blindly. She continued to smile, eyes crinkling at the edges ever so beautifully that he yearned for her even more. The suddenness of seeing her was all too much for him to bear that his knees became weak and wobbly. Their eyes continued to concentrate on each other so much that it would be deemed a scandal if any gossip author saw them now.

At last, the words left his mouth. "You look - he started, but was swiftly interrupted by the arrival of Lord Kenford and the Dowager Countess. He was dressed in garish black and white - stark colors that were ever so popular among the ton. His hair was swept over to one side and in his hand was a bouquet of almost all kinds of flowers . Seeing him interrupt James filled the latter with so much venom but he held his ground. His father had taught him to be civil, and he would carry that knowledge with him at all times.

"Your Grace," he bowed and handed the flowers to the Duchess. "It was meant to be a bouquet of your favourite flower, but since I had no knowledge of it, I just purchased the whole collection."

The Duchess smiled, genuinely that her eyes crinkled at the

edges just like Lady Genevieve's. But where they were different was where the Duchess' still felt forced, Lady Genevieve's was dazzling.

"Thank you," she said. "I should show you around myself," she continued and handed the flowers to a maid.

Together with the Countess, they disappeared down the hallway. James continued to stand there even after his family had been welcomed by the Duke. In public, it was scandalous to look at a lady for so long, but he could not help that she was looking at him as well.

"Welcome, my lord," she said finally with a curtsy. "I hope you find the ball to your exquisite tastes."

He smiled and nodded in reply, stepping into the hallway and down into the throng of people. Since the event that led to the scarring of his face, James had been terrified of going out of the manor. For weeks on end, he was holed up in the study, working on the wages of the servants and the upkeep of the home. He did not even want to see his sister for he feared that she might hate him because of how he looked. Like everyone did.

But like Alice, Lady Genevieve did not hate him. Instead, she sent him knowing smiles and hinted at dances, talked about literature, and fawned over art. Among the throng of people, James could feel his insecurities returning with a devastating force. It suddenly felt like everyone was watching at the same time, waiting for a misstep. He was quite sure that if he were a common man and not the second son of a viscount, he might have been thrown out for the ton fed on avarice and pretentious looks.

When James felt his throat closing up from the terror sinking into his heart, he gravitated towards the farthest end of the ballroom. It was a place of peace for him - a place where he could think and breathe properly without feeling like everyone was after his life.

He helped himself to a glass of iced punch, and the first sip calmed his mind and belly. The taste of wine and rum exploded in his gut and he smiled, knowing that it must have been the Duke's handiwork to add so much alcohol to the evening's punch.

Hanging near the tapestries calmed his raging thoughts, and from there, he could see everything that was happening. Miss Hannah was fiddling with her dress of green gauze, eyes searching for the perfect gentleman she could hold a conversation with the hopes that it might blossom into something; Lady Williams was sending flirtatious glances to Lord Candlethorpe, Miss Eleanor looked like an overripe berry in her purple muslin and Lord Fernsby was making small talk with some other bachelors.

The sight of normalcy gave James some comfort as he took yet another sip of the punch. He withdrew from the crowd even more and turned to see a small crowd of gentlemen forming near the floor-to-ceiling windows in the atrium.

James did not miss the sandy hair of Lord Kenford, nor did he miss the bespectacled face of Lord Abercrombie - the Marquess of Will Harbor. They were almost all surrounding Lady Genevieve, asking to claim at least one dance with her before the end of the evening.

"I should go," he muttered, knowing fully well that Lady Genevieve already wanted to have a dance with him.

He decided that he could no longer wait as other love-struck gentlemen were gathering and before long, her dance card would be full. James set down the glass of iced punch with a thunk and a smile came to his face at the thought of dancing with Lady Genevieve yet again.

Slowly, he started to cross through the sea of people, making sure to hang around the tapestries on the far walls. But just as soon as he started, James saw the Duchess right before him.

She was painfully beautiful and incredibly straight, so much so that James felt threatened by her presence. A false smile was on her face just like the first time they met and it did not reach her eyes unlike before.

"Stay away from Genevieve," the duchess said in a tone so low and venomous that it caught James off guard.

He wanted to reply, to say something but his mouth would not work.

"You do not wish to cross me, Lord Hamilton. So stay far away from my daughter."

And with another false smile, she was gone just as fast as she came. James stood there watching her leave in the direction of the mamas standing as chaperones beside the lemonade bowls.

# Chapter 23

If there was any word that Genevieve could use to describe what she was feeling at the moment, it would have been exhausting. But the word would not have sufficed. While Jenny was right about the gown being light and better to dance with than all the muslins in her closet, it made Genevieve the center of attention. Just like her mother wanted.

She had just taken a break from all of the dances that evening and she was glad that the orchestra finally thought to settle on some slow, melodic music that did not involve dance steps. It was a medley of songs, really, and Genevieve might have been interested if she was not so tired.

On the not-so-distant side of the ballroom, Genevieve could see her mother talking excitedly with the Countess and some other mamas. She was sure that they were spouting their disbelief and admiration at the gown she wore. A few hours ago, Genevieve had fallen in love with the silk fabric, but she wanted nothing more now than to loosen the cords and fall into her bed for a sound sleep.

The dress turned all the gentlemen into love-struck puppies and even Lord Tywin had come to speak to her about the enormity of his estate in the countryside. Genevieve turned the flimsy piece of card tied with a fancy lilac ribbon to her wrist, reading through all of the names. One would think that she was merely admiring all the names on her card while trying to pick one of them that would court her.

But Genevieve was doing more of that. All she was doing was turning the card around under the light, hoping to see a familiar name. She read through the list again, trying to find the name: Lords Tywin, Fernsby, Kenford, Wetherby, Berbrooke, His Grace, the Duke of Gloucester, The viscounts Gough, Melville, and Hampden. But nothing about Lord Hamilton.

Turning around and sipping some of the iced lemonade, Genevieve tried to think about what might have happened. Different thoughts ruminated through her mind as she wanted to know if any issue had arisen that had taken Lord Hamilton's attention. She had purposely hinted at them dancing a few hours earlier and now, his name was not even on the dance card.

They had met at the door when she waited there to receive the visitors and amid the stream of compliments from eligible bachelors and ladies alike, Genevieve saw him stride towards the main entrance. Under the cover of darkness, he moved swiftly and with purpose and urgency that it reminded her of the painting they saw at the gallery. From the stride and slight slouch in his rather tall frame, Genevieve already knew that he was the one arriving.

At the thought of him that way, she blushed heavily and averted her face so that he did not see it. By the time Genevieve turned around, Lord Hamilton was striding toward them. His body was wreathed in light from the brass chandeliers and he was not eschewed in the garish and stark colors of black and white like the other gentlemen.

He wore a cobalt waistcoat, accentuated by silver buttons and a grey cravat that was elegantly made. His tailcoat was an indigo-grey, mesmerizing and bringing out the intense blue of his eyes. Broad shoulders strained in the coat and his hair was carefully trimmed and fluffed, making his face slightly boyish.

Genevieve wanted to move, but her body remained frozen, dancing to the tunes of Lord Hamilton. She had wanted to give him her dance card there and then to fill in his name. But her father was just beside her and she did not want to do anything that might cause even the slightest bit of trouble. While the mischievous part of her wanted to do just that, Genevieve could not help but imagine her mother's heartbreak when the ball would end abruptly because of a scandal in which she would be right in the middle.

"It has been almost an hour," she said to herself, dabbing a perfumed cotton ball on her wrists.

She craned her neck to the side a little, searching for the viscount's scarred face that she had grown used to but he was nowhere to be found. As her eyes continued to pass over the crowd, her disappointment started to grow within her heart. She had been waiting for him to ask her for a dance so that they could finally talk without being bothered. There were so many things she wanted to say to the viscount. About how she preferred staying in the library to gadding around Hyde Park like all the other ladies, how she liked books over any kind of flowers, and how her love for literature even almost pushed her to write a book.

"My lady," Lord Abercrombie said, bowing and jolting Genevieve out of her reverie. "Do I have the honour of sharing this dance with you?"

Genevieve's disappointment grew even more as the orchestra began afresh with the sound of a waltz thrumming from the instruments. She let Lord Abercrombie lead her to the dance floor and she assumed her position without much thought while trying to look for Lord Hamilton.

The music started anew, concordant and beautiful, just like she envisioned. Only that she was not dancing with Lord Hamilton. Lord Abercrombie was a brilliant dancer as well, moving gracefully despite his size as he was almost a head shorter than she was. The spectacles on his face kept slipping and as they tilted close to the windows, Genevieve could swear that she heard a sigh of relief from him.

"Am I making you uncomfortable, Lord Abercrombie?" she asked, stepping back and forth.

He shook his head. "I have merely had one too many dances tonight. But I assure you that this is the best yet."

"Ah," Genevieve said flatly without sounding rude. "I see."

She glanced behind her, looking for the viscount's ash-blonde hair but she did not see him anywhere in sight.

"I have been trying to seek an audience with you, my lady, for quite some time. Did you not receive my letters?"

Genevieve shook her head, not wanting to be sucked into the conversation but the marquess continued. "I know that you have been quite busy with the Season's preparations, and that is why I have taken up the opportunity to make use of this time."

"Whatever you need, my lord," she said with a small sigh that was obscured by the sound of music.

"Lady Genevieve, so tell me, do you prefer London or the countryside?"

Genevieve was taken aback by the question but she was so distracted that she did not want to waste any precious time thinking. "I have never really thought of it, my lord. But if I must, the countryside it is."

He nodded softly. "Very well, then. I shall make arrangements for you to visit, my lady. If you truly like the countryside, then be rest assured that you will like the estate."

"And why would that be, my lord?"

"My ancestral estate is nestled in more than forty acres of greenery and far larger than most others in the area. If you are partial to the country, then every square foot will be worth exploring."

"It will be most pleasant," she declared, trying her best not to be rude.

Thankfully, the music was coming to a close now as the pianist let loose the last set of keys. While it might have been a rather eventful evening for Lord Abercrombie, it was definitely worth much less to Genevieve as the man she was looking for was nowhere to be found.

In the end, Genevieve gave up her search. But she kept the last line of her dance card empty in case Lord Hamilton decided to change his mind. The dance ended and she briskly moved to the other part of the room where Elizabeth, Alice, and Kitty were standing. She did not want anyone asking her about her supper dance because she was saving it for the viscount.

"Alice," Genevieve said, exasperated and in a snit. "By chance, do you know -

A familiar perfume that was so heavy that it was almost choking interrupted her. Genevieve had smelled it at the door and here it was again - scotch, labdanum, and leather. Even if she decidedly had her eyes closed, Genevieve could tell at once that Lord Kenford was standing just beside them.

His brown eyes were murky with intention and he let loose a soft smile as he meandered his way toward them. Elizabeth and Kitty were giggling like they had just been presented with lemon muffins and chocolate ganache. Genevieve could see her mother walking beside him as well, her ivory dress becoming painfully regal.

"Lady Genevieve," he said rather quietly, his eyes smiling. "Might I ask the honour of sharing your supper dance?"

Just then, Genevieve saw Lord Hamilton step into the room. Her heart thudded in her chest and she stopped for a moment. She wanted to push past the worst dancer she had ever known and march straight to meet the viscount.

"I-I-I..." she stuttered and trailed off, mind elsewhere.

"She would be delighted to dance the supper set with you,

Lord Kenford," Genevieve heard her mother say before she even had a chance to answer.

And the world ceased to exist at the painful thought of dancing with Lord Kenford yet again.

\*\*\*

James' mind was clear despite how much he had to drink that night. He could still taste the rum in his mouth and the wine on his breath, but never had he been so angry. Not just because of what happened with the duchess but with the world in general. Nothing felt right, and even his time in the garden was met with the same attitude that every member of the ton gave him.

He had seen some mamas in the orangery chaperoning the young ladies and the look on their faces when he passed with the drink in his hands was somewhat similar to what he had seen on the duchess' face. Except that the duchess' face had been twisted in anger and immense disgust that he had not waited to say anything else when she passed by him to the other women in the ballroom.

When James found the right spot in the garden to relax, he hoped he would feel different because of the scar on his face. A few months ago, those words from the duchess would have hurt him so much that he might have never sought the light of day.

But when he closed his eyes to think, all James saw was a challenge of sorts. His days at Oxford were quite pleasant, and a few mamas had warned him off their daughters with the vilest of looks on their faces. They dropped threats but never acted on them despite the fact that James was ruthless with his philandering.

Some part of him wanted to take the duchess' threats seriously. She was immensely wealthy, a woman of both affluence and influence. But James was a man. He might not have the best of looks or the best books in London, but he knew that a woman could not talk to him that way and expect him to back off without so much of a fight.

Soon, James forgot all about the duchess and his mind rested on Lady Genevieve. She had been in the ballroom, the center of admiration for all the gentlemen present. He even heard a few envious comments from the debutants in the garden and judging from the feathers in their hair, they were not that beautiful.

What men valued more than beauty in London was knowledge. At least, that was what Ned told him and what his preferences had been. James never despoiled women that were without a brain of their own. He wanted someone he could talk to freely and that for a known fact, was scarce in London. Perhaps he might find if he looked to Somerset, but James did not want to look that far when he already had someone in mind.

And there she was again: Lady Genevieve.

She was bewitching by all standards, enough to get James on his feet and strengthen his resolve about dancing with her. His mind was still spinning with thoughts of Lady Genevieve and the disgust on the duchess' face when he stepped back into the ballroom. Outside, the stars were winking into existence and the evening turned darker with every passing minute.

The orchestra struck a chord just as he stepped into the ballroom signaling the start of the supper dance. It was a fast melody, and he watched as the dancers stepped to the floor to have their last dance of the evening. And that was when he saw it.

Lady Genevieve was being led to the dance floor by Lord Kenford. He looked happy, eyes gleaming with pride for sharing the last dance of the day with her. It took everything from James to keep the roaring anger in the pit of his stomach from lurching out. All of the composure he had been building through the night almost crumbled and was only held by a sliver of a thread.

"Since you have no one to dance with, dear brother, would you like to dance with me?" Alice asked beside him, her face bright with excitement.

"Has Lord Lorwood left you to your antics or because you do not know how to dance?" he shot back in a bid to tease his sister. "Or perhaps, he has grown rather tired for he has the stiff back of an old man?"

Alice snorted with laughter. "These insults will not get you a dance tonight, James. Every lady here is with a dance partner. Lord Lorwood has had his fill of dance for the evening and was called for an urgent matter at his manor. And here you are with an empty dance card."

James rolled his eyes, his sense of humor returning. "Empty, just like yours. I believe that only Lord Lorwood has asked you to dance tonight."

She sighed, thrusting her hand to his face. "Quite the contrary. I have only one slot left and I want to pencil you in as a gesture of goodwill."

His sister was right after all. Her dance card was filled with names like Lord Lorwood, Lord Wimborne, Lord Devonport, Lord Camden, Bristol, and some others. Shame curled up in James' gut but he was happy as well. That his sister had a great evening.

"So, shall we?" Alice asked. "Before the orchestra ends."

They took to the dance floor together, their movements matching just like when they were children. Alice had the most crooked of dance steps when they were children, but she glided smoothly over the polished floors.

"You seem rather troubled," she said, pulling his attention away from Lady Genevieve who was at the other end of the ballroom. "Something is always the matter with you, is it not?"

James shook his head and lied. "It is merely a bad headache. Perhaps I have had too much to drink."

"Too much?" she snickered. "Reminds me of when you and Ned went to father's study. A bunch of misfits you were back in the day."

He smiled, the memory coming into place. "I did - he began, but the dance ended faster than he had anticipated.

As the orchestra began playing a soulful tune, the duchess started to lead everyone into the main dining hall for supper. And Lady Genevieve was lost to the crowd once more.

# Chapter 24

Genevieve's disappointment grew even more as the duchess led them to the long linen-covered tables in the main dining hall that was set aside for balls. It was beautifully decorated with flowers and heavy tapestries that provided heat. The maids had prepared the food when they were having their first dance of the evening just like her mother planned it so that there were steaming bowls of food for the guests.

All of the decorations and polished chandeliers only made Genevieve angrier because everything she saw in the dining hall reminded her of her mother and the way she interfered in her decision to refuse Lord Kenford's request to dance. They had danced earlier, and it had been the worst time of Genevieve's life.

She was doing all she could to maintain her composure on the dance floor. For someone so well-born, she could not imagine him not knowing how to even move properly to the music. Their first dance was a melange of rickety movement and the scent of leather was so overpowering that Genevieve was nauseated. Lord Kenford tripped so many times that it would have been obvious to all the other dancers if she had not saved him so many times.

In the end, trying to lead him through the music was futile. At some point, he even began to step on her toes and with every moment, Genevieve was in pain. When she twirled, it was a welcome reprieve from the agony she was feeling. She could not wait for the orchestra to end so that she could take her seat far away from Lord Kenford.

As they danced, he was trying his way through a conversation, but Genevieve was too distracted by his dance that she had no idea what he was trying to tell her. Overall, it was a dissatisfactory performance that when the music finally ended, Genevieve did not wait for him to escort her. She walked away as fast as she could, avoiding the eyes of the mamas that winked surreptitiously at her.

She relaxed on the plush seat, her eyes gazing and searching for Lord Hamilton. He was the only person that could at least save her from the boiled leather stench coming from Lord Kenford. When her eyes finally found him, he was helping himself to some mashed potatoes and a piece of roast duck.

Even when he forked a helping of mashed potatoes into his mouth, Genevieve had never seen anything that beautiful. He was having a conversation with his sister and he had a bright smile on his face. At some point, he threw his head back and laughed lightly and Genevieve felt her mind leave her body. She suddenly wanted to leave her seat and talk to Lord Hamilton.

"Are you paying any attention, Lady Genevieve?" Lord Kenford's airy voice interrupted Genevieve's train of thought.

A small sigh escaped her lips and she turned to face him. His eyes were filled with avarice, just as they had been from the moment he walked through the door. From where Genevieve was sitting, she could see the bouquet he presented to her mother and her heart sank even more. Perhaps if he had brought a book, she might have overlooked all the missteps on the dance floor.

"The mines in Georgia are flourishing quite well, I tell you. Nothing is better than a ruby gemstone sitting beautifully on the curve of your neck, my lady."

Genevieve could barely hold herself together anymore. Since they arrived at the main dining hall, Lord Kenford had not stopped talking and she wondered how a man could talk so much. She was trying so much to be polite and all he could talk about was himself.

"I can only imagine, my lord," she replied through her teeth, almost seething. She sent a dark look to her mother but sadly, the duchess was chatting away with the countess.

"It is a delicate affair, I tell you. Just like I purchased my first set of carriages and barouches fresh out of Oxford."

"That is rather astonishing, my lord," she offered in contempt while trying not to let the false smile on her face slip. "Fresh out of Oxford you say?"

He nodded proudly. "But with so many business interests, it was hard to stay in one place. That was the main reason why I travelled so much. And looking over the estate and my ancestral home was tedious. So, my mother wanted to help."

Genevieve just nodded silently, the smile slipping by the minute.

"What are your thoughts on family, my lady?" Lord Kenford asked, setting down his cutleries ever so delicately that one would think he was that graceful on his feet.

"Family, my lord? I should rather be asking you that question," she replied, not ready to speak about her thoughts to someone who was obviously not willing to listen.

The only attribute of Lord Kenford was the fact that he was handsome. More than most gentlemen in London. But he liked to hear himself speak, and when he did, no other opinions mattered. Through both dances that they shared, he was the one doing all the talking. He was also arrogant and repulsive.

"I want a rather large family. I have enough to take care of a family of twelve if the need be," he boasted. "At least, I am a sordid investor in several business interests that have brought me quite the fortune. If anything, I want to use that fortune to take good care of my family. Like any good man would."

"And what is your opinion on books, Lord Kenford?" she asked derisively on purpose.

"An excellent question!" he exclaimed with a nervous laugh. "Virgil's Aenid was one of my very first and the words still reside in my heart to this day, my lady."

"Virgil's Aeneid? Have you read any other literary work besides that?" she asked, pushing this time.

She wanted to show the rest of the ton the kind of man that Lord Kenford was.

"I suppose I have been too busy to stop and read, my lady. Business calls me on all fronts and I must serve. One must have food in his belly before he can read, is that not?" he replied, his tone shaky.

Genevieve could almost swear that a thin sheen of sweat had covered the earl's forehead. She smiled and looked away, already tired of the back and forth. Her eyes searched again and she found Lord Hamilton smiling. From where she sat, all Genevieve could see was a handsome man who had all the qualities she wanted in a husband. And beside her was the perfect opposite.

"Where do you see yourself settling, Lady Genevieve? I have an estate in Bath if that is where you wish to retire every year. There is also a lot of land in Somerset and quite a few places."

Genevieve sighed. Her head was ringing from the information that all she wanted to do was get away. She had lost appetite earlier and was merely picking at the peas now.

"As far as it is conducive to live in," she replied and at last, dinner was over.

Genevieve got out of her seat as fast as she could, tired of even being near the earl. Before he could say another word, she was out of her seat and heading toward the withdrawing room. Tired and angry, she set out to find her friends in the hopes of finding solace in their conversation.

Kitty and Elizabeth were chatting and giggling when Genevieve arrived. She plopped gauchely on the damask sofa, her ears ringing.

"You should have told us about your new dress beforehand," Kitty said smiling. "Maybe we would not look like simple handmaids."

Genevieve did not even have the strength to smile. She just nodded and threw her head back, exhausted from the day's troubles.

"Tell us everything," Elizabeth giggled assuredly, eyes filled with guilty gossip.

"Will you stop looking at me like that, Liz?" Genevieve muttered. "I do not have the vigor to deal with your ridiculous appetite for gossip."

Elizabeth frowned. "Do not talk like I do not have a good amount of sense. I am merely curious, Genevieve. You got to dance with the earl!"

The last words came out as a squeal and Genevieve bit her tongue in anger.

"It must have been marvelous," Kitty crooned, her eyes dreamy. "I wonder what kind of chemistry has blossomed between you two."

"Trust me," Genevieve said, her voice straight and steady as an arrow. "I have felt more chemistry at the shoemaker's. What you all see is what the earl wants you all to see."

Even Alice was taken aback. "What does that mean, Genevieve? He is the perfect gentleman that every lady here wants for themselves."

"I would not wish him upon my enemies," she answered. "The dance was less than pleasant as the earl was nothing more than a waddling, clumsy child. My toes still ache from where he stepped all over my feet."

"He moved rather gracefully," Elizabeth argued. "Perhaps you have been mistaken."

"I am not mistaken," Genevieve bit out the words. "I was the one pulling him along like a puppeteer. Even then, he did not follow my movements."

"Anyone can learn to dance," Alice said with a small dreamy smile on her small oval face. "Even Lord Lorwood learned in a few weeks."

Kitty nodded in agreement but Genevieve was not through. All the anger and disappointment came spilling out.

"I will never wish for the earl to be any of your suitors because it will be only pain and suffering from there on out. Under the good looks, the earl is nothing but a conceited, egotistical, and arrogant gentleman. Nothing else!"

She had not anticipated that her words would carry so much weight. Kitty's mouth was gaping and Elizabeth's face was twisted in surprise. Alice was trying not to look astounded, but she could not hide it for long. The stunned looks on their faces gladdened Genevieve's heart. At least, her friends would not fall for his charms.

\*\*\*

James felt like if he spent any more time at the Montmere manor, he might go mad. Alice's presence had been comforting all through the night, but for some reason, he could not take the duchess' words out of his mind. Even when Alice was speaking to him about some lady's ridiculous dressing, all James could see was the duchess in her ivory dress, staring at him with eyes burning like hot coals.

A sigh escaped his lips as he straightened on the jacquard sofa, his eyes heavy with disdain. In the dining hall, he had seen the looks that some mamas had given him, particularly the earl's mother. She stared a little too much, her eyes brimming with disgust. For one, James cared little about her thoughts of him. But she kept staring in a way that made him uncomfortable unless he concentrated on Alice.

In the parlor, James was glad to be left alone. He sat on the furthest chair in the room, guarded by shadows and darkness. The light from the grate made shadows dance on the walls, and in more ways than one, James relished the solitude. It was a welcome reprieve from the noise and music in the ballroom followed by the almost endless chatter in the dining hall.

The women had retired to the withdrawing room after dinner and the men had been led to the parlor by their hosts so that they could at least relax for a bit before taking their leave. James flipped his pocket watch open, itching to go home. It had been a rather uneventful night despite everything he planned in his head and he hated when his plans fell through.

He tipped the decanter on the table beside him and poured himself some well-needed scotch. The chattering in the parlor was growing as more gentlemen thronged in, and it was getting to James. He relaxed further, loosening his composure, and poured the golden brown liquid into his mouth. The heat loosened his tongue and warmed his belly but dampened his awareness of everything around him. James was never one to get drunk outside of his home and he would not allow it here. Not when many people were watching.

"Ah!" A boisterous voice exclaimed a few meters away and James almost jumped. "I have been looking everywhere for you, viscount."

From their first encounter, James had not forgotten the Duke's voice. He was a large man, heavyset with a neatly trimmed beard and his presence swallowed the room. When James turned to look at the man, he saw his blue-green eyes shimmering, just like Lady Genevieve's.

James cleared his throat and took to his feet. "Your Grace."

The Duke's mouth grew hard. "Enough with the formalities, Lord Hamilton. There is a lot to be discussed tonight."

The other men were looking at him now and James cursed under his breath. For the first time in hours, he was grateful that no one paid any attention to him. He liked it when he could disappear in a crowd despite him being at least a head taller than the tallest man in the room. But the Duke's presence shattered it all.

"A lot, you say?" James asked, eyebrows arched questioningly. "About what if I may ask?"

"It is nothing serious," he replied. "Just gentlemen talk about business interests and propositions. Nothing you have not heard before. It is a matter that should be taken with careful deliberation."

James reclined slightly, eager to get comfortable and hide in the darkness once more. The Duke's face was obscured by the shadows, but James tilted himself in such a way that he could see the older man's expressions. That way, he would know how to make proper decisions and appeal to him.

"You must have wondered why I am only coming to you now after so long has passed," the Duke said, pouring himself some scotch as well.

James had his suspicions but he did not give voice. Like almost every other gentleman in London with a fortune in their pockets, the Duke was afraid of something. Whether it was the risks involved in business or he was frightened by James. Like the women were. But he doubted the latter because the Duke had been friendly ever since the first time they met at the Arlington manor.

"I suppose you have had your reasons, Your Grace. Just like every other gentleman I met at White's. One must think properly before entering a new business venture."

The Duke nodded thoughtfully for a moment. "Well said. For someone who does not say much at meetings and balls, you have a certain way with words."

James smiled at the compliment. "I believe that merely being an observer gives you the chance to think objectively and without selfishness. It has always been one of my greatest strengths, Your Grace."

He frowned slightly. "Do you remember our first time together, Lord Hamilton? We agreed to lose the formalities and get to know one another. As potential business partners and as friends."

"I can still remember, Your Grace," he said. "As clear as day. That you will call me James only if I decide to call you Edmund?"

"Such a great memory is surely a tool when you go through the books of account, is it not? The wages of the servants must have been seared into your mind after looking through them just once."

A smile covered James' face. "Not as important as when you are trying to recall the business accounts, I suppose. A lot is poured into the trade and profits must be gotten."

179

"Enough about household accounts and pleasantries," the Duke, Edmund, said suddenly and sat straight after a sip of scotch. "I have more pressing concerns to be attended to."

James never had any trouble speaking with people. It was how he got the title of being the worst rake in all of London that year. Like Ned, he had a way with words that charmed even the most sensible of ladies. Barely out of Eton, he helped his father secure investors for the wheat trade before leaving for Oxford. But even he knew that he had his limits. Alice was a better speaker than he was and for that, he suddenly wished that she were here.

The Duke - Edmund - looked agitated about something from his bodily expressions and James could not seem to find out what it was. So when Edmund waved away their discussion and talked about pressing concerns, it startled James.

"Pressing concerns?" he asked politely. "And what might those be?"

"I need you, James," The Duke said finally, slouching once more. "A great need."

"I am yours to command, Your Grace," James replied as calmly as he could even though his body was taut with apprehension.

Suddenly, the duke burst into laughter. "I sometimes forget that you were conscripted into the Army. Perhaps, you might need some loosening up. Frequent visits to White's will help resolve your penchant for solitude."

"A man only has many friends when he is wealthy, Your Grace," he said. "For affluence comes with the need for associations. But more often than not, affluence is best kept concealed for it may waste away without one's knowledge."

In more ways than one, James felt like an old man. His mind was trickling with words unformed, twisting and turning. He could see Edmund's face brightening up now, eyes filled with some vague sense of joy.

"Well, I must say that you are correct in that sense, James. But I want to talk to you about matters other than the sage advice you have just given."

James smiled and allowed Edmund to continue speaking as he massaged the day's old stubble on his chin. "It is quite imperative that I ask you this question, James. What are your plans for the future?"

Dumbstruck, James felt all the words leave his head. Different thoughts raced through his mind as he tried to make sense of the situation. He wondered if perhaps the duke knew that he was in love with Lady Genevieve. But another part of him was ruminating why Edmund had come under the guise of business.

"Oh,by all means, no!" Edmund exclaimed with a sharp laugh. "I did not ask you about your plans about being a bachelor."

James felt relieved and the quick thud of his heart hammering against his chest dissipated. "If this is about the tea trade, then I have a lot of plans for the future. First, there needs to be an expansion and I was hoping to look at lands beyond Cornwall. Perhaps Somerset as its grounds are good for planting."

The duke nodded solemnly and had another sip of scotch. "Good idea as always. You seem to know a lot about the trade, then. It is only best that I put my fortune in the trade than with some witless sycophant."

James looked at Edmund again, at the shadows dancing across his face and the blue-green eyes that reminded him of a certain person. Suddenly, the world faded out in one sweep and the discussion he was having with the duke suddenly gave way to thoughts about Lady Genevieve.

A few hours ago, James could only think about her. But when thoughts of her crossed his mind now, he could see the image of the duchess shimmering just behind his eyes. Her words were painfully raw now, like hornet stings he had endured as a child when he climbed out the tree beside his window.

"... do you have any idea of what kind of money will be great for a start? One has to count his pounds and pennies."

James only nodded with a sigh, trying to focus on the business deal he was about to make with Edmund. Everyone in London knew how wealthy he was, and it was great that he wanted to spend a fortune on the tea trade. Usually, James would have been proud of himself, but other thoughts were plaguing his mind.

"Anything you feel is substantial," James whispered as a reply and the duke continued speaking.

The world faded out again, and he was back in the garden mulling over the duchess' words.

'Maybe she is right,' he told himself, his resolve wavering.

The time he had danced with Lady Genevieve, the gossip columns had talked about it endlessly. James knew that she was not the kind of person that loved unwanted attention even though she did not worry about what the gossip columnists said about them. And more than anything, James wanted to give Lady Genevieve the kind of life she wanted.

Quiet and peaceful, filled with all the books the world could offer. He could give her all the books, but James knew that he could never provide her with the peace she wanted. Lady Genevieve deserved someone better than he was. Someone who society accepted and loved. Like the Earl of Kenford.

James knew that he would only offer her a bad stigma because of the scar on his face. His hand wandered to his face and he felt the scar prickle and sting like thorns under his fingers. The only person that was not right for Lady Genevieve was himself, and he was having a hard time coming to that.

Because with a sudden realization, James knew that he had fallen in love.

# Chapter 25

Genevieve roused from the chair beside the window and sauntered back to the comfort of her bed, sending the pigeons to flight in a flurry of wings and talons. Her body ached from the travails of the previous night and she did not get good sleep either because of the clattering of servants in the house as they tried to clear up the manor and bring everything back to normalcy.

Early that morning, her mother's voice roused her from the bed as she barked out orders to the maids. She grunted softly as she turned around, trying to find the best position to sleep that would not disturb her even further. But the walls of the house were somewhat thin, and her mother's voice was so high-pitched that it left like someone was screeching right into Genevieve's ears.

She had been awake from the crack of dawn when the skies were just a sore purple - the color of a bad bruise - and she had been unable to get back to sleep. Genevieve's eyes were heavy with exhaustion but whenever she tried to close them in a bid to rest, her mother's rambling floated through the walls and into her ears.

But the noise was not the only thing that rankled Genevieve. The disappointment in her grew larger as the night went by and the stifling air of the ballroom had only made it worse. When she finally left the dining hall and retired to the withdrawing room with all the other ladies and their mamas, Genevieve was sullen. Her mind fell and she searched for Lord Hamilton to no avail.

It felt like he vanished into thin air, his blue tailcoat shimmering behind him. There was something about the whole scenario that annoyed her, and her friends only made it worse. They chattered all evening long about the earl of Kenford's gracefulness, his sandy hair, and mannerisms. All of these culminated into a melancholy far greater than anything Genevieve had ever been in.

Her head started to hurt that evening as she ascended the flight of marble stairs that led to her room. She supported herself with the railing as she went, nausea swooping in to hug her like a lost lover. And now in the morning, the headaches came again with a dizzying intensity, threatening to crash the world around her.

Genevieve righted herself in bed, staring at the dust motes swirling in the golden light of the morning. They danced and pirouetted, dusty fingers clinging to the air in a bid to remain afloat. The motes danced so much that it hurt and a lone tear slipped from her eyes. She wiped it immediately with her linen sheets, anger pulsing through her mind.

She tried to find explanations for why the viscount had not come to request a dance of her. If she could, Genevieve was sure that she would have given him the honor of dancing with her the entire night even though it might not have been acceptable under the scrutinous eyes of the ton.

"Perhaps I pushed too much?" she asked herself, sinking into the soft eiderdown.

Genevieve closed her eyes and recalled the bright smile on his face when she hinted at the dance they might have in the evening. She had been bold, she knew that, but not too bold. At least, not enough to evoke emotions of revulsion. He seemed pleased with her words, eyes bright with light happiness that told Genevieve everything she wanted to know. He would dance with her.

"Maybe he did not see me," she said, breaking the heavy silence that had become ever so dreadful.

She wanted to think that, but they had met at the door. Genevieve had been transfixed by him, and he smiled again to acknowledge her. He attended the ball, and she had seen him enter the ballroom, eyes searching. She wanted to go to him, to let him hold her as they danced. Genevieve wanted everything to fade to nothing as they moved in tandem, nothing between them but the conversation of books and everything in between.

Through the course of the night, Genevieve had come up with a dozen hundred explanations about why the viscount did not come to ask her for a dance. She was still thinking so hard that she did not hear the door open. Only when Jenny called her name did she know that she was consumed with her thoughts.

"Good morning, my lady," Jenny said warmly. "It is almost time for breakfast. Should I draw you a bath?"

Genevieve shook her head and she immediately regretted it. The headaches came pulsing back, throbbing and writhing in her head. She held a delicate hand to it and pressed lightly, hoping that it might yet take away some of the pain.

"I have no appetite for food this morning, Jenny," she said, resting her head slowly on the pillows. "I feel the onset of a megrim and I wish to rest. Please, let Mother know that I will not be coming down for breakfast."

Jenny nodded. "It was a busy evening and I quite understand, my lady. Should I bring some tea for you? Perhaps some chamomile and ginger to help you relax?"

"That will be most pleasant," Genevieve replied and forced a light smile. "Thank you, Jenny."

As Jenny closed the door behind her, Genevieve traveled back to her thoughts of the previous evening. The viscount's obvious disappointment, the earl's arrogance and ineptitude on the dance floor, the dizzying dance steps of Lord Abercrombie, and the uncomfortable meal with the earl. It had all been so annoying that she wanted to scream. And then, there was her mother's decision to make her have the supper dance with Lord Kenford. It had been the most annoying moment of the evening and when the earl smiled to show pearly white teeth, Genevieve was suffused with so much anger that she stepped away for a moment to collect herself.

She was so lost in thought about everything going on that she did not hear her mother enter.

"Genevieve," her mother's high-pitched voice filled the room. "Jenny informed me that you did not want to come down for breakfast. Is everything okay?"

Genevieve nodded softly. "Yes, Mother. I wish to spend the rest of the day resting. But seeing as I am supposed to have an outing with the earl today, word will have to be sent to inform him of my situation that I will not be able to attend the theatre."

Genevieve saw her mother's eyes widen like she had just seen a terrible thing. And then, the look was gone like it never even happened. She touched Genevieve's head with her fingers to feel for a fever.

The duchess let out a little sigh and her lips were set in a grim, straight line. "You have to keep up appearances with the earl, Genevieve. He is a man of great standing in the society and if given the chance, all the mamas will swarm towards him with their ambition for him to wed their daughters."

Genevieve's eyes darkened slightly. "I am not feeling too well for an appearance, Mother. Any more movements and my limbs will fall off."

She felt her mother's hand tighten around her arm. "Jenny will bring in some tea for the headaches and you will feel better by the time scheduled for your meeting with the earl."

Her mother's statements caught Genevieve with surprise. She was genuinely tired and wanted a break from everything. Meeting the earl was only going to worsen her malady. His conceit would only drive her mad, and his perfume which made him smell like boiled leather would only make her nauseous. Also, she had seen the performance so many times that it would be nothing short of a bore for her to see it again.

"I doubt that I will feel better so soon, Mother," Genevieve disagreed, turning to make herself comfortable amongst the heavy linens. "I might even have to close the windows now for my eyes are painfully tired."

And Genevieve saw her mother snap for the first time in a few years. Her perfect features contorted into a mask of anger and her grasp tightened on Genevieve's arm. Fire flashed in her eyes and soon, she was shaking with fury and resentment.

"Tell me Genevieve, is this sickness related anyhow to that Viscount Hamilton?!" her mother's voice was raised impossibly high. "Did he tell you to feign an illness so that you could do something as foolish as not going with the earl to the theatre?"

Genevieve was at a loss for words. The string of sentences formed in her head, but none of them made enough sense to become her mother's reply. For one, she did not have the energy to keep up with her mother's sudden change of mood. Secondly, the whole situation had just become a whole lot more confusing.

"What?" Genevieve asked, genuinely surprised. "Viscount Hamilton? What are you talking about, Mother?"

"Do not dare lie to me, Genevieve. I did not raise you to tell falsities to my face! Such insolence will not be tolerated!"

Genevieve felt as if a rock was lodged in her throat and she felt all the blood drain from her skin. "What falsities?"

"I have seen your bloody list, Genevieve," her mother cursed for the first time in a few years. "And I know everything you have been up to this Season."

Genevieve began to edge away slowly, her stomach twisting into knots. Her face went white with her mother's words. Her chest heaved with astonishment and her headache seemed to leave at that moment.

"You need to forget about the viscount, Genevieve! He is not of our social standing, so you need to stop wasting time on his horrible appearance! The earl is a much better match for you than anyone else!"

She just gaped at her mother for a moment, the words in her heart erupting in flames. Her knuckles went white because of how hard she folded them and how her nails dug into her palm.

Her voice was tremulous when she spoke. "Why?"

"Before I leave, there is one thing we need to make clear. You are going to the theatre with the earl this evening and that is not negotiable. Whether or not you feel better, a date has been set and we are not going back on it!"

Shortly after, her mother left, leaving Genevieve angry and flustered.

# Chapter 26

Standing in front of the mirror with the elegant pink roses, Genevieve felt nauseous. The tea that Jenny brought had made her better, but not enough to be completely well. Her eyes were still swimming with pain and her head was no better.

The earl had sent the bouquet of pink roses earlier that morning and Jenny had been there to receive it but from what her lady's maid said, the duchess had beat her to it and told the earl that she would still be holding up the invitation to come to the theatre with him. As Jenny told her all of these things, Genevieve could almost not hide the anger and repulsion she felt for both her mother and the earl himself.

Genevieve was tired of acting polite and courteous and she wished that the earl had taken the hint that she wanted nothing to do with him. But he kept coming like a bee to a flower, sending elaborate flowers and carefully handwritten cards her way. But even Genevieve could not refute that the flowers were beautiful. They were not fully opened, and they lent a thick perfume to the air.

Jenny was smiling as she made Genevieve's hair into an elegantly coiffed hairstyle and twisted it in some lace and ribbons that the modiste had sent in a mere few hours ago. A sigh left Genevieve's lips at the thought of her mother's words and she wondered how she had gotten hold of her list. It was personal to her, and for that purpose, Genevieve kept the list under the inkwell and out of sight from anyone. Even Jenny despite how close they had grown to become.

"The earl is a good man, my lady," Jenny said behind her, smoothing some oil into a part of Genevieve's hair. "And a brilliant suitor no less. His Lordship sends flowers almost every day, declaring his intentions."

Genevieve waved her hand dismissively, trying not to sound like she was denigrating the earl's intentions. "I have no use for these flowers, dear Jenny. There are other things more worthwhile than flowers to me."

Jenny was silent for a moment, her face turned towards the window in deep thought. Then she finally spoke. "That might explain why you detest Lennox Gardens and Hyde Park."

"Not necessarily," Genevieve replied dryly. "The men and their horses prove to be nuisances every time I step into the park. And the bees never let me rest!"

A small laugh erupted from Jenny and soon, Genevieve started laughing too. Even though her lady's maid was siding heavily with her mother matchmaking her with Lord Kenford, she was glad that Jenny had a sense of humor at least. None of which the earl possessed.

"Should I call in the gardener to have these flowers planted before they start to wilt? Her Grace would like that very much as it will add to the collection blooming in the orangery."

Genevieve smiled at the thought of the orangery. She had not been there in a long time and while she detested the flowers, she loved the climbing vines that ran along the glass walls and the stream of sunlight that arced into the conservatory when she sat close to the daffodils and lilies. It was where she loved to read and with a sickening alarm, Genevieve noticed that she had not been reading much.

"The gardener would have other things on his mind, I assure you," Genevieve said dismissively. "Though elegant, are not worth being planted in the orangery."

Jenny looked aghast as she held the last part of Genevieve's hair with a pearl comb that the duchess provided. "I believe that these types of roses are quite rare, my lady. It will be such a waste to have them thrown out when they wilt."

Genevieve was already tired of arguing about flowers. Some other matters were enmeshed in her mind and she wanted to figure them all out before she left the house. At least, it was not negotiable.

She wanted to know what her mother knew about the viscount and what she thought even though deep down, Genevieve knew the answers to her question. From the very first day at the Arlington manor, her mother had openly shown her great dislike for the viscount and Genevieve was sure that it was because of the scarring on his face.

But what she had come to understand was that the scarring told her a story about the viscount. About his past and how he might have wriggled into enemy ranks, his soft smile and ardent love of literature, how much he loved to disappear into the shadows at societal functions. Even though other people saw the scarring as a deformity.

"I am rather tired of this farce with Lord Kenford," Genevieve said, crestfallen.

The headache had started once more and Genevieve wanted to lay in bed and have a good amount of rest instead of going to the theatre where all the noise and music would only make her megrim worse.

She turned in the mirror, smiling a little about how beautiful she looked. As always, Jenny made a statement with her dress. A soft satin dress clung to Genevieve's body, the soft material curving into small but beautiful folds at her bosom. It was a pale green and it brought out the color of her eyes. The dress was cinched higher, just a few inches below her bosom, and flared out wonderfully in a mix of velvet and tulle. The materials were light and soft, and her hair was elegantly coiffed and held together by a small pearl comb that gleamed in the mirror.

"You look stunning, Lady Genevieve," Jenny said softly before exiting the room.

Even with how stunning she might have looked, Genevieve was in no mood to even step out of her room let alone attend the theatre with the earl who was the most arrogant person she had ever seen. But Genevieve did not have a choice now.

As she stepped out of her room and walked down the stairs, she could see Lord Kenford's sandy hair and wiry frame at the end of the stairs. As always, he was immaculately clad in a dark tailcoat and white ruffled linen shirt with a dark blue cravat that had gold embroidery. His attire reminded Genevieve of one late-night discussion she was chanced to have with her father about the latest men's dandyism among the ton.

Eschewed in those colors, Genevieve felt a bit revolted. He was speaking in hushed tones with her mother and she was laughing slightly. Genevieve felt like a glorified accessory that her mother had total control over. And she hated it, but she had no other choice.

The slight clack of her shoes on the marble alerted the earl and her mother's attention. The earl - Henry - smiled at her, his face in a wide grin. Out of politeness, Genevieve smiled back at him only slightly and wished that the ground would open up and swallow her. Just seeing him sent another spasm of pain through her head and a frustrated sigh escaped her lips.

"Good day, my lord," Genevieve curtseyed when she got off the staircase. "I hope you have had a pleasant afternoon."

"Indeed, Lady Genevieve," he whispered, his breath hot and clammy that it made her feel nauseous. "The day has been pleasant indeed. Did my gift get to you?"

Genevieve wanted to scream at him to leave her alone but her mother's presence stopped her from doing anything boisterous. "The pink roses were a delight, my lord. I believe it was gotten specially."

Lord Kenford smiled, exposing his teeth. "I had to go past the florist on Piccadilly and Milner Street, Kensington gardens, and down the Serpentine. It was a hard find, but befitting someone of your beauty."

"While this discussion had been particularly interesting, you do not want to miss the performance at the theatre," her mother said, ushering them out of the drawing room and into the wallpapered corridor.

"My carriage is waiting outside," he said and turned to the duchess. "Thank you for your never-ending hospitality, Your Grace. It is always a pleasure to have a conversation with you."

Genevieve saw her mother blush so hard that she almost turned the color of beetroot from embarrassment. Before she could say anything else, Genevieve was out the door and into the crisp London air. Like Lord Kenford had said, the carriage was truly waiting outside the manor and the slight smell of flowers from the garden assaulted her nostrils.

The earl was walking briskly to the carriage and Jenny pulled her along, acting as a chaperone. Genevieve wanted to break free of Jenny's light grip and dash towards the orangery to lock herself in and watch the clouds float over her. But there was no escape this time. She wanted no scandal attached to her name, and in London, even the trees had eyes and ears.

In merely a short amount of time, Genevieve and Jenny were seated near one another with Lord Kenford sitting opposite them. The carriage's interior was plush enough for Genevieve to relax slightly and close her eyes but not enough for her to miss the smell of alcohol on the earl's breath.

He reached into his tailcoat and brought out a silver flask. Genevieve watched his every move as he uncorked the flask and tilted the contents in his mouth. The liquid sloshed out of the flask, dark in the dimly-lit carriage. They hit a bump then and some of the liquid poured on the earl and dripped down the lavish brocade cushions.

The rancid stench of alcohol filled Genevieve's breath and the nausea became even worse. The carriage lurched and bumped, disconcerting her even more. The earl fumbled for a handkerchief to clean the cushions but it only made things worse. He spilled some of the drink away and some of it got on Genevieve's shoes.

They had only been in the carriage for less than an hour, but Genevieve could already tell that the earl was foxed. The carriage smelled of alcohol and his eyes were bloodshot as if he were having a tough time keeping them open.

"M-May-be, you d-d-do look ra-th-rather beautiful, Lady Genevieve," he slurred and stuttered, spittle coming out of his mouth. "Such a beautiful w-woman lik-like you will h-have a handsome dowry."

Genevieve turned to look at Jenny and saw the look of concern on her face. But there was nothing they could do now. Telling the earl that he was drunk might beget some rather unfortunate incident as her father had once told her not to speak to a man who had his nose in a glass for any incitement might spur vexation.

"What do you mean?" she asked politely with a nod of her head. "Dowry?"

"I am s-sure you m-mu-st have l-ll-ooked through the account books," he growled and swallowed some more alcohol from the flask. "Per-perhaps you can tell me of it?"

"I beg your pardon?" Genevieve shot back, repulsed.

At once, she wanted to go back home. To enter the sanctuary of her room and not leave until she was feeling better. But there was no going back now. They had already left the house and Genevieve berated herself for not noticing the earl's bloodshot eyes sooner. But even if she wanted to go home, Lord Kenford was completely drunk. She wondered how she would even broach the subject to him that they should turn back and return to the manor.

Also, if she returned home now, her mother would be fuming and furious. She would definitely not understand their situation and no matter what Genevieve might say, it would only look like she was lying. Different thoughts started running through her mind about what she should do.

At first, she considered answering his question about the dowry in such an impolite manner that it would bring him back to his senses, but she knew that might not work. She had seen drunk people at balls when the host added too much wine and scotch to the punch and it was usually never a good sight. Though they almost never ended in gossip columns, their scandal was remembered by the ton. And no one forgot that.

Genevieve wondered whether to just go back home and explain everything to her mother. But her mother was under the impression that she only wanted Lord Hamilton as a suitor. Even though it was somewhat true, Genevieve preferred the arrogant earl to this drunken state. And she hoped to evade her mother's wrath.

She turned to Jenny and nodded. "Perhaps we should turn back now? I do not feel comfortable with this outing."

Jenny nodded, her eyes morose. "We should, my lady. We cannot go to the theatre now. Not in this state."

Genevieve was glad that someone finally agreed with her. The earl was muttering now, his hot breath filling the carriage and it was so stifling that Genevieve knocked on the heavy wood. No one answered and she knocked again.

"Take us back please," she called out, but the carriage kept moving.

She wanted to speak again when they were launched into the air. The carriage landed with a heavy thunk and there was a loud screech on the cobblestones as one of the wheels came off the axle. Jenny screamed as the carriage continued to run down the street. Genevieve felt her heart thud powerfully, fear rising in her throat. She knocked at the wood, hoping the coachman might hear them.

The carriage started to swerve around and Genevieve was flung to the other side, hitting her head hard on the carriage. Warmth blossomed on her forehead, but she did not care at the moment. She pushed herself, ignoring the pain that flared up in her shoulders and arms. Jenny was screaming profusely, hitting the carriage. From where they were seated, Genevieve could see sparks flying around.

"He - she wanted to scream, but the carriage was suddenly thrust forward and she was weightless.

Everything seemed to pass by slowly and Genevieve saw the world flash before her eyes. Wood splintered and smashed into her as she slid through the carriage. She could still hear the troubled neighing of horses, but the pain that bloomed in her chest was too much for her to even breathe.

So, she just lay there, watching the purple sky. Beside her, she could hear the earl groaning in pain as well, and she bit the insides of her cheek. If only she had stayed home, then this might not have happened. Fear crushed her insides and she wanted to scream, but her voice was lost to the thud of her own heart. Genevieve felt her blood being soaked up by her dress and the terror in her heart only grew larger as the seconds passed.

She tried to shift but the wood pinned her down even harder and she groaned helplessly. The pile on top of her creaked, echoing into her ears like the moan of death. Her vision swam in blue and ash, fear and bile rising in her throat. She saw the viscount's eyes above hers, but Genevieve knew that it was just a dream. One that she wanted to return to.

Different emotions battled for dominance in her mind and heart. Fear. Pain. Panic. Desperation. Regret. Confusion. Winding through all of that was the feeling of utter hopelessness and terror that if she closed her eyes, it might be the very end.

Tired from pain, heavy blood loss, and exhaustion, Genevieve finally closed her eyes to dream about the future that would never happen as the cold hands of death stroked her cheek and guided her.

# Chapter 27

"We need to make this clear, Alice," James growled as the horses broke into a trot. "I will no longer be your chaperone. You have our mother for that. Or better still, you can take Wylla, your lady's maid."

Alice rolled her eyes. "Why take either of them when I can have the company of my kind-hearted brother for the rest of the evening? Tell me, where is the fun in making you sit at home all night long with no company but brandy and account books?"

James was almost seething now, thinking about all of the things he could be doing if he were not in the bloody carriage. There were accounts to be sorted, bills to be managed, and signatures to be appended. He had no such time for frivolities like attending the theatre and watching awful performances. James was truly tired of gallivanting around town like Alice's father. It was taking a huge chunk of his time and he could see in his sister's eyes that she loved to torment him.

"There are a lot of things to be done back home, Alice. If only you had not connived and schemed with mother to parade me in front of those audacious mamas and their witless daughters, maybe I might be getting some work done!"

Alice smiled, her lips twisting into a childish pout. "That is rather insulting, dear brother. Not all of the debutantes are witless widgeons."

James rolled his eyes and his hand grabbed a fistful of fabric from his rosewood tailcoat. His mother had been trying all week for him to get out of the house, but James wanted nothing to do outside. Most times, he spent the day in the study and went horseriding in the evenings along the fields of the estate to ponder on matters that arose in his mind when he was in the study.

He liked the way the air tasted after he rode. Like plums and melons ripe to bursting, the sweet smell of blueberry tart from the kitchens when he rode too close to the manor. More than anything, James loved his horse - Tar. His father had given him when he was young and the horse was a mere filly. They had grown together, and James watched her grow over the years.

She was as dark as midnight, her coat a soft sheen like coal.

When James gave her even the lightest nudge, Tar became a burst of motion. She moved with a rather silken gait, smooth like a waterfall. They went around the estate so many times, prancing around until James' behind was chafing raw from the saddle.

His sister brought his focus to the present. "Brother, I want you to see this outing as a blessing in disguise."

James snorted derisively. "Blessing? More like a disappointment, Alice. I would rather sleep at home than go to a theatre. It is quite the crowd in the opera."

"Lord Lorwood has told me that it can be quite interesting," she replied sweetly. "And I am determined to try it out. He followed me to the gallery after all."

James sighed and dropped his gaze to the polished oak floor of the carriage. Over the days, his sister's interest in Lord Lorwood had grown. And it was the same for the young lord as well. His cards came in almost every day with gifts and flowers. More suitors had started to come in, but Alice only had her eyes on Lord Lorwood. And for that, James was happy.

Thinking about his sister's blossoming relationship, James was once again reminded of the very person he wanted to forget more than anything else. The previous night, he drank himself into a stupor while hoping that he could chase his problems away. But when the haze of drunkenness left him, James was filled with a deep melancholy about the very problems he tried to get rid of.

Lady Genevieve.

When he closed his eyes to sleep, James could see her behind his eyelids. Everything that happened reminded him of her. When he ran his fingers over the spines of the books in the study, when Robert dropped off roses and the thick perfume of it reached his nostrils, the lilac tapestries that reminded him of the dress she had worn for the ball. Even Tar reminded James of Lady Genevieve. Of how her hair shone like Tar's, combed to perfection.

"I know that you have a motive for asking me to accompany you, Alice. It is not merely chaperone duty, but rather, something else entirely," he said, straightening his back on the soft pillows that served as cushions.

Alice blushed slightly, her neck turning a bright shade of red. "It is nothing, dear brother. The theatre has its secrets and it is better you unlock them yourself."

James shook his head. "If this is another motive to matchmake me with some unsuspecting lady, I will make sure that your dowry is delayed. Then, we will see how Robert reacts."

At the threat, Alice guffawed. "Resorting to threats like some common hooligan. I wonder what else you have up your sleeve."

"Hooligan or not, I am in possession of your dowry. Do what suits you with that information. Perhaps, we should play this out and watch where it ends."

Alice finally gave in after a few minutes to ponder on her decision. "Fine! But I will tell Mother of how you wrung this information out of me with a threat! We shall see what she has to say about that."

James laughed, glad that his machination was working. "We both know Mother will not do anything beyond shrill screams and heavy silence. Whatever comes, I have grown fond of both."

They burst into laughter, bending over and chortling so hard that their faces were red and hurting when they finally stopped.

"Mother informed me that a certain Lady Genevieve will be attending the theatre this evening in the company of -

"Henry, the earl of Kenford," James finished miserably.

"I have been tasked with delivering you to Lady Genevieve while using Robert to distract the earl. A rather nice tactic, is it not?"

James sighed, once again seeing Lady Genevieve in his mind. Her voice resounded in his head, melodious and beautiful. He could still recall her laughter in the gallery. High-pitched, sonorous, and wonderful that it sent flutters through his veins.

Hearing that she was also attending the theatre brought joy to his heart but at the thought of seeing her with the earl, an intense vexation flooded him. So much so that he did not know how he would react when he saw her. James could see her already in his mind: her hair elegantly coiffed, blue-green eyes shimmering with the hints of a laugh, pale skin accentuated with a slight blush, mouth spilling out words that brought his mind to a sudden halt.

James shook himself awake, wondering what was happening to him. He had fallen in love with Lady Genevieve when he should not have. He knew that he should have stayed away from the very first day, meandering his way through the achingly boring balls, and not followed his mother's advice to ask her for a dance. But here they were, and he was smitten by her. A budding feeling that should have been quashed long ago.

He rested his head on one of the pillows, inhaling the cool scent of lavender that remained from where the maids sprinkled perfume on the seats. James reminded himself once more that he was not the right person for Lady Genevieve. She needed someone who her family accepted and he had decided long enough that he was not that person. Whoever it was that would become her husband would be a very lucky man.

When he returned from the ball at the Montmere manor, James had gone riding to clear his head. His mind was a tumult, filled with thoughts of what could have been if only he did not have the scar on his face. Tar whinnied, soaring over the lawn and kicking up clumps of dirt in her wake. After riding around for hours, James returned to the gazebo and sat there, letting his mind wander beneath the curling ivy with its bursting blossoms.

In the end, James could only come to one decision. He would stay far away from Lady Genevieve as long as the Season was still underway. That meant only leaving the house when he wanted to chaperone Alice and spending all of his time in the house. He knew that the duchess would not allow her to come to their residence, so it put his mind at peace.

Also, he would make sure to stay hidden in the heavy tapestries and decorations of ballrooms, smearing himself to the wall like a fly and not bother her with his words even if his mother went on her knees while asking. Having been through some relationships when he was younger, James knew how to cut people off when his heart started fluttering. But it was different with Lady Genevieve and while he did not want to, it was the best thing to do.

James would only attend the few balls that sent invitations to him, and he would ask his mother to go in his stead as a chaperone for Alice. All of this was just his way of waiting till his sister got married to Robert. Once they were married, James already planned to leave London and retire to the countryside for the rest of his life. At least, he would have fond memories of Lady Genevieve even though he was foolish to ever have considered that there was a chance something might happen between them. He was only being childish, wrapped up in his affectations to even consider the reality of the society that they lived in.

A small sigh escaped his lips at the thought of Alice's marriage. She was looking outside the window now, her eyes starry with the night's expectations. Lord Lorwood had voiced his intentions, and so far, James could see that Robert and his sister were smitten with each other. One time, he had overheard him asking her what kind of family she wanted and Alice blushed so hard that James thought her face might never be the same.

For his sister, he wished her everything that he might never have. Love, peace, and everything in between. James did not doubt in his mind anymore that Robert was the perfect fit for his sister. They burned bright, talking late into the evenings, taking walks along the Serpentine and down to Hyde Park, riding through Kensington in a curricle, and sitting under the large tree to talk about the things they loved. It was beautiful to see them, and James was already wishing Alice a happy life while he retired to their ancestral home in the country.

"Brother, is everything okay?" Alice asked in a small voice, tapping his hand to get his attention. "You look rather pale."

James did not want her to worry. So he smiled as wide as he could, a goofy grin plastering on his face. "I merely have a lot on my mind, Alice. It is nothing for you to worry about."

"But it is getting worrisome that you get lost in your cogitations," she answered. "I know it must be something else for books of account do not send you this deep into your thoughts."

"Do not worry for me, Alice. It is nothing out of the ordinary."

Alice groaned. "Since I know that your thoughts are not about the account books or your tea trade, it must be about Lady Genevieve. I take it that it has something to do with her, yes?"

James exhaled deeply. "I do not want to talk about these matters, Alice. I will be most pleased if we could talk about something else."

He tried to hide the pain in his voice, and he hoped that it had escaped Alice. But he doubted it for he saw the look of pity on her face for just a second before it melted into a heartwarming smile.

"Well, if you must know, Lord Lorwood is rather interested in horses. An athlete, no doubt," Alice said with fervor, changing the topic just as quickly. "A quintessential sportsman, you might say."

James groaned, his eyes sparking with pride. "Then maybe I shall challenge him to a match and see how well he fares since you sing praises of him every minute."

"He has challenged almost all the bachelors in London. Last I heard, he won a huge purse from Lord Suffolk."

Their carriage came to a sudden halt that made James jolt in his seat. He sat up, worried.

"Is anything the matter?" he asked the coachman after he slipped the small window open.

The door to the carriage opened to let in the sour-sweet smell of the London air as a footman bowed before him.

"There has been a rather terrible carriage accident, my lord. Wheels and axle have filled the road and there is nowhere for us to pass for now," the footman said, bringing them abreast of the situation.

"Then let us make a detour," James said to the footman. "We shall ride through -

"Good Lord!" Alice exclaimed, gasping, and James stopped mid-speech.

"Alice?" he asked, worry creasing his features. "What is the matter?"

He could see that his sister was trying to speak, but her mind could not form the words. All she could do was point out of the carriage, her shoulders heaving and shaking.

James turned his head in the direction Alice was pointing and his eyes widened at the sight. Fear coursed through his stomach, knotting them out. Jenny was standing by the side of the road, waving violently at passers-by but no one seemed inclined to help them. He stuck his head out at an awkward angle and he could see the carriage, almost turned upside down.

He prayed hard in his heart that no harm should ever come to Lady Genevieve. Power pumped through his muscles and soon he was running towards Jenny with all of his might, the London air rushing towards his face.

"Where is Lady Genevieve?" he asked, whipping his head around. "Jenny, where is she?"

The lady's maid was stricken with fear, tears slipping from her eyes.

"The earl..." she cried and stuttered, trailing off and pointing in the direction of the carriage. "Lady Genevieve!"

James felt his ears ring at the words and he could see her smiling face behind his eyes. Full of life and happiness and joy.

"Where is she? At home?"

After crying and stuttering the first few words, Jenny finally spoke. "Lady Genevieve is still in there, my lord. I think she has been hurt quite badly and she pushed me out of the carriage before it toppled."

His heart fractured into a thousand pieces at the words. His mind tried to search for a reason why Lady Genevieve was still inside the carriage.

"No one is willing to risk their lives to climb in there and help her," Jenny cried. "It is no longer stable and it might topple soon, my lord. It is -

But James was no longer listening. In a moment, he was sprinting towards the carriage, his legs running as fast as he could.

# Chapter 28

James rushed to the carriage, his heart racing. His mind was praying boundlessly, hoping that no harm would come to Lady Genevieve. He could not bear to see her hurt as it would shatter his mind.

The carriage was in a terrible state, completely toppled over and creaking loudly with every touch. Having not been in a situation like this before, James knew that the best line of action was to try and bring Lady Genevieve to safety from the carriage without toppling it. Any movement out of line and everything would fall into a downward spiral. One where he might lose Lady Genevieve for life.

His breathing hitched as he fell to his knees, his eyes searching for her familiar golden hair. Adrenaline trickled through his veins as he called out her name softly, hoping for a reply. Anything that might help him to know her position so that he might bring her out without a hassle.

But there was nothing. Except for the creak of the carriage as the cold wind blew past. Fear clawed into his gut and bile rose to his throat. He searched through the small opening and that was when he saw her.

She was lying there, her midsection covered by piles of broken wood. Her hair was matted to her head with blood. There was a huge gash on her forehead and James winced at the sight. She was at the opposite end of the carriage - the hardest place for her to be.

James planted his hand on the cobblestone and crawled through the wreckage. She was so close, yet so far away that he wanted to just push away all the wreckage but he knew that he could not. So instead, he let the cold bite into his hand as he continued to crawl, eyes alert for his surroundings.

When he rested his body too close, he heard the carriage creak badly. So he propped himself up softly, trying as much as possible to stay still while the carriage creaked. Once the terrible sound was gone, James shifted again, pushing past the fallen splinters. By the time he was beside Genevieve, he was sweating profusely despite the cold air. His body shook with pain and pity at the same time, as the pale green dress she wore was already matted with blood. He put his hand on her arm and he felt the slight life-giving pulse. Happiness bloomed in his heart as he cleared the wreckage off her.

The carriage creaked again and James knew that there was no time to waste. It was now or never. In one fluid motion, he propped Lady Genevieve in his arms, his body pulsing with power. He pushed through the way he came, carefully and delicately.

When he got out, he hefted her higher, cradling her close to his body for fear that she might break. Alice was running over to him now and the passers-by already burst into raucous applause but James did not mind all of that. Lady Genevieve was in a bad state, and for that, he would do anything to save her.

An elderly man shuffled forward, his eyes milky behind heavy spectacles. "I am a physician," he said. "And I would very much love to help."

James was happy. The physician pressed her arm and felt her pulse. He nodded, and James took it as a good sign. Everything was going to be okay. He knew at least that much. Lady Genevieve was alive and that was all that mattered.

"My lord," the physician said, "you have to be careful about moving her too much. She is in a rather more dangerous state than I imagined."

His heart dropped to his stomach. "What?"

"She is in dire need of urgent care. Where does she live?"

"Montmere Manor," James replied softly, his heart beating faster than he could talk. "On the mere outskirts of London."

The physician shook his head sadly and let out a sigh. "Before we get there, this lady would have lost a lot of blood. If -

James did not even have to think. "I live not too far away. We can take her there, right?"

"Of course, my lord," the elderly man replied. "Then we must go there at once! For we have no time to waste."

Cradling her closer, James carried Lady Genevieve into his carriage, and off they went at full speed to the Hamilton manor.

\*\*\*

Time was crawling by and the moon was only a sliver in the sky when James got to the house. His shirt was matted with Lady Genevieve's blood but none of that mattered at the moment. He just wanted to see her open her blue-green eyes again and smile at him.

They rushed into the drawing room with Alice trailing closely behind. The physician brought out his bag and asked for some space while he set to work. James did not want to agree, but he saw the look of utter discomfort on Lady Genevieve's face and it melted his resolve.

"What is going on?" James' mother, Marcia asked, her voice ringing through the house.

She was consoling a hysterical Alice and James was trying not to break down himself. He had met Lady Genevieve in a bad state and all he wondered was why something like that could happen to someone he cared so much about. Without answering his mother, he marched out to arrange for the coachman to take Jenny back home to inform the Duke and Duchess about the current situation.

When he got back, Alice was rocking in a corner, wiping her tears with a satin handkerchief. His mother was with her, trying to ask what happened, but his sister was too disoriented to talk. The physician was not out yet, and James was getting really worried.

He started to pace outside the drawing room, worry gnawing at his heart. Fear and panic coursed through him at once and he felt utter helplessness at the situation. James berated himself for not being able to help more and he wished that he had some knowledge pertaining to the situation.

Just when everything looked bleak, the physician stepped out with his grey hair matted to his forehead. James jumped, crossing the distance between them in merely a second.

"I have wiped down most of the blood, and there are only a few complications. The lady has a broken arm and the injury on her head might result in memory loss, but we are hoping for the best. I will set her arm soon and give her something to dull the pain that might come after."

James nodded, unsure of what to say or do. "Please, save her life," he pleaded.

The physician nodded sullenly and drifted back into the drawing room. At that moment, the doors burst open and James saw Edmund barreling towards him. The Duchess was not far behind as well in her lurid purple satin.

"What is the situation?" Edmund asked, his voice shaky. "Where is my daughter?"

"She was involved in an accident, Your Grace, and the physician said that the injury sustained to her head might lead to memory loss."

The duchess screamed and her eyes rolled to the back of her head, but James caught her before she could reach the floor. Edmund was aghast, pale as a ghost as he tried to piece the information together.

"Will she be alright?" The duke asked, but James had no answer for that. At least, not for now.

# Chapter 29

Grunting in her sleep, Genevieve sank into the soft underlinens and velvet where she lay. The tangy scent of lemons floated to her nose and it made her smile. She no longer felt like she was falling, and it was marvelous. At least, she was safe.

She opened her eyes to a large bed, slightly larger than her own but definitely not hers. It was bedecked in dark blue - wallpaper and silk curtains with silver accents on the pillows and sheet lining. Her head was still swimming, but it felt better. At least, better than it had been.

Genevieve wondered where she was, and she turned to see an unfamiliar face staring at her. The world tilted at first, blurry and fuzzy but after a moment, Genevieve saw the petite face and dark hair, green eyes glazed with worry.

"Alice?" she called out, weak with exhaustion but hanging on to the waking world. "Is that you?"

"Thank goodness," Alice whimpered, tears streaming down her face. "I thought you might never wake up."

The room tilted sideways, brimming with unfamiliarity to Genevieve. "Where am I?"

Alice smiled softly. "You are at our residence. There was a terrible accident on the way to the theatre, Genevieve."

Worry creased Genevieve's featured. "Is everybody okay? How is Jenny?"

"Everyone is fine," Alice answered assuredly. "Jenny is in the drawing room with everyone else and the earl survived with only a few scrapes and bruises. Nothing fatal that you need to worry about."

Genevieve was still confused. The last thing she remembered was the pile of wood on her body, the icy tiredness seeping into her body, and the pain that burst through her eyes when she hit her head against the carriage. How she got to the Hamilton manor, she had no idea.

"James brought you here," Alice said, noticing her confusion. "We were on our way to the theatre as well to meet Lord Lorwood when we were informed about the accident blocking the way. I saw Jenny and before I could even say a word, my brother was out and running towards the carriage even though it was threatening to collapse at any second."

Genevieve felt a stab of guilt in her heart. "He risked his own life?"

Alice smiled. "I do not think that James sees it that way. He was consumed that he just ran headlong into the crash to retrieve you."

Genevieve felt a warm tingle work through her veins as her heart thudded. She was not happy to have gotten into an accident, but she was excited about the viscount. He had been there when she needed him the most; without complaint or anything. Instead, he ran headfirst into the situation, his mind bent on rescuing her.

"I should call his Grace," Alice said softly. "He asked me to send for him if anything happens."

Genevieve nodded and immediately wished she had not. Pain ran through her head, stinging and raw, and she placed her head on the soft pillows. She turned around to make herself comfortable when the door opened and her father walked in.

"Genevieve," he called out, his voice hoarse with emotion. "How are you fairing? Is everything alright? Do I need to call the physician?"

She smiled at her father, at his blue-green eyes and greying hair. "I am alright, father. And you do not need to call the physician."

"You had us all worried," he said, covering her hand with his. "If not for the viscount, I wonder what might have happened. He has been beside himself with worry about your wellbeing that he sat here all night. I just told him to get some rest."

Genevieve felt her heart thud as a softness made her body vibrate. It gave her an assurance, something to hold on to. That he had been there for her. His blue eyes swam into her vision, filling her body with strength.

"The viscount has been very kind, and I have been talking to him all night, unable to get even a wink of sleep," her father began. "I spent the last several hours speaking with him about the future, and it was never about business. Instead, it was personal, like a father to son."

Surprise was etched on Genevieve's face as her father continued to speak. Never once did she think her father would speak to the viscount that way. They spoke about business from time to time, but that was it. Hearing her father say that they spoke about the future made Genevieve oddly excited.

"The viscount is a good man, Genevieve. And from what I gathered, he is very much smitten and in love with you. Not in some moony-eyed suitor way, but in the way I love your mother."

Genevieve felt her heart hurt at the words. Tears gathered in her eyes as her father continued to speak. Her heart continued to beat rapidly in excitement as she listened.

"I can very well say that he is an excellent man of the highest standards so far. I do not know how you feel about him, but I just wanted you to know that he loves you so much that he was willing to let you go because of his standing in society. Selfless, decent, and compassionate."

Genevieve felt a lone tear slip past her eyes and pain blossomed in her head. "I want to see him, Father. I want to speak with the viscount."

He nodded softly and got to his feet. "He will be here in a moment."

# Chapter 30

James' head was lolled back on the brocade sofa on the parlor from exhaustion, his eyes threatening to close. He was tired from staying up all night, but he vowed that he would not sleep as long as Lady Genevieve was not yet awake. He wanted to see her okay first, to see the smile on her face before he could allow himself some sleep.

All through the night, Edmund had sat with him and asked him a lot of questions that James felt no need to lie. He spoke about everything that had happened that Season, about how he had met Lady Genevieve, their growing affection for books, and everything in between. For the first time, James accepted that he was in love. And it felt rather beautiful.

Edmund had not criticized him for it, a fact for which James was grateful. In more ways than one, he was glad that the duke only listened. He sighed at intervals, asking questions, but never did he make James foolish, and at the end of their discussion, he felt at peace much more than he ever had.

"Genevieve is asking for you," Edmund said, breaking the silence that James had come to associate with tranquility. "I should follow you, but I think it best if I break the rules of propriety just this once. For I think that she wants to say something that is best kept private."

James muttered his thanks and got up from his seat. Different thoughts rummaged through his mind as he moved towards the door of his room. Every step brought him closer and made him more alive than he had felt in a few days. After not getting the chance to speak or dance with Lady Genevieve at the ball in their manor, he missed talking to her.

He longed for her delicate smiles and when he opened the door, the world seemed to stop for that moment. She had a smile etched on her face, but behind all of that, James could still see the pain in her eyes. Her head was wrapped in clean gauze and linen and some of her hair was matted to her forehead.

"Please, sit," she said, her eyes gleaming. "I have something important to tell you."

At the sound of this, James felt his heart deflate. Some part of him knew that she might reject him. And that time was here. Soon, he would return to the country and leave the rest of his life in misery.

"Back home," she started, her melodious voice cracking slightly. "I have a list with all of the qualities I wanted in a gentleman. I was the diamond of the Season, yet I was without a husband by the Season's end. I had no idea what I was doing on my debut, but I guess that I was simply preparing.

"This Season, I came knowing what I wanted. I wanted a gentleman who was honorable and kind, who shared my devout interest in literature and poetry, who loved the little things as much as I did, who danced so well that they became my lodestar on the dance floor. Also, I wanted a gentleman whose eyes were so rare that I would look at them every morning and smile from ear to ear.

"And you have far exceeded all the expectations I wanted in a gentleman, Lord Hamilton. I -

He interrupted her. "James. Call me James."

"James," she said, her voice high and sweet, "You have crossed all of the qualities and beyond. I know this might come across as bold after everything, but I do not care anymore. I love you, James. So much that my heart explodes when I set my eyes on you. And I hope you feel the same way about me."

He could not believe his ears. James shook himself, trying to check if it was all a dream. But it was not. She was right there in front of him, eyes gleaming with unshed tears.

"I love you too," he said softly, a tear slipping past his defenses. "I have been captivated by you ever since the first time we met at Arlington Manor. I have been in love with you every second of the day and it cripples my ability to do things well, Genevieve. I really am in love with you."

The heat of her body seeped into his clothes as he leaned toward her. She was leaning in too, eyes shut tight with expectation. And then the kiss had come, uninterrupted and more beautiful than James had ever imagined.

He felt the slow swirling heat in his head, the prickles of desire stinging his chest. The sound of her breath was melodic, every rise and fall pushing James toward the edge. The pull between them grew strong and James leaned in further into the kiss.

Someone cleared their throat and they pulled away, eyes

filled with need and warmth. Alice was standing there, smiling at them.

"Get out, Alice," James moaned and threw a pillow her way.

Then they all burst into laughter.

Genevieve how to ride despite her remarkable ineptitude, read poems in Hyde Park, watching the ducks glide across the waters of the Serpentine while trying to find new ways to properly describe them. The nights were spent with thoughts of how much knowledge she had, her wits and preference for landscapes, staining her hands with watercolors and painting James' face with it and so much more. It amazed how the love in his heart became an explosion of flames and want.

They were in the midst of their wedding breakfast, and Genevieve could not think about anyone else. Their wedding was the grandest in all of London and almost every member of the peerage was present. That morning, Genevieve had been terrified, but in a happy way. She recalled how quickly time passed when she was with James, how he spoke with such knowledge that it sometimes amazed her, how her heart fluttered when he called at the door.

When she walked down the aisle in the large church on Byward Street, he was standing at the altar, bathed in incandescent light that shone through the stained glass windows. His tailcoat of white became a smattering of crimson and yellow, cobalt and green and white.So colorful that it was beautiful. And he had the kindest smile on his face.

As they recited the vows, James took every word slowly and carefully. Every word was an affirmation to Genevieve, her heart fluttering at the soft baritone of his voice. She hung on to every word, repeating them in her heart until they were seared into her mind. It was beautiful and wonderful at the same time, every echo of his word reaching the depths of her heart.

And she she finally cradled his face to kiss him, the desire worked through her veins like holy fire. Genevieve no longer cared about the scar on his face. It told a story of his sufferings and battles, of how he became stronger and better. She kissed him with such ferocity that he was taken by surprise and when the innocent look on his face withered away and gave way for passion, Genevieve knew that she made the right choice with James.

"Who knew that all he wanted was Genevieve's dowry to make headway through his mess of misfortune?" Edmund said, laughing conceitedly.

"News about him was all over the gossip column," Marcia stated. "Of how he spent his money in clubs and betting pools. Serves him quite right."

"He only wanted to captivate us with his good looks and arrogance," Sybil laughed. "It would have been a terrible decision for him to even court Genevieve in the first place."

When Sybil heard about everything that happened, she was terribly sorry for her daughter. The accident was all her fault. If only she had listened to Genevieve, things might have turned out differently. For Sybil, the accident was a turning point. She started listening effectively to her daughter instead of imposing rules on her. They became closer than ever and she apologized to James.

Since then, she had become like Edmund. They started to find joy in the little things again. In their conversation and small talk, chats about accounts and plays, the opera and performers. For the first time in a while, she stopped seeing the imperfections in little things and focused on seeing the bright side. Since then, she remained happier than ever.

*Clank. Clank.*

The sound of silverware on glass roused everyone from their conversations and thoughts. Robert was on his feet, his heart beating so hard that he thought it might explode. But he was tired of waiting and longing. He spent the whole day with Alice every day, but it was not enough. It was never enough.

His hand rolled over the metal in his pocket and a nervous smile burst on his face at the silence in the large room. Slowly, he closed his fingers around the ring and brought it out of his pocket before going to his knees.

"Alice, I know we have only known one another for a short time, but I want to keep knowing you for the rest of my life. I love you, Alice and with that, I pose the question. Will you marry me?"

All heads turned to Alice at that point and she squealed. "Gladly!"

James had never seen his sister that happy. She hugged him tight after pulling Robert from his knees and they all laughed so hard at the baron's shyness. He wished her everything he had with

Genevieve. Passion, peace, intense happiness and overwhelming love.

And the celebrations continued in two fold!

# Epiloque

"I heard that Lord Kenford is now in the country despite the Season having not ended," Marcia said from her place at the table, her fingers fiddling with the linen napkins. "Serves him right, yes?"

The Duchess, Sybil, shook her head with a small laugh. "I find entertainment in reading the gossip columns, Marcia. He has definitely brought aspersions to his parentage."

"I am sure that his mother would be stricken with shame," Alice said, turning to glance at Robert. "It is only a matter of time before she returns to the country as well."

James just watched them all as they spoke, his fingers twined with Genevieve's under the table. Ever since they both confessed their love for one another, they had been inseparable. They spoke about everything possible. Settling down, poetry, starting a family, business, and the flourishing tea trade and potential investors, how the stars winked in and out of existence when they spoke in the gazebo.

The past month had been beyond wondrous for James, and it was by far the most exciting time of his life. Getting to know Genevieve was a smooth task, enlivened by her smooth jokes and soothing talk, her melodious voice and soft laughs that filled the mid-afternoon air. Together, they had visited the bookstore in Piccadilly and bought a large amount of books from various authors, drank tea with lime and biscuits while they looked out of amber glass windows and laughed at the passers-by.

James had talked much more than he anticipated and he loved every moment of it. He spent the days laughing and jesting, trying to teach

# Extended Epilogue

"Sometimes, it is hard for me to envision this marriage," Kitty said excitedly, patting her husband's shoulder. "Or do you?"

Everyone was happier than ever, but none than James and Genevieve. It had been two years since their wedding and every day was more blissful than the last. Brandon, their first child was crawling around between the legs of the visitors and he giggled when Marcia reached out to hold him. Genevieve had taken in again, and they were expecting a second child.

Each day was marvelous after they moved to the countryside on the evening of their wedding, and Genevieve did not ever want to leave. The halls were quite at first, empty passageways where her and James would laugh and read and make love. It was a beautiful experience, and continued to be blissfully so.

"Is this merely a party?" Elizabeth asked, her husband in tow as they walked into the house. "And why am I not seeing cake and lemonade?"

Genevieve laughed and hugged her friend. "It has been long, has it not?"

Elizabeth smiled. "Barely three months since we saw one another, Genevieve. Not really a long time."

James carried his son from his mother and tickled him. He placed a light kiss on his child's head, his eyes filled with love and relief. He had never loved anyone as much as his family. And that family was only going to grow bigger as the years passed by them.

"Have you read the gossip columns?" Alice said, her hands thrown out in amazement. "We have been termed London's best couple of the Season! Even though we have been married for two years."

James laughed. "You never used to care about these columns, Alice. Tell me, what changed? And do not let your excuse be Robert's indulgence."

Everyone burst into laughter. "It is only a particular author, dear brother. And she has always caught my attentions. I just never revealed it to you."

"Ha!" James exclaimed. "So that explains where all the pennies were going! I should have known earlier!"

"You read gossip columns too," Genevieve said, pointing an accusing finger at James. "Or do you not?"

Everyone laughed as James sputtered. Finally, he caught his voice. "Usually, you read it a lot more than I do."

"That does explain a lot," she replied, every word dripping with sarcasm. "I have once caught you intensely studying one of those gossip sheets. Perhaps you would like to explain to everyone?"

Everyone present started to laugh and James blushed so hard that his face turned red. And he was happy. Genevieve teased him about everything, and he loved it.

He pulled her close with one hand while supporting Brandon with the other. "This teasing has to stop."

She smiled wickedly. "Oh, it will not. As long as I love you, James. For the rest of my life."

And then he kissed her lightly, his heart filling with relief and excitement.

**The End**

Printed in Great Britain
by Amazon

22332098R00126